OPERATION
FRANKENSTEIN

GET BITTEN BY THE FIRST

CODE NAME: LONEWOLF THRILLER

BITE

OF THE

WOLF

AVAILABLE IN KINDLE, PAPERBACK &

HARDCOVER

A CODE NAME: LONEWOLF THRILLER

OPERATION FRANKENSTEIN

WADE WALKER

World Mythic Entertainment

World Mythic Entertainment

Any references to historical events, real people, or real places are used fictitiously. Other names, characters, places and events are products of the author's imagination, and any resemblance to actual events, places or persons, living, dead or reanimated, is entirely coincidental.

Operation Frankenstein ©2023 World Mythic Entertainment (WME) and M.G. Larson. All rights reserved. No part of this book may be reproduced, stored in a retrieval system, or transmitted in any form or by any means, electronic, mechanical, photocopying, recording, or otherwise, without the prior written permission of the author, except as provided by U.S.A. copyright law.

Based on characters created by Mary Shelley.

First printing, October 2023

ISBN: 979-8-9871084-3-7

1:	HEADS UP	1
2:	SHE'S A LADY	10
3:	FRANKENBALL	22
4:	NOBODY CALLS IT "THE ORKNEYS"	34
5:	DEVIL OF THE SEA	45
6:	"NOPE. I'M JUST GOING TO KILL YOU."	58
7:	UNHAPPY RETURN	68
8:	SNOOPING ABOUT	75
9:	CROSSPLOT	88
10:	FRAU STIGLITZ'S FINISHING SCHOOL FOR GIRLS	101
11:	PISTE-OFF	114
12:	BRIDE'S HEAD REVISITED	124
13:	TO THE VICTOR	129
14:	LADY'S NIGHT	140
15:	MAROONED	148
16:	YELLOW JACKETS REQUIRED	160
17:	THE DANGER ZONE	166
18:	BALLOONED	177
19:	BRING ME THE HEAD OF VICTOR FRANKENSTEIN	185
20:	THE LORD AND THE NEW CREATURES	196
21:	STITCHING THE PIECES TOGETHER	204
22:	BELT BRAWL	212
23:	HERE COME THE BRIDES	222
24:	LIGHTNING STRIKES	231
25:	MONSTER CLASH	239
26:	BEWARE! THE BLOBULUS	248

27: NEVERMORE 255
28: ANIMAL VITALITY 265

OPERATION FRANKENSTEIN

Author's Note:

The dossier containing top-secret data on the ParaCommand mission officially designated "Operation Frankenstein" was, as are all the CryptoFiles, received by a transmission from a Q-Wave quantum computer, wherein these documents, classified as beyond top secret at the highest level, were leaked.

Compiled from a staggering file of verifiable incidents, official records, shocking reports never before uncovered, and transcribed from the testimony of the very credible witnesses involved, the evidence is here within these pages.

The facts that will be presented are true.

This may be the most shocking story you will ever read.

1: HEADS UP

The man who had followed Val West for the last three blocks stood at five-foot-nine, weighed one hundred eighty-six pounds, had a slight deformity in his left foot, suffered from halitosis due to a rotting molar, and dealt with chronic bowel incontinence compounded by the wearing of semi-soiled undergarments.

That was just from what West had been able to pick up by scent.

The man momentarily lost West's trail in a grimy London backstreet alley. This was by design as West lurked in the shadows, waiting for the man to pass by. He didn't have time to deal with someone tailing him—especially if this fellow was after the same target and just looking to piggyback on his efforts.

Suddenly, the man stopped mid-stride—he didn't need a werewolf's supernatural sense of smell to realize he was now the one being stalked. In an attempt to look like he was just out for a stroll, he glanced over at West and nodded. "Do you have the time?" he asked.

"No," West replied, his voice taking on an increasingly irritated rasp. "I don't."

The man lunged.

West's eyes flashed a beastly red glow.

The lunge came to a screeching halt. He stood frozen, unsure of what he had just seen, the way one doesn't quite know what to do when stumbling upon a predator in the wild.

West let out a low growl, which grew in volume and intensity until the man's fight-or-flight instinct decisively chose "flight," and he ran off faster than he thought possible on a gimpy foot.

Something was off, though. West couldn't quite put his finger on it, but he sensed there was more to this. He chased after the man and quickly had him by the scruff of the neck.

"Turns out I do have the time after all," West said, baring his fangs. He could smell the fear rising and the man's leaky bowels losing control.

He had him.

"You're not just a typical street hood. You wouldn't happen to be employed by, say, HIVE, would you?"

"Nuh…no… I don't know anything about that."

"And you're a lousy liar. Let's try again." He grabbed the man by the throat and threw him into the brick wall of the alleyway. There was no further reply as the body went limp and crumpled to the ground—not dead, but West had overdone it.

"Tremendous," West muttered to himself. He still found it difficult to control his animalistic tendencies, and in this case, he wasn't going to get anything out of someone unconscious from both fear and excessive force.

Inside the man's jacket, West found what could be considered identification: a modified PF9 plastic pocket pistol. 3-D printed and untraceable, this was the weapon of choice issued to HIVE agents. There was one more thing to check, to be certain.

He lifted the man's limp left arm, turning it to the underside of the wrist. Under the sleeve cuff, there it was—a round, red-outlined circle with a red dot in the center. It was some sort of tattoo or scarification, a mark he had seen on the few HIVE agents he'd been unlucky enough to have encountered. The agents weren't quite brazen enough to carry business cards, but this was the next best thing.

And who, or what, was HIVE?

HIVE was the latest secret organization infecting the world with schemes of domination—or, at the very least, causing problems professionally for profit. They had first come up when West still worked for the counter-espionage unit of International Command and, since working for Commander 7 at ParaCommand, they continued to come up in association with international threats.

West let the sleeping thug lie. With this distraction now out of the way, he could get back to the task at hand. So far, he had managed to get through the day without being punched in the face, but the night was still young.

He stayed on the track of the new trail he had started following—thankfully, one that didn't resemble the smell of fifty-year-old cat piss. Moments later, his sense and scent detected something lurking behind him, hidden in the thickening fog rolling through the London night. It had a strong scent, like the mustiness of the grave.

Whatever it was, he caught the whiff of scent too late. Through the mist, a monstrous hand punched him straight in the face, followed by giant fingers wrapping around his throat. These HIVE agents were getting bigger... much bigger. This one must be nearly eight-foot.

West squeezed his fingers tight to activate a button on his glove, sending an electric shock through the gauntlet, which transferred to the massive attacker. It only provided a momentary distraction, just long enough for the fingers to loosen their grip, dropping West to the ground. Sparks arced off the giant's face. He couldn't see his attacker clearly in the foggy darkness, but in the brief flashes of light, he saw enough to know it was ugly.

As peculiar as all of this was, West didn't have time to continue fighting, either as a human or relying on the tactical advantage of his just happening to be a werewolf. He ran off, already late in following his quarry, and not about to be further detained by a giant-sized hitman with a lower jaw apparently made of steel.

Ten blocks away, where the scent trail ended, West found himself staring up at a luxurious brownstone apartment building near Oxford and Piccadilly Circus. The top floor penthouse looked to have a splendid view overlooking London. The young lady on the rooftop terrace provided nice scenery as well.

Ossie Weiner could hardly believe his luck.

He watched the teeming nightlife from the balcony of his seventh-floor penthouse at Whitechapel Court. All the lights twinkling over London, all the people coming and going, all the glamorous women going to the nightclubs, couldn't compare to the sight he had just seen—all five foot five of her, long, silken auburn hair, and with curves so dangerous he was not only willing to risk a fiery crash—he welcomed it.

That delicious fate was still in the bathroom, but would soon be out, and his heart was counting every second with its throbbing beats. He still couldn't believe his luck. Here he was, sixty-two years old, picking up this stunning girl who was certainly no more than thirty. Maybe she was more like twenty-two, at most. He couldn't tell. He didn't care.

The bathroom door opened, its sound alone sending a wave of ecstasy through him. She was all that mattered now. He wondered what her name was, but then quickly decided not to worry about such trivial matters. Her scent made him go lightheaded from the rapid rush of blood to his overheated loins. To say her fragrance was intoxicating was to do it a grave disservice and assumed other intoxicants were even close to being on its level.

She was now his everything. Although they had only met moments ago, he knew she was the one he had to have every moment, every waking moment of his life. Nothing would deny him.

He would die for her.

She would be his bride.

West watched this rather bizarre interaction from his perch beneath the balcony railing. He was only supposed to be keeping an eye on things, not peeping on a quite lucky old man and his lovely date. Still, he had seen enough in his time to know it was highly probable she was more interested in something other than a romantic affair with this man and thought it wise to keep watching.

Weiner swallowed hard, panting slightly as she stood before him, her slender fingers slowly, tantalizingly, reaching up to caress his face. Her touch made him tingle like he was connected to an overloaded electric current. Even if he could pull out the words stuck in his throat, he knew he could never formulate anything but babble for this vision of absolute loveliness. His uncontrollable fever for her was so strong, he wagged his salivating tongue, and it felt like his eyes were going to pop out.

And then his eyes popped out.

West watched in horror as the woman squeezed Weiner's head with such force that his eyes popped from his skull and were dangling grotesquely from their sockets. Then, with cold precision, she twisted his neck so smoothly, so efficiently, that his head spun around and was still spinning atop the spinal column as the limp body crumpled lifelessly to the stone floor.

It's going to be one of those nights, West thought as he vaulted up onto the balcony. The woman turned to face him and hissed before leaping straight onto the rooftop above.

It was definitely going to be one of those nights.

West then turned his attention to transforming himself into his werewolf form, Code Name: LoneWolf. Since gaining the wolfskin belt known as der Wolfsgürtel (see *Bite of the Wolf-- Editor),* he had been able to control his lycanthropy. Through practice, he learned to trigger his transformations with thought, emotion, and controlled breathing, while also maintaining his mental faculties in werewolf form.

The rush of hormones and adrenaline surged through him as the physical metamorphosis began: his ears became pointed, his human features shifted to wolf-like and fur-covered, and his eyes glowed a fierce red above a fang-filled mouth announcing itself with a fang-filled snarl.

LoneWolf leaped onto the rooftop in pursuit. The girl was already half a block ahead, bounding effortlessly over the buildings overlooking Piccadilly Street. Although he wasn't judging, there was something undeniably inhuman about her movements—which only fueled his curiosity. Originally, his mission was to track Weiner, but now, he would be tracking her, and she was leading him on quite an unexpected chase.

With impressive agility, she vaulted across wide gaps, clearing the Royal Academy of Arts entrance and Old Bond Street without breaking pace. Even with LoneWolf's near-boundless energy, West found it grueling, but he doggedly pushed himself to keep up.

As fast as she was, she would have to slow down as she neared the edge of the roof ahead, so he took this chance to narrow the gap with a forceful leap. Unfortunately for LoneWolf, as he soared through the air, she caught sight of him. With razor-sharp reflexes, she grabbed him mid-leap and hurled him into a glass greenhouse that shattered beneath him.

LoneWolf sprang to his feet, shaking off the shards as he grabbed her leg, yanking her back just as she attempted to cross to the next rooftop. Her powerful leg swung him off balance, sending them both sliding down the slick, slanted metal roof. She managed to stop her fall at the ledge, taking the opportunity to kick him over the side. He cursed her as he tumbled over, becoming entangled in a string of bistro lights strung between the buildings.

Now he was losing his cool. The animalistic tendencies of LoneWolf took over, rage bubbling just beneath the surface. The snarling beast tore at the tangled lights, bulbs bursting as he thrashed. Gripping a cable, he ripped it free from the wall in a burst of bolts and swung it like a lasso, catching a chimney on the opposite building. Aware he was losing her, he swung himself across, landing hard on the next rooftop just in time to see the girl's shadow vanishing ahead. With a grunt, he pushed forward with all the speed he could muster.

She was fast—too fast. With the distance she had on him, he needed a shortcut, and running along rooftops didn't offer many. He had only one option left—one he'd hoped to avoid. His official armorer, Dr. Hector Borge, had issued him what he called "Wolfapult Boots." Apart from informing Borge that the name was an affront to any sort of taste or professional dignity, West had deep reservations about the cybernetic spring-loaded devices built into his boot heels, designed for rapid propulsion. At best, he thought the physics seemed dubious. Still, if he was to catch up to this woman, catapulting himself at an unknown rate of speed and distance was the only chance he had, slim as it was.

The blocks-long stretch of buildings ended at Piccadilly Circus. Once she reached the open square below, he would never find her. Even with his keen sense of smell, it would be impossible to track her among the competing scents of the nighttime crowd.

LoneWolf clenched his jaw. *Okay, Borge,* he thought, *here's your test, in the name of science and necessity.*

He stopped, leaned back on his heels, and with a click, heard the microprocessors booting up. A high-pitched beep signaled they were ready. He ran forward, and with another click, he was launched into the sky at high velocity.

For a heart-pounding moment, he soared above the rooftops, unsure where—or how—he'd land, desperately hoping it wouldn't be face down in the plaza of Piccadilly. The woman was still racing along below him, nearing the last roof. He needed to come down now, and to ensure it, he twisted into a swan dive, placing his hands along his buttocks as if directing his speed in a freefall, diving toward his target.

The mystery woman looked up just in time to see a werewolf barreling towards her before they both collided hard on the surface of the rooftop. He had to hand it to Borge. The damn things actually worked, but there was no time to celebrate. The woman flung him off and tore a nearby television antenna from its base, wielding it like a sword.

She lunged at him, and LoneWolf dodged, barely escaping the swing. The antenna suddenly glowed with a greenish hue, electricity crackling along its surface. She aimed it at him, and a charged lightning burst erupted from the tip. He rolled, dodging the deadly bolts, his mind racing, wondering what the hell kind of reception she was picking up.

He was deciding what he would do next, apart from praying these boots had rubber insoles, when the woman stopped abruptly. The antenna clattered to the ground, its electrical glow fading to static and leaving only the scent of ozone. She held her arms straight in front of her, stumbling toward him in what seemed to be an attempt at continuing the attack. He watched curiously as she shambled, then collapsed into a fall.

As he leaned in to catch her—and to his stunned surprise—her body dropped to the ground, leaving only her head in his hands. He certainly didn't know what to think as he stared at the severed head. The face, still beautiful but marred by visible stitches, was separated at the neck. What appeared to be metal clamps, still glowing and hot to the touch, protruded from the torn flesh, and the skin had begun to shift, turning a sickly green. At his feet, her body oozed, dissolving into a bubbling, pea-green puddle of slime.

West inhaled deeply, his mind clearing as he shifted back from LoneWolf to his human form. He gazed down at the disembodied head, trying to make sense of what he was dealing with. This wasn't a robot, although there appeared to be small metal parts dissolving in the puddle of green goo that had once been her body. He needed to preserve some of it if he could, and bring a sample back to ParaCommand for Borge to analyze.

He cradled the head in his left arm and squatted down to see what he could retrieve from the bubbling mess. What he found was a swift boot to the face. Caught completely off guard and understandably surprised, he fell backward, the head tumbling across the ground.

"Don't move," an angry female voice commanded.

"I wouldn't dream of it. Let me guess… or you'll shoot?"

"You are smarter than you look," the voice said, moving behind him. From the ground, the severed head stared up at them.

West turned to explain, then stopped when he felt the hard steel of the gun jab into his back.

"Make another move and I *will* shoot. And just so you don't get any ideas…

"The bullet is silver."

2: SHE'S A LADY

Walking with a gun trained on your back always adds a little nervous tension, particularly when it's loaded with the only type of bullet that can kill you. How did this woman know about his lycanthropy? This was West's most vexing thought at the moment. She would have to have known in advance in order to be prepared with silver bullets, a decidedly unusual item to be armed with.

Just minutes earlier, she had forced him at gunpoint into her black 1965 Jaguar E-Type, parked near Piccadilly Circus. This wasn't the first time he'd been forced into a car, and he was curious as to what kind of ride she was taking him on. He had attempted to get a closer look at her through the shadows but was blinded by her deliberately angled dome light.

As this mysterious woman drove far too fast through London's winding backstreets, West considered his predicament. The man who had tailed him on the way to Ossie Weiner's apartment was certainly a HIVE agent. And the behemoth—he had to be, as well.

What about her? The obvious answer would be "yes," but in the world of espionage, obvious answers were few and far between. Still, HIVE was an organization in expansion mode and becoming too prominent a force in the underworld to underestimate.

The car pulled into a darkened alley. With a shove, he was out and on the march again.

She jabbed him with the handgun, ordering him to round the next corner. Should he make a move now? No, it was better to see where this was going. It was a pleasant night for a walk, with spring finally springing in London. Under different circumstances, it would have been truly enjoyable.

Moments later, they rounded another corner and entered the familiar grounds of Highgate Cemetery. This made him more nervous than knowing there was a silver bullet chambered in the gun pointed at his back. He played it cool, though his curiosity was at a fever pitch as they stood before the Gothic mausoleum hiding the secret ParaCommand base entrance.

"Open it," she snapped.

"Open what, my dear?"

"Let's not be difficult." Her voice was sharp, with an undisguised posh English accent. "I've been very restrained so far. Now, open the damn door."

"I have no idea what you're talking about. Are you sure you're in the right cemetery?"

She muttered an obscenity under her breath, then, keeping him in her sights, stepped aside. Her free hand reached over to flip open the moss-covered marble gargoyle's head, revealing its hidden keypad. The fingers with the expensively polished nails typed a series of numbers. To his surprise, as well as growing annoyance, the mausoleum doors swung open.

West turned toward the figure in the shadows (who had a rather lovely scent at that, though he wisely kept this thought to himself). "We really need to change those locks."

She responded only by poking him in the side with the gun, pushing him ahead. He thought this was the time to take a chance and make a move. How did she know any of what she had just demonstrated? Surely,

Borge had seen her by now on his cameras. Why hadn't he activated lockdown procedures?

Once inside, they moved through the secret door disguised by a false wall burial vault marker, descending the carved stone steps to Borge's laboratory. West looked past the walls of monitor screens and cabinets of blinking computers spitting out streams of data and saw Borge at work, hunched over his desk. If he made his move now, the silver bullet would undoubtedly kill him.

But… should Borge activate security and stop her, he could theoretically remove the silver bullets and revive him with a dose of artificial WLF lunar rays. Better still, if he did this right, he might not even get shot. If he was going to act, the time was now.

"Good evening, Kendra," Borge said, looking up from the electronic device he was soldering.

"Your dog was loose, so I brought him back." She gave West a final shove forward before holstering her handgun.

West spun around to see the face of a beautiful young woman glaring at him. He was impressed by what he saw. She wore a black, skin-tight, form-fitting catsuit… and what a form for it to fit!

Her blonde hair was swept up in a bouffant style, with long tresses falling over her shoulders in a little dance, framing a face he'd be damned if he'd ever forget. The glittering green eyes were piercing, and the sinful lips were an invitation to a mouth with mean and dangerous intentions.

Whoever she was, she could be both bad news and good news at the same time. He shot a sharp glance at Borge. "You know her?"

"Yes, of course." He realized the awkwardness of the situation and began to stammer. "This… uh, this is Kendra. Um, I mean… Lady Kendra. Lady Kendra Kenton."

West's mouth dropped open. "As in Cedric's daughter?"

Kendra narrowed her eyes at him. "You really are quite the detective. No wonder they keep you around, aside from having a murderous beast to play fetch with."

"Hey, now that's—" West's retort was interrupted by the hum and crackle of the speaker box and waveform monitor. The leader of the ParaCommand team, Commander 7, was tuning in. The voice transmission came through with the usual speaker hiss and tinny-sound, always seeming distant—especially since West had never met the Commander in person.

"Lady Kenton. So glad you could join us."

She turned toward the speaker as if addressing someone actually present. "Always a pleasure, Commander. Well, almost always."

"I know you don't know Agent West, but I assure you he is of the highest caliber."

The mean mouth turned meaner. "He almost got a .38-caliber silver slug sent into him tonight."

West walked over to her and pointed at her holster. "How did you think to pack silver bullets in that .38?"

She looked him straight in the eye with an icy stare. "You don't think I know how my father was actually killed?"*

West winced. "That's not fair. I don't know what you think you know, but I didn't kill your father."

"Maybe not directly. But it is because of you that my father is dead."

Commander 7 broke in. "Your father believed in what we are doing here, and he also worked extremely hard on the LoneWolf program with Mr. West, Dr. Borge, and me. His death was in the line of duty, and it was a brave and honorable one at that."

West tried his best to be understanding, although part of him was seething. He could feel his fangs emerging and fought to hold back. Looking at her with glowing red eyes wouldn't do him any favors—and could also still get him a silver bullet on top of it.

Borge, finding the tension unbearable, slunk back to the side room laboratory and busied himself, keeping one ear on the situation.

---

*see *Bite of the Wolf*—if you haven't, what are you waiting for? -- *Editor.*

"Kendra," West said in his calmest tone, "Cedric was my friend and, at one time, a mentor. If I could have saved him, I would have, despite the fact that he always said he wanted to be carried off the battlefield on his shield. My being a werewolf doesn't put me in the same category as the one who killed your father."

"Yes... the one who killed him—oh, you mean your partner, Agent Wildebeest? Actually, you and he were quite alike. I should know. I was once partnered with him on an assignment in Thailand. And if it could happen to him, it could happen to you. You're dangerous. I know you're the 'Lone-Wolf' but once you're gone, then there's 'No-Wolf.' Meaning no more werewolves. Threat eliminated."

West didn't think he could reason with her. There was still too much grief and anger flowing through her veins. He was still hoping to avoid being shot with a silver bullet this night, so he decided to change the subject. "I assume you didn't follow me onto the rooftops of Piccadilly just to threaten to shoot me?"

"Don't flatter yourself—I always keep a silver bullet loaded just for you. I was at a soiree being held at the Hemlock House."

Commander 7 rejoined the conversation. "You didn't happen to be there because of the Hemlock Diamond, by any chance?"

She hesitated before replying. "I don't steal anymore... at least not from anyone who doesn't deserve it."

The Commander was well aware of the Hemlocks' less-than-sterling unofficial reputation. "So... you were there for the diamond, then."

"That's neither here nor there. What does matter is that I saw a familiar face—a friend, and after she left the party, she ended up on a rooftop, where I found your pet, Mr. West, with her head in his hands."

"Listen," West said. "I didn't kill her."

"That, I believe. Because she's been dead for a year."

At this, Borge's ears perked up. He decided he did want to hear this conversation after all.

So did West. "If you would care to, by all means, please elaborate."

She let out a heavy sigh and finally lowered her guard enough to join West and Borge at the round table where they held their briefings.

Borge brought her a glass of freshly squeezed beet juice, which she refused.

West offered a glass of freshly crushed ice with a double jigger of gin, which she did not.

"My friend, Lynda Callahan, died in a car accident a year ago, in March. Tonight, I was at the Hemlock House—by invitation, I might add—and was making my way through the crowd across the main floor when I looked over and saw her on the far side. I moved closer to get a better look, thinking it obviously had to be someone bearing a striking resemblance.

"Once I got closer, I could see the faint scar above her left eyebrow. I knew about it because I gave it to her—accidentally, of course—in grade school. There was no doubt it was her, and, understandably, I was at a loss for an explanation. I decided to keep an eye on her and followed a few steps behind."

She took a big gulp of her gin, gathering her thoughts before she continued.

"Then I saw her talking to Igor Zelensky from Frankentech. I couldn't hear what they were saying. He stayed close to her and whatever was said was whispered into her ear. Then she went over to another man, the man she left with. After a very brief conversation, she took him by the arm and they were gone. I then tailed them to the penthouse at Piccadilly."

West took a moment to process all she had told him. As expected, he had some questions about this whole bizarre affair. "The man Miss Calloway left with…"

She interrupted sharply. "Callahan. She was Irish, not English. Americans never know the difference."

"My apologies. And I'm Canadian, actually."

"Hmph. Then you really have no excuse."

West ignored her and continued. "Miss Callahan left with a man named Ossie Weiner. Have you heard of him?"

Kendra shook her head slowly. "No, can't say that I have. Neither by face nor name."

"He's American. Publicly, he is known as a physics professor. Secretly, he was an engineering scientist involved in a highly classified government project. We think there's a connection with HIVE. We're just not sure what it is."

She downed the last of her drink. "I don't know anything about that. What I do know is that she was involved with Zelensky, and that's enough for me to know Frankentech is somehow involved. And you know the reputation the Frankensteins have."

"Had," Commander 7 said. "Victor Frankenstein has spent considerable time and effort overcoming his family's historical reputation. Despite any misgivings you may have about Frankentech or Igor Zelensky or even the rubbish that persists to this day about the Frankenstein family, Victor Frankenstein is a man of good character. There is, without a doubt, more than meets the eye here."

Borge leaned in. "Kendra, I know what you think you saw, but how can you be sure this is actually your friend, and not just a case of someone looking remarkably like her, scar and all?"

She stood and reached into the bag slung over her shoulder, tossing the head at Borge. "Check this for an ID," she said through gritted teeth. "Lynda won't need it anymore."

Borge had caught the head reflexively and quickly dropped it on the table when he saw what it was. He let out an exasperated sigh. "Why are people always throwing disembodied appendages at me?"

"Commander," she said. "My family has known you for a long time and I trust you like I trusted my father. However, trust in others can often be misplaced. For example, I still don't trust your judgment of secret agent wolf-man, here. And until I say otherwise, Frankenstein—and his organization—is number one on my list."

Kendra stormed to the exit and punched the sensor, opening the sliding doors. "I'm going after whoever is behind this."

She paused in the doorway. "Keep your pet on a leash," she said, glaring at West, "and out of my way, or next time you'll be picking silver bullets out of him."

As the doors slid shut, she added, "Thanks for the drink."

A baffled West stopped to think about his new acquaintance. He was at a loss. "What a delight," he said. "No wonder Cedric drank so much."

"She can actually be quite charming when she wants to be," Borge replied. "Tonight was not one of those times."

Commander 7 agreed. "Kendra is the only daughter from Cedric's brief fourth marriage. They had grown closer only in recent years. With his death last autumn and her belief that her dead friend was somehow resurrected by Frankentech… well, she has been through a lot, and quite frankly, I'm worried about her."

"Sir," West replied. "I think whoever gets in her way should be worried."

What a night. The strange fight with a giant henchman and an electrically charged stitched-together woman possibly made of dead body parts would normally be enough to qualify as one of "those" nights.

Then he finally meets the daughter of his long-time spy friend, Sir Cedric Kenton, and their introduction begins with her immediately threatening to kill him. He knew Cedric had children from the aforementioned multiple marriages, but Cedric had largely kept his personal life private—at least as much as a publicly known aristocrat could.

He found her infuriating. He also found her intriguing. And with that, he found himself anticipating their next meeting, of which he was certain there would be one. For now, there was still the matter of her visit.

West walked to the heavy security doors that acted as a protective barrier between the lab and the hidden entrance in the mausoleum above. "Borge… Cedric's daughter or not, don't you think we should change the access codes so she can't just waltz in whenever she pleases?"

Borge looked up and grinned. "Val, we could change the codes every day and she could still waltz in whenever she liked. Security measures wouldn't stop someone like her. Wouldn't stop you either."

West thought about it for a moment and could only shrug in agreement. It was true. "Aside from receiving an education in spycraft from Cedric, what's the rest of her story? Professionally, I mean."

Commander 7 answered. "Lady Kenton, despite her noble heritage and status as a member of the Kenton family, is what you would call an 'adventuress.' She is a freelance operative now but has trained and worked with the best throughout the world. International Command wanted to bring her in, but she has never pledged her allegiance to anyone except her own cause."

The commander paused before continuing. "That's not entirely fair. She has helped many people all over the globe for her own reasons. And while she was formerly—and occasionally still—a high-level thief, she typically steals only from, as she likes to put it, 'those who deserve it.' And right now, with more on her mind than just theft, I don't think Baron Victor Frankenstein deserves what she intends to bring him."

"Sir," West said. "This man, Ossie Weiner—in the briefing files, you mentioned he was working on a top secret government project, but you didn't say what. Is there any reason to suspect Frankentech's involvement, along with HIVE?"

It was a fair question. Commander 7 had told him all he needed to know so far, but now, at a dead end, more disclosure was needed. As a growing secret global terror organization, the true extent of HIVE's infiltration into the international business world was unknown. West explained his run-ins with the HIVE agents who were tailing him.

"HIVE—yes. Frankentech... possibly, but perhaps not directly. That's what I want you to find out. Weiner was working on the Quantum Collider project. With its potential ability to manipulate neutrons, photons, electrons, and protons, the implications of this device are world changing... or world-threatening, depending on its use. He was the only physicist able to work out the equations needed to make it operational. Although there were other complications with the required hardware, for security purposes, he was the only one with knowledge of its construction."

Commander 7 continued. "I don't believe Kendra is entirely incorrect in her line of thinking. Someone within Frankentech is working with HIVE, but I don't believe it is Victor Frankenstein. It could be Zelensky, but before pursuing someone that connected, you better damn well have something solid, not just a woman's intuition."

"Or a woman's scorn," West added.

"Indeed. Italian intelligence has a contact inside Frankentech. I have associates in the Italian AISE, and I have been receiving reports with bits and pieces of information. Borge will get you a file so you can catch up while you're on your way."

"On my way, sir?"

"Yes. Tomorrow night is the annual Frankenball in Geneva. Victor sent me an invitation, as he does each year, even though I am unable to attend. I have already RSVP'd with you attending on my behalf. I thought it best for you to meet the baron… socially.

"And know—it will be difficult to connect HIVE or any other operatives to anyone right now. Geneva is crawling with spies like it's Tangier in 1964. Most likely, if HIVE has any involvement with Frankentech, this business is being conducted elsewhere. Hopefully, you can sniff out a lead."

With that, Commander 7 tuned out, and the speaker and monitor powered down.

West sat in silence, deep in thought. He was interrupted when Dr. Borge plopped a box down on the table in front of him.

"Before you leave, I do have some new items for you. May I have your belt, please?"

He removed the wolfskin belt and placed it on the table, its gold wolf's head faceplate glistening under the work lights while Borge ran a scanner over it. As it made a range of 'bleeping' and 'blooping' noises, West wondered what this was all about.

"Excellent!" Borge said. He continued to examine the belt. This continued for several minutes. West grew irritated.

"Borge," he said, doing his best to remain patient, "are you going to explain what is so 'excellent' or am I to be left in eternal suspense?"

"Oh, yes, my apologies." Borge began explaining excitedly, his Dutch accent growing thicker the faster he spoke. "I have been working with a tissue sample from the belt. Quite curious it is, and I can only deduce that it employs some sort of interdimensional hypersonic transmutation. You understand that this works in conjunction with a type of internal algorithmic semi-sentience to…"

West gave him a blank stare.

"Meaning… it works much like the biometrics used on a fingerprint encoded gun you know, like the type you've had that only responds to your fingerprint scan?"

"Yes," West responded dryly. "Or like, say, an iPhone?"

"A crude example, but yes. Using the sample, I was able to bioengineer the wolfskin belt's biometric system to match with your DNA. Should one of your many enemies get hold of it, they won't be able to wear it and use it against you."

West gave him a smile of approval. "Very nice work, doctor. Once we got past the language barrier, I see what you did, and that is a tremendous development."

"And that's not all—if you have a couple of minutes, let me show you a few more things."

Three hours later, West left for his new flat near Regent's Park to get some much-needed rest. Instead of sleeping, he lay in bed, reflecting on what had transpired, one thought dominating the others: the entrancing Lady Kendra Kenton, the hot-tempered spitfire who had threatened to kill him and knew how to go about doing it.

She was going to be a problem… a trifling bitch.

Whether he wanted to admit it or not, he was also tremendously turned on.

3: FRANKENBALL

Spring's arrival in Geneva's Old Town is marked by a tree along the Promenade de la Treille whose first bud makes it official. For the elites, it is officially marked by the annual Frankenball, this year being held at Switzerland's most famous castle, the twelfth-century Château de Chillon on the shores of Lake Geneva.

The driver sent by Commander 7 pulled the limousine up to the lavishly decorated entrance. Val West stepped out into the warm springtime air, tinged by the cool mist coming off the lake. The setting sun gave the water a soothing golden glow, and West found it hard to imagine trouble could ever break its serenity. But he knew better. The hardened cynic in him knew that usually, the greater the beauty, the uglier the secrets.

He paused to take in the view of the towering Alps glowering over the lake, still holding the shadows of winter in their snow-capped peaks. After tipping the valet, he walked up to the entrance of the beautiful yet imposing medieval fortress. He hoped to glean some information about Victor Frankenstein, his right-hand man Igor Zelensky, and if there was any connection between Frankentech and HIVE.

Frankentech had come a long way in both reputation and corporate mission since its founding in the early 1950s by Baron Hans Frankenstein, the father of the current baron, Victor III. There were many rumors about the family's interests and allegiances during World War II, and whispers of what Baron Victor Frankenstein I had created in his laboratory decades before. Dark stories had circulated all across Europe from Geneva to Karlstadt, Visaria to Transylvania, and all points in between.

However, Frankentech was another matter. Under Baron Victor III's leadership, it had evolved from a chemical and pharmaceutical conglomerate involved in controversial bio-weaponry and arms manufacturing to a highly respected biotech manufacturer. Among their interests was a dedication to solving world hunger problems through genetically modified agricultural products. Still, it was not without its detractors, with the term *Frankenfoods* often being used to criticize these efforts.

Despite this, Victor Frankenstein sought to prove his intentions with his actions and created one of the world's largest charitable organizations, the Frankenstein Foundation. Now in his fifties, Victor had successfully rehabilitated the family name, rebranding it away from its top-of-mind association with monstrous experiments and what he dismissed as "old folk tales" and "rumors and innuendo."

West had been briefed on all of this and while he trusted Commander 7's judgement of Victor Frankenstein's character, he still needed to make his own assessment. Igor Zelensky, however, did not have the same type of voucher for his character, or, as some would say, lack thereof. Zelensky was known for his unwavering loyalty to the Frankenstein family, dating back to his early days working for Hans Frankenstein. Most organizations have a hatchet-man, and Igor Zelensky was Frankentech's. Cold, ruthless, and efficient, Zelensky made the tough, sometimes unpopular decisions that had built Frankentech into a global business empire.

Now West would have a chance to meet them both. For such a successful and renowned organization, it seemed unnecessary to involve itself with HIVE. Yet, West knew that the unquenchable thirst for power was addicting. He had seen it corrupt men of once good standing before, and he was certain he would see it rear its ugly head again.

Inside the entrance threshold, West paused to read the room, by both sight and scent. While standing in the archway, he knew he was also being checked out. He was glad it was of the mostly female variety, although there certainly would be more nefarious types interested in his movements.

For such a grand occasion, he was clad in a white tuxedo jacket with satin-striped black tuxedo trousers and a black cummerbund—which also doubled nicely as a cover for the wolfskin belt underneath.

The interior of the medieval castle was decorated extravagantly for the event, festooned with large golden sculptures of mythological characters. Atlas, Gaia, Prometheus, Uranus, and other Greek Titans towered over the throngs of the glamorous, along with illuminated champagne fountains, diamond-encrusted chandeliers and other glitzy items which were impressive, but in West's opinion, also of dubious taste.

He took his time observing the ballroom while sipping the excellent Moët & Chandon Imperial Vintage '46 served by the wait staff. This was not the kind of gala that skimped on its champagne. So far, he had noticed nothing out of the ordinary. The standard array of security cameras mounted high above monitored the proceedings, with any other security measures being undetectable.

What wasn't undetectable was his contact. Dressed in a tuxedo that might have last been worn to a 1979 high school prom, this middle-aged, mustachioed man was the contact he was here to meet: Gino Primavera of the AISE.*

West watched him fumbling about, trying to toss a few crumpled Swiss francs on the waiter's serving tray. Amused by the faux pas, he strolled over and stood next to him. "Mr. Primavera, I presume?"

---

*Agenzia Informazioni e Sicurezza Esterna– Italy's foreign intelligence agency-- *Editor.*

Primavera froze like a deer in headlights. "The weather in Zurich is…"

West cut him off mid-sentence.

"Yes. 'Quite atrocious, but Geneva is having an early spring.'" Primavera began to perspire. "I'm Val West."

"But… but the *code phrase*."

"I think we're past that point." West stuck his hand out to the still-aghast Primavera. As if recovering from a daze, the portly Italian slowly shook West's hand.

"Gino Primavera." He took his hand back, pulled out a soiled handkerchief, and mopped the anxious sweat off his clammy forehead. "Forgive me, Mr. West. It's just… we have protocols. In fact, I'm here undercover, here to blend in with the rest of the flossy-flossy glamoratti."

"Yes, I do apologize if I compromised your cover."

Primavera's attempts to play at this level were laughable, but West immediately liked him, and being mindful of his own snobbery, he made sure to put Primavera at ease for both of their sakes. He already looked ridiculously suspicious and, by acting so nervous, was likely to create a sense of nervousness in others—people who were already likely paranoid due to their less-than-legal professions.

"Listen," West said, patting him on the shoulder. "Let's call an audible. You are… Antonio… Antonio Margheriti, from the Italian Press Corps, here to cover the charitable contributions of the Frankenball."

Primavera thought for a moment, stroking his thick black mustache. "Yes… yes, I do like that. That is molto bene… uh, how you say, 'quite good.' You may not believe this, but I don't get out into the field much. With this assignment, I said, 'Gino. You sit at the office too long. You grow into a soft, fat, doughy bitch. Time to get back out and show the younger generation—like you—how this business is done.'"

"Tremendous. Now, let's—" West's attention was stopped in its tracks by a scent he wanted a better sniff of. Walking across the ballroom floor was a tall, dark-haired woman in a crème-colored evening dress bedazzled with glittering sparkles. She certainly bedazzled West. Needless to say, he thought she was quite a lovely creature. So much for work, but he would be happy to investigate her thoroughly for any useful information. Primavera may be the official contact, but as far as West was concerned, he was on his own. Gino meant well, but stood out worse than a handful of sore left thumbs.

"Mr. West, this…"

"Hold that thought, Gino… uh, Antonio. Duty calls."

West crossed the room to introduce himself. Along the way, he picked two fresh glasses of champagne from the roving waiter's tray and swirled around to meet her gaze.

"Good evening, Miss—"

Before she could answer, or accept the offered glass of champagne, a stern Slavic-accented voice came between them.

"Excuse me, are you supposed to be here?"

West turned to face the speaker. He was a man in his early sixties, with gray-white hair creeping up on the still-brown hair on top of his head, combed in a dignified side part. The face was long, with hard lines defining it and a hawk-like nose that gave him the appearance of being perpetually grouchy. Perhaps he was.

West knew the face from the file photo. *Pleased to meet you, Mr. Igor Zelensky.*

"I say," Igor continued. "How did you and your so-curiously dressed friend manage to get in here? This is the Frankenball, you know."

Another voice broke in. "By my invitation."

West, the woman, and Igor Zelensky stopped and looked toward the speaker. Baron Victor Frankenstein III descended the nearby staircase and walked toward them.

Dressed resplendently in elegant formal evening wear, the baron also wore a big smile on his handsome face, the clear blue eyes only somewhat hidden behind his tinted aviator eyeglasses. His slicked-back blonde hair betrayed a small scar along the top of his forehead, the usual telltale sign of some cosmetic work. Nonetheless, his friendly aura was quite welcome, and the tall, broad-shouldered Frankenstein offered a warm handshake to West.

"Victor Frankenstein," he said, as if an introduction was needed, especially at a party called the Frankenball. "Our mutual friend, the Commander, rang me that you would be attending on his behalf."

He turned toward Igor. "My apologies for not letting you know about the arrangement."

Igor nodded.

"Mr. West, I hope you are finding the Frankenball enjoyable. It is Frankentech—and the Frankenstein Foundation's—premier event of the season. After a long Swiss winter, it really is the only way to usher in spring."

West found his host a bit difficult to read. He was polite and charming, with his educated European-accented voice, but also had a slightly eccentric delivery common to exceptionally intelligent people. Geniuses. If that label could be applied accurately, Victor Frankenstein certainly qualified.

"I am very much enjoying the evening so far," West said. "Mr. Zelensky—now that we've been introduced, I do hope we can have a drink together at some point this evening."

"I would be delighted," Igor said, sounding anything but delighted. He excused himself with a polite bow and disappeared into the crowd of partygoers.

Frankenstein gestured toward the radiant woman West had been so keen on meeting. "Mr. West, allow me to introduce you to my publicist and personal assistant, Miss Volta Elettrica."

She offered her hand, and West took it in his, brushing his lips against it in a courteous kiss.

"I'm sure the two of you will have a chance to connect throughout the evening. For now, Miss Elettrica, I want to borrow Mr. West."

The two men excused themselves and walked down a marble-floored hallway leading to a winding stone staircase.

"This is quite an extraordinary place," West remarked. "It is, of course, quite historic, but until now I've never had the pleasure of visiting it. It's a wonderful place to be able to get for the Frankenball."

They walked into a darkened area. "Thanks," Frankenstein said, unlocking a large wooden door. "I just bought it."

"I assumed it was owned by the State, as a cultural landmark. I didn't even know it was for sale."

"Everything, Mr. West," Frankenstein said with a smile, "is for sale." They entered a large, luxuriously furnished office. Frankenstein gestured to West to take a seat in front of an absurdly huge oak desk. Frankenstein sat down in his office chair and continued. "That also means that something is for sale in my organization, something I may not want to be selling to a certain party. Is that right, and the reason you are here, Mr. West? I knew the Commander wouldn't be attending, but he usually doesn't send a top agent in his place."

"Quite right, Lord Frankenstein." West paused. Commander 7 had told him of Victor Frankenstein's discomfort and aversion to being addressed as a baron and the terms, such as "Lord," which came with it. He much preferred to be called Victor, though so far, he had made no correction.

However, he had just met the man, and was here on official business. "The Commander has some concerns based on information received from intelligence sources that Frankentech, and you by extension, may be of interest to the group called HIVE. Are you familiar with them?"

Frankenstein grimaced. "By name, yes. By implication with them, no."

"Please don't misunderstand me, sir. I'm not suggesting you are working with HIVE, but that they may have designs on you and your organization. They may have already infiltrated."

"That is quite impossible. We have a very strict vetting of all company officials."

"Does that include Igor Zelensky?"

Frankenstein grew concerned. "My God, you can't be serious. Igor has been a loyal and dedicated part of this organization for decades. He is practically part of the family. I would trust him with my life."

The air was thick with discomfort, and West found himself fidgeting. Frankenstein rose from the desk and paced the room. He stopped at a window covered by blinds and opened them, revealing a two-way mirror overlooking the ballroom below. "Mr. West. Besides these assuredly baseless accusations made of Igor Zelensky, I—"

He turned to West and looked him in the eyes. "It's just that it's taken a long time to restore honor and integrity to the Frankenstein name after being so unfairly smeared for so many years, the very name itself being synonymous with being some kind of a… monster. Igor may come across as unfriendly, but it is a social awkwardness and should not be taken personally. I sincerely hope you are wrong, as something like this, should it get out, could be very damaging to Frankentech, as well as my foundation's efforts."

West thought he should soften the implication. He was losing Frankenstein and needed to ensure his continued cooperation. "With the way this HIVE organization operates, it is possible that Igor is unwittingly involved." He decided to shift the subject. "This came up due to the death of Professor Ossie Weiner. Are you familiar with him?"

Frankenstein paused to think. "No… no, I can't say I have heard of him. Should I have?"

"Perhaps. But more importantly, Igor was seen with the same woman Weiner left with at a recent party in London."

"Well… he is not entirely unsocial. I'm sure a man like you can understand that."

"Yes," West agreed. Frankenstein did have a point. Perhaps there was no connection here at all, despite Kendra's insistence. There was nothing at this time to suggest further investigation of Igor, except one thing: a nagging gut feeling. Probably the same scientific method Kendra was employing. West stood up, extending a hand to Frankenstein. "Baron, thank you very much for your time."

Frankenstein graciously accepted the handshake with a warm smile. "You are welcome. Please keep me apprised of any developments and if there is anything I can do, please don't hesitate to ask." West nodded and, with a polite bow, walked toward the office door.

"And Mr. West—"

West stopped and turned back. "Yes, sir?"

"Please. Call me Victor."

...

In the ballroom, Gino Primavera was arguing with security that he was on the guest list and was indeed the society columnist for Il Mattino ("*the* most read Neapolitan newspaper"). West was descending the staircase in time to see Primavera being escorted out. He sped up his pace with the idea of intervening when he bumped into Volta Elettrica.

"Mr. West." She spoke in a sensual Italian-accented purr. "I hope you're not leaving so soon."

"I wouldn't dream of it."

West took another look, up and down, of the voluptuous Miss Elettrica, treating his eyes to her long, swept up black hair, the wintry blue eyes, and the oval, wonderfully angular angelic face.

She wore a green ribbon choker necklace adorned with a sparkling heart-shaped diamond pendant, which matched the sparkling gown worn over her svelte and shapely figure—at least being worn for the moment.

West had some thoughts about that for later in the evening.

She made a fanning motion which (as if he needed encouragement) led his eyes from her hand to her also-shapely breasts. "It is getting hot in here... and a bit too stuffy. Care to join me out on the balcony?"

"That sounds like a tremendous idea," West smiled agreeably. "I'm glad I thought of it." Taking her by the hand, he led her out onto the stone balcony. The chateau itself was a man-made peninsula, jutting out over the waters of Lake Geneva.

From the balcony, the colorful lights of the city danced on the surface of the lake. Framed by the white outline of the mountains glowing in the moonlight, the view was nothing less than magnificent. And even though West had—or at least told himself so—full control over his lycanthropy, the power of the growing moon and the scent of Volta was bringing out his inner beast.

She gazed out over the lake, taking in the picturesque scene. "It is a wonderful view, yes?"

"Yes, it's great," West replied with disinterest. He moved closer, bringing his arm toward her back to bring her nearer.

"Geneva is having an early spring…"

"Yes, it is." West pulled her toward him. "Wait, what?"

She stared at him in silence. He didn't know what to say. Actually, he did.

"The weather in Zurich is quite atrocious?"

Her pleasant, expectant expression melted into a frown. "Is that a question or a statement, Agent West?"

"It was, uh, a statement. But I thought…"

"…Gino was your contact? He is, at least for your commander. He is my superior officer in the AISE and tonight he came here as a diversion. There have been rumors swirling that there is an AISE agent inside of Frankentech. Gino came here tonight to be shown the door and let them think they found who they were looking for."

"Well, well. I have to say I very much look forward to working more closely with you."

"Down, boy," she said, her demeanor becoming cold and professional. "Our contact is to be limited. I'll tell you what I know now, but then it's back to my cover, which doesn't include you... unfortunately," she added with a sly smile.

West did the mental equivalent of dumping an entire ice chest down his pants and regained his focus. "Right. Give me what you got."

"Mostly it's what I would term as 'irregularities.' There have been some strangers involved in Frankentech business as of late."

"HIVE."

"Yes, I think it is, but can't confirm."

"I think it's possible Igor Zelensky and HIVE are in league. I think there's some plot to oust Victor Frankenstein from Frankentech. How that is to be accomplished, I don't know. Killing him, of course, could be an option. In the report Commander 7 received, an island was mentioned. What else can you tell me about it?"

Volta thought for a moment. "There is a secret Frankentech lab in the Orkney Islands. I don't have the exact location."

"That's something, at least. Whatever they are doing on the island could hold the key to how HIVE is involved, and the reason for killing Ossie Weiner."

West stopped Volta from speaking. Anyone else would have heard only the gentle lapping of water and the soft rustling of the breeze through the treetops. However, he detected the sound of scattering pebbles falling from a cluster of rocks along the bank near the chateau. This noise came from a tiny amount of loose gravel—almost dust—tumbling from a footfall moving between rocks. He focused his eyes and saw the faintest outline of a shadow slipping along the rocky shore.

His heightened scenting abilities caught the faintest whiff of something, but then it was gone—carried away by the cool lake breeze. It had been too quick to place. Still, someone was out there... watching, or perhaps listening, from below.

West decided this was their exit cue, and he and Volta made their way back into the party and went their separate ways for the rest of the evening.

"*Whatever they are doing on the island could hold the key to how HIVE is involved, and the reason for killing Ossie Weiner.*"

The audio of West and Volta's conversation was played again on a tape machine.

The recording was then stopped and contemplated by a figure in the shadows, watching the partygoers on a video monitor from a darkened office.

4: NOBODY CALLS IT "THE ORKNEYS"

"No, no, a thousand times no! Listen, West, this is still untested. You can't take it."

Dr. Borge was incensed. A lot of difficult and meticulous work had gone into the new ThunderBird vehicle and even though it was meant for West's use on assignments, he would be damned if it was going out before it was perfected.

"Borge, the only true test is in the field. You know that." West very well remembered his first experiences as a partially bionic werewolf secret agent, with Borge controlling him like he was a real-life video game character.

Borge knew this was true as well, and though he felt defeated, he had to agree with West.

Reluctantly.

"Besides," West added, "you can't just keep working on it forever. We'll work out the bugs as we go."

Throwing his hands up in the air, Borge led West into the large underground cavern which served as a testing lab and hangar for the ThunderBird. He powered on the lights, giving West his first glimpse of the new and improved vehicle. It resembled the ThunderBird he remembered and had used on his previous assignment. A two-seat microjet no larger than a mid-sized sedan, its sleek black finish was augmented by bird-like design flourishes meant to suggest it could be the Thunderbird of legend—the giant, supernatural bird described by the American Indians.

"Before you go jetting off to the Orkney Islands, let me give you a briefing on the new ThunderBird." Borge walked around the vehicle, with a control module in hand. "Once only a supersonic speed microjet, the ThunderBird 2.0 is much more."

He activated the controls, and the ThunderBird began moving, its parts changing their shape. "As you can see, you are no longer the only shapeshifter here. The ThunderBird now shape-shifts from microjet to car…" He clicked the controller again and it quickly drew in its wheels and the parts seemed to melt and reform. "…to a watercraft," he continued. "It uses subatomic molecular photons—you know, the type that bunch together in clumps."

West nodded like he understood. He did not.

Borge broke it down in what he thought may be more relatable terms. "The properties of these identical particles can be changed depending on the order in which they are arranged. Just like how the molecular arrangement that makes up your appearance shifts its shape when you turn into a werewolf."

He activated the controls again, shifting the ThunderBird back into automobile form.

"This is quite incredible, Borge. If I wasn't seeing it happen in front of me, I really wouldn't believe it. When it's shifted into a car, what type is it modeled after? It looks familiar."

Borge beamed at the question. "Yes, I'm glad you asked. If you know your cars like I know my cars, you can see I have programmed the particles to arrange themselves and lock into the design of a 1955 Ford Thunderbird of the hot rod variety." He ran his hand along the sleek, rounded tail fins up to the large scoop sticking up through the hood. "You no doubt notice this monstrous hood scoop. But it's what's under the hood that really counts. '55 T-Birds normally came with a 292 Y-block V8. This one is designed with a 409." He popped up the hood and showed off the gleaming chromed engine. "And not just any 409… a four-speed dual-quad, positraction 409."

"She's real fine," West said, looking the vehicle up and down. "And being that it's not actually a vintage classic car, it won't be so catastrophic when some enemy eventually shoots it full of holes or blows it up or it gets sent off a cliff."

Borge cringed at the thought. "Luckily for you, the photons can be reprogrammed, albeit with much painstaking work. Unluckily for you, we are going to spend the next few hours training you on the ins and outs of how to use it as a car, a plane and as both submersible and non-submersible boat, so buckle up."

West let out a groan, then went off to do his duty learning under the tutelage of Dr. Borge.

Hours later, West was piloting the Thunderbird over the North Sea. Located roughly ten miles off the northeastern coast of Scotland, the Orkney Islands are composed of seventy small islands, with only twenty of them inhabited. The month of March is always said to either come in like a lion or a lamb. It was now late April and weather-wise, the Orkney Islands could still be both lamb and lion on any given day. The locals would say any given hour.

The weather on this day couldn't have been any more idyllic and lamb-like as West skimmed across the mirrored surface of the Bay of Kirkwall. He transitioned the ThunderBird from aircraft to seacraft and boated in toward the shoreline of Mainland, which is, just as it sounds, Orkney's main island, with plans to head on to its largest town and *de facto* capital, Kirkwall.

With seemingly no one around, he took a chance and shifted the ThunderBird to automobile mode when he reached the concrete boat launch ramp on the shore of Kirkwall Harbour. The sleek black vehicle prowled the still-quiet streets, beads of water glistening off it in the first rays of the morning sun. Even though the design was that of a '55 T-Bird with a monstrous engine, Borge did have the sense to at least give it a silent running mode and West employed this feature while driving during these early hours.

Looking for his first destination—finding breakfast—he cruised past block after block of charming old sea-village buildings until stopping at a little seaside restaurant called Clark's Landing. It was a bit unusual for a '55 T-Bird to be on the mainland, and the early-risers gawked as West pulled into the small parking lot.

Minutes later, he was sipping the local coffee and awaiting a traditional breakfast of hen eggs, smoked haddock with sheep scrotum, and black pudding. He had been expectedly eyed-up by the regular patrons from the moment he strolled in. Despite this, he still felt he was being watched in a different manner.

It was a sort-of sixth sense he noticed he had developed since becoming a werewolf, not exactly something he could pin down. It was more of a heightened gut feeling, or perhaps the instincts animals possessed that he could now access.

A frumpy-but-friendly-waitress brought his breakfast. He found Orcadian cuisine to be to his liking. At least, he thought he did. The truth was, he was so hungry he could have eaten Orcadian roadkill, and when he was LoneWolf, this would not necessarily be out of the question.

Who was he when he was LoneWolf, anyway? This question had vexed him since he had become able to maintain consciousness while in werewolf form through the use of the wolfskin belt. He was certainly more aggressive, and, as expected, more animalistic. But *he* was different somehow. Was it even really him?

West still dwelled on these thoughts upon exiting the restaurant. He walked along the sidewalks, the bright warm morning sun making it a pleasant start to the day in Kirkwall. West was where he was supposed to be, but did not know his next move. Commander 7's contact would send a meeting location, but he was yet to receive it.

The sidewalk brought him to the town square where people were now milling about. He thought the block he was walking down had a lovely scent—early spring flowers blooming, perhaps? No, it was stronger. A flower of a different sort.

His senses began to pulse. It was a garden… a lady garden. He felt a sensation as a woman brushed against him while passing by. There it was: scent pinpointed.

"Good morning," West said, with a politely insincere smile, "Lady Kenton."

The woman stopped and turned back to him, confirming her identity. He held out his hand. She turned up her nose.

"Oh, if it isn't Mr. West… what brings you to the Orkneys?"

"You mean *Orkney* or the *Orkney Islands*. Nobody calls it 'the Orkneys.' Number one mistake tourists make that annoys the locals—the *Orcadians*, as I'm sure you know. And I was just about to ask you the same thing. Crazy coincidence, just bumping into each other like this. Perhaps we should consider bumping into each other more often, in a different manner?"

She hated his know-it-all quips. She hated it even more that she thought about him enough to hate him.

"You might like that too much, so no. Did you enjoy Frankenstein's balls?"

"It was just the one ball, thank you. And I would also ask you the same. After all, you were there, albeit just skulking about, uninvited."

She was surprised he had noticed her there. It must be a guess. How could he possibly know?

"Oh, you're probably wondering right now how I could possibly know?"

She hated him even more now.

"Well, my dear, it's not just my keen eyesight." He pointed at his nostrils and inhaled some more of her scent. He could smell her temperature, and her temper, rising. "The nose, knows. The night we first met, you were certainly wearing too much perfume. But even under all that, I was able to pick up your natural scent—much more pleasant, I might add. The same scent of the lurker outside the Chateau de Chillon."

"So, I was there. It's called 'gathering intelligence.' Something you always seem to be short on."

"Am I? In that case, thank you for confirming it was you. It was just a guess on my part. With the wind coming off the glorious view of Lake Geneva, I hadn't caught enough scent to be sure. Also, you should watch your step with loose sand."

Kendra was annoyed. "What a delight this is. I mean, being here, not being with you."

"If you don't mind, please enlighten me on how exactly I'm supposed to 'stay the hell out of your way' when you keep coming to me?"

"I'm not," she lied. "Although with such charm," she said while stifling a yawn, "how could I ever resist? But now that you're here, and I know I can't trust you, I'm going to have to stay close by to keep an eye on you."

West was annoyed. "I was hoping you'd say that," he lied. "But now that *you're* here, maybe we should—"

The funereal tones of *Toccata and Fugue in D Minor* interrupted their conversation. The sound came from West's wristwatch. Borge was calling over the encrypted frequency. West entered the decoding sequence. This used to be easier before the encrypted secret intelligence frequency, Channel D, was repurposed as the frequency now used for everyday cellular phones. After going through all the steps, he opened the antenna and turned away from Kendra, holding his wrist toward his ear.

"West," the tinny-sounding voice of Borge called out, "I have a location for you. Sorry it's late, but the Commander just received it from our contact in the Orkneys."

"Yes," West replied, attempting to muffle his voice with his other hand. Before he continued, he felt Kendra creeping closer over his shoulder.

"Dr. Borge," she interjected. "Nobody calls it 'the Orkneys.'"

West shot her a glare and moved a few steps away. "Now, Borge, about—"

"Is that Lady Kenton with you?"

"Yes, now about the location—"

"Kendra!" Borge raised his voice for her to hear him more clearly through the watch speaker. "So wonderful that you're there with West."

"Actually," West said through his teeth, "It's not wonderful. Now, if you please, where is the contact meeting location?" He gave up on trying to conceal the information and moved his wrist closer to her so they could both hear. She flashed him a glare paired with a smirk and leaned in.

"Oh, yes, yes, of course. You are to meet at the ruins of Bishop's & Earl's Palaces, on Watergate. Twenty minutes from now. Climb to the top of the round tower."

"Is that all, then?"

"That's all for now. And Kendra, please—"

West cut off the communication. Kendra glared at him.

"You can get your own watch if you want to talk to Borge."

"I have one. My father's, remember? You know, the one he was still wearing when he was mauled to death by a werewolf?"

"And we were just starting to get along so well. Anyway, you heard the man. I wouldn't even dream of trying to have this meeting without you, but at least try to keep the hell out of the way."

He thought maybe she smiled, but it may have been a wince of pain. It was hard to tell with her.

The ruins of the twelfth-century Bishop's & Earl's Palaces were on Watergate Street to the south, in the shadow of the towering nine-hundred-year-old St. Magnus Cathedral. West and Kendra entered through the gate as tourists, although they seemed to be the only ones so far this morning.

As they walked in silence through the open-air remnants of the medieval castle, the only sound came from the echoes of their footsteps falling on the ancient stones. They stopped at a placard on a stand for directions to the round tower.

Kendra started to speak. West put up his hand to stop her.

After they had stopped, he noticed there had been one extra footfall coming from a short distance behind them. Kendra nodded that she understood. He signaled her with his eyes to follow, and they quickly moved ahead through an archway, ducking around a corner. They then flattened against a wall and waited.

A few seconds later, the source of the following footsteps drew nearer, coming to a stop at the archway. A few more seconds elapsed, and West realized they were in a following standoff. He decided to bite, noting he hadn't been attacked yet today, so he might as well get things underway.

West motioned to Kendra to stay against the wall and moved back along the edge of the archway. He spun out from the wall, ready for a fight.

"Ah-ha!" a voice called out. Gino Primavera leaped out in front of him. He laughed and pointed at his head. "Desk job… ha! I still got it, and you, my friend, maybe never *had* it!"

He slapped West on the back and entered the archway. Upon seeing Kendra, he fawned over her, and even she was not immune to his gregarious charm.

"Nice to see you again, Gino," said West. "And choosing Watergate as a meeting location—quite appropriate for a meeting about a conspiracy."

"Conspiracy, sì, but what do you mean about the Watergate?"

West thought perhaps it was a language barrier issue. "Surely you know the story of Watergate, when—"

"Oh yes, Watergate! I love the Kevin Costner... with the gills to breathe, drinking his own piss... splendido!" Primavera touched his fingers to lips in a "chef's kiss" gesture. "I do not see what expensive picture about flooded Earth has to do with this, however. Do you think there is maybe HIVE plot to melt the polar ice caps or something?"

West bit his tongue as best he could and decided against explaining the not-so-subtle differences between the Watergate scandal and the film, *Waterworld*. "Listen, Gino. Let's move on. I think you're a likeable fellow and I don't want to change that. Now, what do you have about the case we're actually working on?"

"Sei fuori! I don't like this so much. It makes me wish maybe I had stayed at my desk job, capito? Anyway, something seems rotten here. I do not like. I talk to contact here and he tells me of body found, drowned but partially eaten. Body of CIA man, it turns out, not tourist here to fish, capisce? So, I go and see old fisherman who catch the body in his net. Fergus Sweyn. Up in Twa—"

Primavera stopped, his eyes opening wide, and his throat stiffened.

"Twaaaaaat."

He forced the word out with a gurgle before falling backwards.

West dove onto Kendra, pushing them both out of sight below the wall's edge. Before she had time to complain about him being on top of her, he rolled to the side and up onto his haunches. Crouching low, West looked through a crack in the stonework and caught sight of a fleeing figure.

"Stay with him," he shouted as he leaped over the ledge in pursuit.

The streets of Kirkwall were getting crowded. West strained to track the faint scent left by the assassin before it was lost in the sea of other smells. It seemed to be just one person. At first glance, it had looked like Primavera had choked or maybe suffered a heart attack. In the normal world, this would be the first suspicion. But the shadow world of espionage was not the normal world, and West had sensed an assassin's presence almost immediately. Now, to find the assassin.

With each step, the scent grew fainter. In the busy seaside streets, it faded almost completely, mixed in with the smells of food, perfumes, toilet water colognes, body odor and the mix other scents wafting from the rows of boats lining the harbor docks. West stopped, scanning the crowd, trying to lock onto the scent trail again.

There—near the concrete breakwall. His quarry. He couldn't see much, only a man in a dark suit.

The man ran into the dockside building of a shipping company. West followed, charging through the entrance, and found himself in a busy scene of dockworkers loading nets of fresh fish. His target was on the other side of a large suspended net. West skidded to a halt, feet slipping on the slimy, fish-oil-slicked floor—just in time to see the gun aimed in his direction.

The assassin fired, but not at West. The shot severed the rope above the net. In an instant, West was buried under a literal ton of fish.

Tremendous.

By the time he clawed his way out of the slippery mess, the man was long gone. Frustrated, West angrily tossed a cod aside and got to his feet, given a hand by a helpful local policeman ready to make his first arrest of the day.

When West finally made it back after telling an elaborate fish story of his own to the authorities, Kendra was still crouched over the fallen Gino Primavera.

"Anything?" she asked, as West hurried over.

"No," West replied, shaking his head. "Whoever it was, I lost them."

Kendra pursed her lips. She decided not to question him, but accepted that whoever it was, was a professional and skilled enough to evade someone with West's peculiar tracking abilities.

"I'm afraid we also lost Gino."

West leaned down and examined the purple-colored circle that had formed on Primavera's throat. He took a knife from his pocket, unfolding a pair of tiny tweezers from its blades, and carefully extracted a miniature lethal dart embedded in the throat. The tip was coated with a lethal dose of concentrated wasp venom. He had seen this before.

The dart was in the shape of a Yellow Jacket wasp—the mark of HIVE.

Kendra closed Gino Primavera's eyes and gently lowered his head to the ground.

"At least we have a name," Kendra said. "And then, 'Twatt.'"

"Yes, and I suspect that wasn't entirely meant for you."

Kendra shot West a withering look. "More likely he was referring to the Village of Twatt, about thirty miles from here. An atlas is your friend, you know, and—"

"Yes, tremendous. And I'm sure he meant both meanings."

She got to her feet, giving him a sharp elbow to the side on her way up.

What a delight, he thought, though now he wasn't sure if he meant it sarcastically or sincerely. The meaning seemed to be shifting.

But she was still more trouble than she was worth.

5: DEVIL OF THE SEA

The sea-lashed Orkney Islands can go from breathtaking beauty to completely *falbh gu clach* and other choice Scottish Gaelic terms very quickly. Val West and Lady Kendra Kenton learned this firsthand as they drove the ThunderBird toward the village of Twatt. The morning's bright sun had retreated behind blackened clouds, and a wicked wind whipped against the windows like an angry ghost.

Inside the vehicle, the atmosphere was equally chilly, with neither saying a word. Kendra spent the drive rebuffing West's attempts to make friendly conversation.

"The weather here seems to match your mood," West quipped. "Perhaps you both should consider therapy."

It was just as well, as it gave him time to mull over the situation. There certainly were strange things happening, and now Gino Primavera was dead. Someone knew they were coming and the only good thing about it was it meant he was on the right track.

Then there was the matter of Kendra. It was hard to believe she was the daughter of Sir Cedric Kenton. Sir Cedric had been the epitome of a perfect intelligence operative—one of the kindest and most cooperative people West had ever worked with. She must take after her mother, he thought.

Still, if he was stuck with her, he might as well try to make peace, though it seemed like a wasted effort. There was no denying that he found her intriguing, though. Her spitfire personality was frustratingly attractive, and all he wanted to do was take her over his knee and work on taming this wildcat. He found it more difficult than he expected to rein in his carnal thoughts and bring his focus back to the mission.

Nestled between the thighs of rolling farmland hills, the village of Twatt lay just ahead. The pleasant countryside was dotted with dozens of small farms, but the one they sought belonged to Fergus Sweyn—a rickety old stone house off Loons Road. West pulled into the rutted clay driveway, and the moment he stepped out, a shotgun blast rang out, kicking up dirt at his feet.

"You're not welcome here," a voice with a thick Scottish brogue called out from inside the open doorway.

"I did get that hint," West replied. "I'm just here to ask you a few questions, Mr. Sweyn."

"No more goddamn reporters, and definitely no more fookin' secret agents. Bugger off."

West held up one of the gold Krugerrands he always carried on missions. "I can make it worth your while."

"Awa' n bile yer heid," the voice shouted back.

West wasn't sure what this meant, but it sounded like another cue to "get lost." Kendra got out of the car and walked toward the house. "Kendra! Stay back." West didn't need this right now. Or maybe he did.

"Mr. Sweyn," she said in a soothing tone, "we don't mean to bother you, but if you could help us, it would be very much appreciated."

Fergus Sweyn stuck his head out the door. He was a thin man, in his seventies, with tufts of white hair curling up around the edges of his brimmed scally cap. His grumpy frown softened into a warm smile. "Well now, that's different," he said, his mood lifting at the attractive sight of Kendra. He lowered the shotgun and waved them inside.

"Okay, you just earned your keep for the day," West told her as they walked up the porch steps.

The teapot whistled away while Fergus Sweyn was launching into yet another fishing story when West finally managed to steer the conversation toward the issue at hand.

"I don't want to talk about that," Sweyn said with a puckered brow. "Ever since I fished that body out of the water, it's been nothing but trouble. And I tried to tell all of them it was the Nuckelavee, but they won't hear of it. Well… I've seen it! Now, I know you, and especially this pretty lady, don't believe in monsters, but I seen it. I do swear by *aal michty God*."

"Mr. Sweyn," West said, deciding to follow this line of conversation and hopefully get to something more useful, "you'd be surprised."

Sweyn scratched himself and considered West's response. "Yeah?"

Kendra looked at him with a warm smile. "I believe you."

"You do?"

"Yes," Kendra added, taking a sip of her tea. "Please tell us more—we've been dying to hear about it."

Fergus Sweyn smiled a toothy grin. "You sweet bonny lass! Well, now, that's more like it. So, you see, this body was partly eaten, but not by any fish or sea creatures you've ever heard of. It was the Nuckelavee. Sure, everyone here knows it's from what they say is just Orcadian myth, but I seen it with my own two eyes while out fishing. Aye, it's a right terrible creature. Nuckelavee is Orcadian for 'Devil of the Sea,' and it is that, without a doubt.

"And I sure as shite seen it, good and clear through the plitter, when I was out fishing out by Faray and got too close to old Rusk Holm. It has the head of a man, but with a lamprey's sucker for a face, and the man's torso is joined to a horse's body. The horse face has just one cyclops eye in its head, and the whole clatty creature is skinless, all its red muscles and sinews a-showin.' And it lets out a horrible screech, one to damn your ears straight to hell, where this beast comes from."

He took a swig from the whiskey bottle he kept alongside his cup of tea. "It ate all the damn sheep, and then it ate the American tourist. Maybe not a tourist, but some kind of American spy, they say. Or an idiot Canadian… I always get them mixed up."

West politely smiled at him, trying very hard not to be an idiot Canadian. "Where is this at?"

"Rusk Holm is a just a wee small island about two miles southwest of the Holm of Faray. It was the home to the 'Holmie Sheep'—that is, until the Nuckelavee ate them all. The place is haunted, without a shadow of a doubt. There is a prehistoric cairn on it—you know, an ancient tomb? I bet the Nuckelavee lives inside it, then comes out through the sea caves to eat the sheep. And now that they're all gone, it's been eating anything else that comes near."

West tossed a gold Krugerrand on the table and thanked Fergus Sweyn for his time. He now knew where their next stop would be.

With seventy islands, narrowing down a location was going to be tricky, but thanks to Primavera's work, they had found something worth pursuing. Regardless of which local legend—the Nuckelavee, sea devil or some other horror—was being used to scare off unwanted visitors, Rusk Holm was about to receive two unexpected guests.

...

"Seventy-five pounds. Same as the last test, I'm afraid." The lab assistant reluctantly gave the news to Baron Victor Frankenstein III, who listened in silence, offering no expression. After what seemed like minutes, he breathed heavily and looked up to compose his thoughts.

"How can this be?" Frankenstein stared through the glass window at the subject. His son, Franklin Frankenstein, was seated on the weight bench, once again being tested again for his bench press max.

A fifteen-year-old boy should be able to bench press at least a hundred-twenty pounds, but Franklin could barely lift an inadequate seventy-five and was showing no signs of improvement. With the intense regimen Frankenstein had put him on, he should be lifting five times that amount—ten, ideally.

Frankenstein stood up abruptly and walked down to the gymnasium. Here in his home, his castle, built beside the historic site of Castle Frankenstein in southern Hesse, Germany, he had constructed a fitness facility equipped with everything needed to develop into a physical specimen, including state-of-the art body monitoring systems and the best nutritional supplements.

It was fine that Franklin was concerned with his studies, but while he was excelling in academics, he was failing in his physical education. And that, to Victor Frankenstein, was unacceptable. He pushed open the gym doors as Franklin stood at attention. He didn't know what to say to the boy.

Franklin had seen his father coming and tried to prepare himself. He didn't know what to say to him. In fact, he wasn't sure about anything anymore. Ever since his father had sent for him to come to Germany, everything had felt off. He knew his parents were having problems. His mother, the Baroness Monique Van Seyton-Frankenstein, was still back home in New England. Were their issues with each other? Or with him?

He leaned toward his father being the cause, but like everything else these days, he wasn't sure. The only thing he was sure of was that things used to be good, and now things were anything but. His father had once taken an interest in him beyond just testing his physical abilities. He had been warm and caring. Now, Victor Frankenstein felt cold and distant. Franklin no longer felt like a son—he felt like just another experiment.

All he had to do was perform at the level his father expected and maybe things would get better. But he couldn't. He wouldn't.

Victor Frankenstein stared at his son with stern eyes and delivered the usual, "you'll have to do better—you're a Frankenstein" speech before dismissing him, then leaving again to return to his work.

Always his work. That was all that seemed to matter anymore. Everything else felt like an interruption.

Franklin thought maybe his father should have to do better.

...

The sea around the Orkney Islands has some of the world's strongest, fastest tides. Val West and Lady Kendra Kenton were learning this the hard way aboard the ThunderBird speedboat—or as West had taken to calling it in this form, the *ThunderBoat*.

The boat was tossed violently as it made its journey toward Faray, and then on to Rusk Holm. West quickly put up the roof to shield them from the spray of crashing waves and the relentlessly harsh, battering winds.

While getting a closer look at the rocky shoreline, West had had several close scrapes as he steered around the towering rock stacks surrounding the craggy red sandstone cliffs, the constant turbulence keeping him on high alert.

A creeping fog rolled in, thick and heavy, casting a dreamlike haze over their vision. The silhouettes of swirling seabirds darted in and out of the thickening mist like ghostly spirits, their foreboding presence feeling like a warning to turn back.

"Lovely day for a boat cruise," West remarked. They passed by a herd of seals lounging about on a flat, jagged rock outcropping, unfazed by the weather conditions. "They look happy now, but I doubt they'll stick around when the Nuckelavee shows up for dinner."

"Do you believe what Fergus said?" Kendra asked.

West paused his answer as he dodged a giant seaweed-covered rock the receding waves had just revealed. "I do. Not entirely, but I think there might be some truth to it. It wouldn't be the first time scare tactics were used to frighten off the locals. At most it's probably a very creatively disguised amphibious vehicle, which, if packed with armed HIVE agents, is intimidating enough."

"You don't believe it is an actual monster? Why not? I mean… what about yourself?"

"There's still a scientific basis for lycanthropy. I'm sure Borge will be happy to explain it to you the next time you have several free hours to spare. He also likes to use the saying, 'behind every superstition, there is a fact,' and I believe that also applies to our Nuckelavee—whatever it may be. It's most likely a myth."

The waves continued their assault against the cliff sides, obscuring the view of any cave openings. West activated the submersible mode, diving the ThunderBoat beneath the churning sea. Even with the headlamps activated, the sea was a briny mess, and they could scarcely see more than a few feet in front of them.

West strained his eyes, trying to see farther ahead. "I don't know that we'll do much better searching down here. It's murkier here than in Loch Ness."

The ThunderBoat jolted violently.

"And there's the monster," Kendra said, pointing at the large sucker-like mouth attached to the rear window.

West became more alarmed when he saw the circular rows of teeth grinding on the glass like a buzz saw.

"Well, definitely not a myth."

The Nuckelavee let out a deafening hypersonic screech that rippled through the water, causing the ThunderBoat's lights to flicker and its gauges to spin wildly. West's sensitive ears were especially affected. He instinctively covered them, attempting to block the piercing sound. Kendra quickly took the controls from the passenger seat, attempting to maneuver them away from the creature.

The Nuckelavee reared back on its horse-like legs, slamming its front hooves down on the ThunderBoat, knocking them around the cockpit.

West's ears recovered from the deafening sonic attack, and he spun the ThunderBoat around, only for the Nuckelavee to attack from the other side.

It grabbed the boat with inhumanly strong, humanoid arms and hurled it with great force. They felt a spine-jolting crash as the boat collided with the base of a sea stack. The rock spire crumbled down, smashing into the hull. Inside, the damage was accumulating.

West had to act fast. The sonar capabilities were damaged. The Nuckelavee was now on the hood, its suction cup–like face latching onto the windshield. Though the glass was specially formulated to be bulletproof, the powerful whirring ring of fangs was grinding through it.

West flipped open the aerial radar scope. It wasn't as accurate as underwater sonar, but he needed to find a route that wouldn't send them smashing straight into a rock wall.

Kendra finally lost her cool and screamed as the first spurt of water sprayed through a spidering crack in the window. The inside of the ThunderBoat tightened, squeezing as if being crushed like a junk car in a compactor. Whatever West was going to do, he had to do it now.

There! The radar pulsed, indicating what had to be an underwater cave opening.

This was it. Do or die.

He powered on the aerial rocket thruster. It wasn't meant for use with the submersible, but West felt he had no choice. The display lit up as the thruster reached full power. Then it went dark.

No, goddamnit, not now!

The long, slimy tongue of the Nuckelavee wormed its way through the dashboard vent, now also spraying water.

Kendra felt the wet, slithering tongue wriggle up her leg. As hard as she tried to suppress a scream, one burst out uncontrollably. Her hand scrambled for the knife strapped to her inner thigh, fingers slipping until they found the handle. She gripped it tightly and began stabbing wildly at the probing tongue as it tightened its own grip.

West's eyes blazed with fury. He pulled his leg back and kicked the thruster controls with all his strength.

The light powered back on. West gripped the steering tightly with both hands and yelled to Kendra to hang on. The jet thrusters shook and roared to life, forcing West and Kendra back into their seats, flinging the stunned Nuckelavee off as they rocketed away.

In a matter of seconds, they were plunged into the mouth of a large underwater cave, pinballing off its walls. West pulled back hard to slow down, but momentum kept propelling them forward. He turned sharply, narrowly missing a jagged outcropping as the hull tore and scraped against the rock.

Light was streaming down just ahead—an opening!

West gripped the steering tightly, pulling it back to launch upward. The ThunderBoat blasted through the stacked rocks of an ancient cairn and was spat out onto the hard ground of Rusk Holm.

When they finally skidded to a halt, upside down, West called for a timeout. Kendra agreed, and they sat in silence for a few moments, just breathing. They would have loved a few moments longer, but were rudely interrupted by something heavy slamming into the ThunderBoat, sending it flipping into the air.

The Nuckelavee was back and, with part of its long tongue now severed from the craft's abrupt departure, it was quite unhappy. Its bloodied mouth emitted a long, horrifying shriek. This time, West was ready for it and covered his ears. He had also had enough. The ThunderBoat had come to rest on its side, and an angered West kicked open the door, climbing out to meet the Rusk Holm Welcome Committee.

The creature was just as Fergus Sweyn had described: a larger-than-average horse body with a human torso and a head with a lamprey's mouth full of sharp teeth. The skinless red musculature glistened with wetness. One red eye pulsed from the horsehead, glaring at West, while the humanoid head gnashed its teeth, blood pouring from its mangled tongue. A gurgling snarl reverberated through its mouthful of spinning fangs.

West closed his eyes, breathed in deeply, and a second later, he bared his fangs and replied with a snarl of his own.

The Nuckelavee reared back and charged with its hooves out. LoneWolf leaped into the air, dodging the attack. It hit the ground hard, making a watery, gurgling, pained whinny. LoneWolf jumped onto its back. It jerked up and shook wildly, trying to throw him off. LoneWolf held on, sinking his claws into its side. The bleeding behemoth bucked and screamed in a vicious agony.

LoneWolf reflexively pulled out his claws to cover his ears from the sonic assault and was thrown to the ground. The Nuckelavee snorted a steaming stream of snot water, pawing the ground in front of it with its hoof. The creature opened its mouth wide. A foul mixture of bile and fish vomit sprayed from the mouth, the spinning saw blade of teeth coming at him like a Cuisinart of death.

With no choice but to ignore the pain, LoneWolf charged toward the advancing beast, claws out and at the ready. He dove into the air and plunged straight down, slashing the Nuckelavee's throat open.

The wounded monster could no longer scream and was choking on the bubbling blood gurgling up through its torn open throat. LoneWolf jumped back on it as if mounting a horse and, to end the creature's suffering, wrapped his arms around its humanoid neck, twisting the head until he heard the familiar crunch that said it was all over. The Nuckelavee went limp and dropped to the ground. To make doubly sure, LoneWolf leaped down and slashed at its equine throat with his claws, sending the cyclopean horse's head sailing. The quivering beast finally stopped moving, lying still in a seeping puddle of its own still-spurting blood and viscera.

LoneWolf calmed his raging animal impulses. Kendra had been watching all of this from inside the ThunderBoat. She was stunned and also found herself terrified at the deadly dangerous beast West had become. Of all the bizarre things she had seen in her life, this was on another level.

She watched with a morbid curiosity as LoneWolf's werewolf features—the pointed ears, fur-covered face with furrowed brow, snout-like nose, and protruding fangs under red-yellow slit-eyes, slowly changed back into the face of Val West. Once the metamorphosis was complete, she dropped her reservations and ran over to him.

West stood over the remains of the Nuckelavee in his black body-clinging spysuit, throwing off the tatters of the rather nice Brioni suit he had been wearing over it.

"Okay," West said, still panting. He spat on the ground and stretched. "Now, let's take a timeout."

Kendra was so happy to have survived she wanted to throw her arms around him. She managed to catch herself in time.

"Come look at this," West said, pointing at the carcass of the Nuckelavee. "What do you make of it?"

Kendra thought it was quite possibly the most revolting thing she had ever seen. She retched from the smell and didn't want to make anything of it.

West leaned down for a closer examination. "I think this is some kind of lab creation, perhaps even a genetic mutation," he said. He felt along the squishy muscle-flesh where the humanoid torso and horse-like body were fused.

"Look here. Sutures. This thing has been operated on. Looks like we have a man-made myth here. Or at least an excessively big and ugly guard dog. Borge would love to dissect this, but I don't think we'll be able to fit it into any of the ThunderBird's formations to bring it back."

Kendra wasn't sure if he was kidding or not, but was relieved to know that either way, the dead Nuckelavee would not be a passenger.

"Okay, break-time is over. Let's see what else is on this island. And what the Nuckelavee was guarding."

Rusk Holm was a drab, treeless speck of an island, just over a mile in length and about fifteen hundred feet at its widest, surrounded by jagged rock cliffs all along its sides. Through the rolling fog in the distance, West glimpsed the outline of some type of structure.

They left the upended ThunderBird and headed off on foot. The weather had not improved—it had somehow worsened, with the black clouds overhead sending down chilly droplets of rain. The green grass and wildflower buds of a new summer season were just starting to poke their heads through the brown and dirty dead turf of last year, although on this day they were ready to retreat in protest.

The remote and barren islands of Orkney have been described by historian and travel writer Mary Shelley as a "desolate and appalling landscape; hardly more than a rock, whose high sides were continually beaten upon by the waves." Ms. Shelley must have chosen a day like this to visit. The mist thickened and the salty sea air was chilled by an icy wind.

After what seemed like an unending walk through the savage elements, they reached their destination. A deserted, crumbling cabin built of wood and moss-covered stone was what they found. This did not seem promising, but they came this far and decided to check it out, if only to get out of the dreadful weather for a few minutes.

The long-abandoned hut's door was off its hinges and inside were just two small, filthy rooms. Parts of the thatch roof had fallen in, and the frigid wind crept in through the decaying, unplastered walls, whistling an eerie refrain.

West looked it over. "Here we are dear… home sweet home."

Kendra was unamused. "I think perhaps we made a wrong turn—in Geneva."

"There must be something, *somewhere* on this island. When we went flying through that underwater cave, I did see the cave kept going past where I turned upward to get us out. Maybe that's where we need to look."

Kendra shuddered. "Are you suggesting a swim? I don't know that the ThunderBird is up for another undersea journey at this point."

"Yes, it has sprung a bit of a leak and is somewhat less than tip-top." West paced the room. What next? They couldn't just turn around and go back. The presence of the Nuckelavee alone meant they were on the right track.

In the corner of the larger room sat a pile of rotting furniture, covered in a thick layer of dust. In this dust, something caught West's eye.

"Hello," he said as he walked across the room. They were in such a hurry to get in, they neglected to see the footprints in the thick dust—footprints that were not their own—leading to the pile of furniture. A broken, upside down chair was covered in dust, except for one clean spot on its spindle legs.

West grabbed the leg, and it shifted, acting as a lever.

"Hello again," he said with satisfaction. A group of stones in the floor moved to the side, revealing they were stone tiles over a metal sliding trapdoor. It opened to a black hole, with carved stone steps leading down into its dark depths.

West waved toward the darkness of the open stairwell.

"After you, my dear."

6: "NOPE. I'M JUST GOING TO KILL YOU."

Val West and Lady Kendra Kenton descended the shadowy steps, unsure of what lay at the bottom. Water trickled down the slimy rock walls, and the clammy air grew chillier with each step. At the bottom stood a metal door that appeared to be of recent construction. It was unlocked.

Aside from the creak of the door, an eerie silence filled the dark cavern, broken only by the echo of their footsteps on the concrete floor. Their flashlight beams sliced through the shadows, revealing only a vast emptiness, save for some scattered scientific equipment. The stale air was thick with a musty foulness that choked their nostrils and clung to their throats.

A shadowy outline on the far wall hinted at an elevator. They reasoned that they must have missed another hidden entrance, likely concealed in the thick scrub-bush blanketing the island.

The less they saw, the more concerned West grew. He stopped and turned to Kendra. "I think I'm starting to see what Primavera thought smelled so rotten, and it's not just the air quality."

"Yes," another voice replied, one with a deep Italian accent, and reeking of past its sell-by date Italian cologne. "We've been expecting you."

The owner of the voice stepped out of the darkness, flanked by a group of HIVE agents, all sharply dressed in their standard black suits with yellow and black horizontally striped neckties. Behind their thick, black-lensed oval sunglasses, the agents fixed their gazes on West. The leader, distinguished by the yellow blazer that marked him as a high-ranking member of HIVE, was the notorious international criminal Romano Orlada. West recognized the slick, bald-headed figure from the thick file detailing Orlada's lengthy list of past criminal activities, as well as the recent intelligence reports from Primavera's team.

"Primavera had been on me since my last venture in Cortina. Now we are rid of him and since we so easily led you here, we will also now be rid of you. You had the right idea, but the wrong time… at least for what you're looking for. However, you are just in time to join in as we close operations here—permanently. I am curious, though… how you managed to get past our Nuckelavee. I do give you kudos for that."

"Well, if you're handing out kudos, that changes everything. Nice to meet you, Orlada. Last I heard, you oversaw HIVE's Central Europe operations. So now you take your orders from Igor Zelensky?"

Orlada scoffed. "Not just Central Europe—*All* of Europe. The so-called intelligence organizations have outdated information, which is why we are always ten steps ahead." He laughed a wheezy laugh. "And *I* give the orders."

Two of his men went to work binding West and Kendra with rope. They made sure to snug the bindings extra tight, feeling up Kendra in the process. Her hands weren't free, so her looks had to kill for her. Both were shoved down onto the cold concrete floor.

Orlada nodded in satisfaction. "This entire installation is rigged with explosives to detonate. Pity. It was a nice laboratory but compromised by too many irksome intelligence outfits. We have already left an evidence trail tying this to the American CIA, so our work at this location is now truly done." He smiled and turned away.

"Wait," West called out, "don't you want to tell me your plans before you kill me?"

Orlada stopped and replied without looking back. "Nope. I'm just going to kill you."

Well, damn, West thought. Usually that worked to gain at least a few more minutes, sometimes a full half-hour, depending on the level of megalomania involved.

Orlada motioned for his men to leave. The only light, cast by their lanterns, shrank away as they climbed into the elevator by the far wall. West and Kendra heard Orlada's words echo through the darkness. "Why take the stairs when you can take the lift? I trust you two will have quite a blast. Ciao."

West was sure he could survive this as LoneWolf, but there was no way Kendra would make it. He had to get her out before the explosives detonated—but how much time did they have? Not enough, no matter what the detonator was set for. He closed his eyes and began the transformation into LoneWolf.

The werewolf's muscles bulged, and the ropes binding him exploded away. In his human form, West's eyesight in the dark was already sharp, but as LoneWolf, it was extraordinary. He sniffed through his snout-nose and growled. He could see both the stairs and the elevator—they would make it to one of them. With his hairy, clawed hand, he groped around—despite Kendra's taking exception—until he freed her from the bindings.

He led her by the hand to the staircase they had come down. Just before they reached it, he screeched to a stop and pushed her back with one arm, sensing incoming danger. An explosion rocked the old stone stairwell, sending a cloud of debris and broken rubble tumbling down, sealing off their exit. With no other choice, they rushed to the opposite side. The elevator hadn't been their first option, as Orlada's men might still be nearby, but it was the next—and last—option.

After bombing the stairway entrance, they would have to be on the move before the whole thing went up. Halfway across, they received the bad news.

With a fiery crash, the remnants of the elevator clattered across the floor in charred pieces of twisted steel, the shaft collapsing in on itself in a barrage of heavy rock.

This was it. They were trapped, and they were doomed. He might survive this, but he couldn't be sure. He would have to hold on to her and comfort her as much as he could while they awaited oblivion.

No.

There was one chance. Actually, a pair of them.

He pulled off his boots—the Wolfapult Boots he was still beta-testing for Borge—and handed one to Kendra. "Put this on," he shouted in his gruff, lycanthropic voice. "Never mind if it doesn't match your outfit. You're going to have to trust me if you want a chance at surviving this."

He took the other boot, then scanned the ceiling, some thirty feet above. His night vision spotted a weakness: a spiderweb of cracks between the girders. There... this one spot would have to do. He clicked the heel back, waited for the sound of it booting up, then gave it a hard chop with his other hand. The Wolfapult Boot shot upward, its coiled force blasting through the ceiling and into the earth above. Dust and dirt rained down, but most importantly—light streamed through the hole.

One chance used... now for the other of the pair.

"Can you hop on one leg?" Kendra nodded. "Good." He reached down and clicked the heel into its full catapult mode setting. "Time to take a leap of faith. When I say go, hop up on that one foot. When you land, get clear... and good luck."

She gulped and avoided looking at him. His werewolf appearance was still unnerving to her. There was no time to protest... she knew that. If he wanted to kill her, he would have just bit her throat out or slashed her to pieces, like what had happened to her father. Would he make it? Was he sacrificing himself for her? Too many questions and not enough time for answers. This place was about to be buried in a blast of collapsing earth.

Ten.

Nine.

Eight.

Seven.

She took one deep breath—perhaps her last—and, putting her best foot forward, hopped into the air.

Six.

Five.

Four.

Kendra couldn't breathe.

The landing on the hard earth had knocked the wind out of her. She forced herself up and glanced at the hole. West was still down there, with no way to climb out.

Three.

Two.

One.

ZERO

The ground rumbled with tremors and then spasmed with a thunderous force. An explosion of earth geysered into the air. Kendra ran faster than she ever thought she could, desperately trying to get as far away as possible. She looked back to see the cabin being chewed up and swallowed by the collapsing crater. Could West have possibly survived this? She didn't know what a werewolf could or could not withstand. Even if he did, would he be trapped, left to suffocate, choking on the dark soil?

Only a cloud of hovering dust remained after the earth had settled. In that moment, she began to wonder what she *really* thought of Val West. Despite being a literal monster, he had just helped her save her own skin. Although he did drive her crazy, in both some good ways as well as bad—she quickly turned those thoughts away. She owed it to him to see if he had made it, and she did her best to focus solely on that.

The icy wind returned, sweeping in a blanket of fog thickened by the lingering dust. Barely able to see in front of her, she fumbled her way toward the edge of the blast zone. An approaching noise brought her to a sudden stop. Two yellow orbs pierced the fog bank, followed by a growl of a different sort—not that of an animal, but the rumble of a motorized engine. An amphibious vehicle emerged, loaded to the gills with armed HIVE agents.

With no sign of West and nowhere to hide, she knew she had to run before they spotted her. This time, she wasn't quite fast enough. The agents caught sight of her and swung the vehicle around to give chase.

She ran ahead, her heart racing, as there was nowhere on the barren landscape that offered any cover. The ThunderBird! It was still functional—she hoped—and was close enough to reach… if the HIVE vehicle didn't run her down first. She plunged into the thick fog, praying she was heading in the right direction while ignoring the bullets zinging past.

As the sound of the vehicle drew nearer, Kendra pushed herself forward, leaping over shrubs and rock piles. There it was! Lying on its side next to the bloody carcass of the Nuckelavee was the ThunderBird, just as they had left it. She had an idea of how it operated by observing West and hoped that was indeed enough.

With all her strength, she charged at the ThunderBird, throwing her shoulder into its roof to rock it upright. The door creaked open, serving as a timely shield from a hail of bullets sent after her. From the headlights, she could tell the agents were only a couple hundred feet away.

The system powered up, and she frantically started mashing buttons to transform its shape from a submersible boat to any of its other forms—either a 1955 T-Bird or a microjet would do in this moment. Bullets rained down, peppering the windshield as the battle-scarred ThunderBird groaned in protest, slowly shifting its shape into automobile mode. As soon as the light on the console flashed, showing transformation was complete, she jammed the shifter into gear.

The ThunderBird spun around, racing in the opposite direction with the pursuing HIVE vehicle directly on her tail. As she approached the steep cliffside, Kendra turned sharply, hoping to send the large amphibious vehicle careening into the sea below. To her dismay, it made the turn, and to add further insult, a second amphibious vehicle loomed straight ahead. She couldn't drive around in circles forever—she needed a better plan.

Her fingers punched the controls until the dashboard readout finally displayed the option: "Microjet." She pushed the button with such force she worried it might break through the console. For a moment, she began to believe that was the case when nothing happened. Three hundred feet ahead, the second vehicle drew closer, while the first one was quickly coming up behind her.

Two hundred feet now, and in seconds, they would meet in a crunching collision. "MICROJET MODE ACTIVATED." It was a sweet sight to Kendra's eyes, and the transformation began even as she barreled toward the amphibious vehicle. The controls flashed the all-clear signal. She quickly rocked back on the steering, the wheels of the ThunderBird running up the hood of the vehicle charging at her as it screeched into the air, sending a few surprised HIVE agents tumbling off in the process.

...

A bruised but not quite entirely beaten LoneWolf slowly and painfully pushed his way up through the clumps of dirt. The earth was still loose from the collapse of the blast, but there was also some thirty feet of it on top of him. Using his claws, he burrowed upward until he felt the relief of breaking through and the rush of air that he took in with even greater relief.

He poked his snout out and sniffed. Once he separated the scents of the damp earth from the surrounding odors, he realized he was alone and climbed to the surface, spitting out a mouthful of the crunchy dirt clinging to his fangs. No scents or sounds of HIVE—or of Kendra.

After a long, slow breath, he transformed back to Val West. Even though the wind had subsided, it was cold, and West would soon have to change back to LoneWolf to keep warm. Even in this situation, he still preferred to be in human form. He had been quite deliberate about this. He was afraid of becoming lost in the beast, like the werewolf who had bitten him, Otto Skorzeny. West was still a man—most of the time—and he would try to maintain his humanity, even if it was easier to live life as a rampaging beast.

All he could see was the misty fog that surrounded him. Kendra was probably waiting by the ThunderBird, and they would soon be on their way.

How long had it been, anyway? After he had transformed into LoneWolf and the blast occurred, he had been knocked unconscious—a feeling he was well acquainted with. He checked his watch to see how long he had been blacked out and found it crushed, with only scraps of the band still hanging on his wrist.

"Tremendous," he muttered.

It was another one of those days.

No watch also meant no wrist-comm either. West swore a few times, then a few more, and then got on with it. Being barefoot, he changed himself back to LoneWolf for the instant fur coat effect and walked back to where they had left the ThunderBird.

As he walked, he thought about how she might have been taken captive by HIVE if she had been seen escaping. Did she even survive the blast? He trusted she did, but couldn't be certain.

The ThunderBird was gone. So was Kendra. The fog was finally lifting, and he looked out over the glassy sea, dotted with distant islands. One of them had to have a phone. An early evening swim wasn't his first choice, but he dove in, nonetheless. At least there wouldn't be a Nuckelavee.

To increase his speed, he swam underwater and nearly swam straight into a hook dangling in front of him. A fishing line! Grabbing it, he followed it to its source and, forgetting himself, excitedly popped out of the water.

Fergus Sweyn had seen many a strange thing in his time, including the legendary Nuckelavee. None of this had prepared him for catching a werewolf while out evening fishing near the Holm of Faray. He screamed so loudly he nearly fell out of the boat and would have, if not for being caught by West's forceful grip on his way over.

When he turned around, he was even more confused. Wasn't this the fellow who had been at his home earlier that day? The one with the pretty girlfriend, the one who had also left him a much-appreciated gold coin? He was certain it had been a bloomin' werewolf he had snagged on his line. And what in the blue hell was this guy doing swimming out here? His trip to Rusk Holm must not have gone so well.

West would have agreed and considered that very much an understatement. After calming the hysterical Fergus Sweyn, West returned to his home with him to use his rarely used rotary phone, earning him another Krugerrand for his cooperation—and silence.

Using his ParaCommand-issued 1990s-era vintage phone calling card with special code, West placed a call directly to the Highgate Cemetery headquarters.

"West, good of you to call." Borge's tone was more of sarcasm than actual relief.

"My apologies, doctor. I'm afraid my watch-comm is a bit worse for wear after the explosion and thousands of pounds of dirt falling on it. But late check-ins aside, I'm worried about Kendra. She was here with me until the blast—"

"Oh, she's quite all right, and gave us a full report. She was good enough to drop off the ThunderBird and even left it with a full tank. I do say, West, the damage you inflicted upon it is another matter, though. Do you know how hard it's going to be to fix the molecular structure damage? It's not a simple task to reprogram and restabilize the particle matrices."

"I'm okay, by the way," West interrupted. "And as for the Thunder-Bird, you have my sympathies."

Borge suspected the sympathy was less than genuine.

"Listen," West continued, biting back his anger, "I don't know what all the marvelous Miss Kenton told you, but this was a setup. That much I confirmed, although something involving Frankentech and HIVE was happening here. Primavera is dead—killed by a HIVE assassin. I think he smelled a swerve in the air, and I think I know where the smell came from. I'm going to sniff it out, by paying a visit… to Castle Frankenstein."

West hung up the phone and climbed into Sweyn's old pickup truck. As they puttered down the winding country road, the fading light of evening cast its long shadows across the landscape.

In the depths of those shadows, a large, hulking figure lurked, watching intently. A chill settled in the air as the figure stared into the distance, waiting… for the next move.

7: UNHAPPY RETURN

Night fell over the Odenwald Mountains of Hesse, Germany, where the skeletal remains of the historic hilltop Castle of Frankenstein stood like broken tombstones, memorializing both the old castle and the old Frankenstein family legacy. Its two enormous towers remained intact, silently glowering over the city of Darmstadt below. The site had become well known for the legends and myths that had grown over the years since its thirteenth-century construction. Tales of ghosts haunting its crypts, a fountain of youth, buried treasure, man-made monsters created from the dead, and even a dragon lurking on the premises, plus the usual sordid romantic intrigues, were all part of the lore surrounding the imperial Barony of Frankenstein.

Next to the castle ruins stood a true monstrosity. All harsh, sharp-angled metal girders and mirrored glass, it had been described as an "expressionist labyrinth of jutting angles" and "Frank Lloyd *Wrong*," among other unflattering remarks, although the architectural community predictably found it brilliant. Its recent construction was commissioned by Baron Victor Frankenstein III, who made his residence in the ten-story building, while generously leaving the historic castle as a sightseeing destination.

Beneath the historic castle was another matter entirely.

During the construction of New Castle Frankenstein, the baron took the opportunity to build not just beneath the new castle, but also extending to an old laboratory hidden under the original castle, creating a vast private research facility. And it truly was private.

No one had ever actually seen this lab facility to provide an accurate report. It was alleged Baron Frankenstein had a decommissioned missile silo transported by his friends at NATO to create the multilevel cylindrical structure underneath the castle, where he spent much of his time.

Victor Frankenstein was just about to take his private elevator to this subterranean superstructure when the doorbell sounded. Curious as to who would be calling at this hour, he pushed the elevator door open and stepped back out. The elderly servant, Minnie, had already gone to bed, and Igor Zelensky was moving toward the door. The night had been stormy, with a wicked whipping wind and a pelting rain. Perhaps someone had become stranded.

Igor pressed a button, unlocking the steel automatic doors. His usual stony expression was replaced by one of frozen shock as he recognized the visitor standing under an umbrella.

"Good evening, Igor. You look like you've seen a ghost."

Igor blinked a few times and forced a smile. "Mr. West. You surprised me. It is quite late, you know."

"And quite nasty out, so I'm sure you won't mind if I come in."

"Well, I—"

West sidestepped Igor and entered the foyer. "Thank you. And quite hospitable of you, I might add."

Igor's polite expression twisted into a grimace. "Now, look here. This is highly irregular, and if I might say, also quite ill-mannered."

"Yes… you are, but I will excuse your behavior this time."

Igor bristled, his temper rising over the banter with this unwelcome guest.

"Igor!" Frankenstein's voice boomed down from the top of the winding open staircase. "Please send Mr. West up. I would like to speak with him."

West tilted his head in acknowledgement, gave a salute, and then handed his overcoat and umbrella to the seething Igor Zelensky before heading up the staircase. "Good of you to see me, Baron."

Frankenstein was concerned. If West was calling at this hour, something peculiar must have been discovered. With rumors swirling, he hoped for some good news, but braced himself for the greater likelihood of more trouble.

At the top of the stairs, Frankenstein beckoned West into his study. The room, like the rest of the house, was all steel and glass, furnished with odd, hard-seated angular chairs that offered little comfort. West sniffed at the style, but once Frankenstein mentioned they were the latest in ergonomic design, he gave their hideousness a pass.

"Now, Mr. West," Frankenstein said in a pleasant tone as he sank into a plush leather seat, "what brings you here at such an hour, and on such a ghastly night?"

"Yes, well, it's been a ghastly couple of days to go with it. I just visited your lab in the Orkney Islands."

Frankenstein's jovial demeanor turned cold. "My lab?"

"A Frankentech lab. Commandeered by HIVE. That is, until they destroyed it."

"Mr. West. I—we... don't have a laboratory installation in the Orkney Islands."

"That you know of, at least. However, someone in your organization does."

Frankenstein winced. "Mr. West, I can't speak to what you're accusing me of—"

"Baron, I'm not accusing you directly—"

Frankenstein raised his hand. "Let me finish. Frankentech is my company and if it is being accused, then I am being accused."

He started to speak again, but hesitated, collecting his thoughts. "There *is* something going on, something complicated, something I was hoping not to involve Commander 7 or any other authorities with, for that matter. It is, shall we say, an… internal matter."

By the stress in Frankenstein's voice alone, West sensed something was very wrong and wondered exactly how it connected to the ambush at Orkney, and by extension, the murder of Ossie Weiner.

The baron fidgeted with the papers on his desk. "If you like, you are welcome to stay here for the night. We can continue our conversation in the morning. As it is, it is late, and I am tired. My housekeeper is already in bed, I'm afraid, but my personal assistant, Miss Elettrica, is also staying here and can show you to a guest chamber."

West's senses heated up. He cocked an eyebrow.

Volta. Staying here.

He had more than one bone to pick with her. The night seemed like it might not be a total loss after all.

…

Franklin Frankenstein lay on the bed of his first-floor bedroom, the music blaring through his headphones in an attempt to drown out his thoughts. It wasn't doing a good enough job, as his tumultuous teenage thoughts kept coming back to his present situation and how different it was here in Germany compared to life back home in the United States. He missed his friends, and more importantly, he missed his mother. Even more importantly, he was worried sick about her.

The Baroness Monique Van Seyton-Frankenstein was still at the family's main home—at least it had been the Frankenstein family's main home when things were still normal in Franklin's world. Now she spent her days alone at the FrankenCrest estate located in historic Seyton Place, Maryland. It was in this lonely mansion that she idled away her time, trying to drown out her own thoughts in an inebriated, tranquilized haze, a constantly crying mess. They had been so happy, the three of them… now it seemed none of them ever were.

Franklin was stuck here, half a world away from the world he knew. The music helped muffle his thoughts but couldn't silence all the feelings. On top of that, he also didn't know what was happening with his body, but he knew enough about puberty to realize that these were not your typical adolescent changes.

Feeling restless, he threw off the headphones and walked over to the very large, very expensive weight set his father had installed in his room. The barbell, resting on its stanchions, was loaded with the full three-hundred pounds of Olympic weights. Franklin picked the bar up with one hand, pressed it overhead ten times, then gently set it back on the rack.

…

Volta Elettrica greeted Val West with a warm smile. For someone who had just sent him into a hornet's nest of HIVE agents, West thought she appeared very calm and casual. As attractive as she was, she had some serious explaining to do, and he couldn't wait to hear it. He had assumed he wouldn't be able to dress her down until the following day, so it was quite fortuitous she had a room here at New Castle Frankenstein.

West responded with a smile of his own, though it was only half as sincere, and followed her up to the guest bedroom. Outside the windowed walls, occasional flashes of lightning illuminated the twisted, wind-bent trees, making the flickering shadows seem to move with a life of their own.

Volta led him down a long hallway to a spacious guest room. She opened the sliding door and clapped to activate the room's lighting system. Once inside, West closed the door before she could give him the grand tour of the room. A look of concern crossed her face, especially after she caught what she thought was a quick flash of red in his eyes.

West stood across the room from her, arms folded across his chest. "Now, dear Volta. Let's talk about my recent holiday getaway, shall we? You know, the one-way death trip to the Orkney Islands?"

She looked at him in confusion. "Whatever do you mean? What happened?"

"Well," West replied, with a hint of venom, "You're out a superior officer now, for a start."

Her expression shifted from simple confusion to stunned surprise. "Gino... he's dead?"

"Yes. And the same fate was planned for me, as well. By your friends at HIVE."

"*My* friends!" Her mouth fell open in disbelief.

West noted her reaction, and her response didn't give anything away. With his heightened senses, he could often detect deception through scent and other subtle tells of human behavior he could now easily read. She seemed genuine, but that didn't exonerate her, exactly.

He moved closer. She turned away from him, her voice shaky. "I can't believe you just said that. Accusing me of being an enemy agent... a traitor."

She turned around and struck him with a lightning-quick slap. "How dare you?"

"You found the information on the island. Someone tipped off HIVE that we were coming, and I don't think it was Gino Primavera since they sent a poison dart straight into his gullet. Who else knew about this? Igor?"

"Nobody else knew. I made sure of it when I looked at the files. There's no way anyone else could have known."

West sharpened his red-eyed glare. "Exactly."

Tears welled up in her eyes. She tried to pull herself together and faced him. "I don't know how this happened. But it wasn't my doing. I've worked with Gino since I was first drafted into the service," she said, her voice breaking as she began to cry softly. "This hurts me more than you can even imagine."

West looked down, realizing he probably just cocked this all up. Tremendous.

Her scent checked out, and she seemed to be telling the truth regardless of how HIVE knew to expect him. And now he had her crying. "Listen, Volta... I'm sorry. All the signs pointed to a setup. And they still do. I'm just choosing to believe it wasn't your doing."

She turned toward him and slowly drew closer. They stood looking at each other for seconds that felt like long minutes until she fell into his arms. As she looked up at him, he let his fingers tenderly caress her face, wiping away her tears. In an instant, the unstoppable magnetic forces of attraction pulled them into a passionate kiss.

Once they came up for air, she whispered, "Are you convinced now?"

"It can't hurt your case," West replied, flipping her onto the bed. "I think it's time we did the rest of the tour."

He clapped his hand to dim the lights. "Open Sesame."

She hungrily grabbed hold of his belt loop, pulling him toward her, beckoning him in.

Far beneath the guest room, a video monitor displayed the image of Val West and Volta Elettrica writhing in the dark, enhanced by the glow of night vision. On a separate machine, the audio of their conversation played again.

Apart from the light from the monitor, the room was dark. A figure in the shadows sat back to watch the quite primal display of lovemaking and reached for a tub of popcorn.

Igor Zelensky always enjoyed a good movie.

8: SNOOPING ABOUT

The clock struck two. West decided he had lain in bed long enough—it was time to prowl. Volta was sound asleep. He'd made sure to wear her out for his eventual exit and allowed himself a final, satisfied look at his efforts. While she peacefully snoozed, he put on his spysuit and quietly padded across the floor.

He gently pried at the door until its electronic motor slid it open with a whispery hiss. The hallway was dimly lit, with only small pools of light emanating from the in-wall nightlights placed throughout. Staying close to the wall, he glided down the corridor toward the room he was most interested in getting a better look at: the baron's study.

Here was the real trick: Was the door locked, locked with an alarm system ready to be triggered, or both? He paused, thinking he saw a shadow move outside the sheer glass windows of the exterior wall. A quick flash of lightning, followed by a low, distant rumbling of thunder, dispelled the idea of the shadow being anything of concern, and he went back to his task.

 Borge had provided a device which could frequency-jam any alarm system, but he wanted to save it for later, as it had limited capability in mimicking the chosen alarm's frequencies. He tried the electronic door's push button. No good. Remembering a trick from an old film, he took a rubber-tipped prong off his boot and attached it to a pen. He ran it along the crease of the door's edge, and it slid open with a light pop. No alarm, which was a relief, seeing he had no plausible story to explain himself. He quickly ducked inside and slid the door shut.

WHAM! The kick to the chest winded him instantly. Judging by its force, it had definitely come from a trained martial artist. He was still sucking wind when the next quick barrage of strikes pummeled him. That scent... it had to be...

Ugh—no!

CRACK! Before he could even think about regaining his composure, he found himself hurled into the wall. A priceless sculpture teetered on the shelf above. West rolled, catching it just in time to keep it from shattering loudly.

Now that his eyes had adjusted to the pitch darkness, he stood up, feeling like he had his wind back. The figure wasted no time, attacking again—this time shoving him into a pedestal upon which sat a rare and valuable fifth-century Aegean Vase.

West snatched the wobbling vase, spinning around only to receive a volley of kicks to the groin for his efforts. Before he crumpled to the floor, he made sure to hold the vase high, keeping it safe as he went down. While taking a second to groan in pain, he thought again about the scent. *Damn it, Kendra. Why here? Why now?*

She went in for the kill, and knowing she couldn't see him, he figured he would try another tactic. He growled at her with a full-on LoneWolf snarl, complete with glowing red eyes. This had the desired effect.

The shadowed figure of Kendra stepped back in stunned silence. "Good evening, Miss Kenton. What's the matter? Wolf got your tongue?"

"More like wolf-breath. You could use a milk bone." She switched on a flashlight, which, not coincidentally, happened to shine directly into his eyes. "However, I doubt you are that well trained. Or even housebroken, for that matter."

West stood up, carefully set the vase back in place, dusted himself off, and turned to take a good long look at his attacker. She was dressed in her usual form-fitting catsuit, this one in sleek dark purple. It was adorned with glittery sparkles for no particular practical reason, and the front zipper was teasingly unzipped, revealing a distracting view of her upper cleavage.

When he finally managed to pry his eyes away, he cleared his throat and gave her a scolding. "I'm not the one who almost destroyed this office, nearly smashing priceless antiquities and waking up the entire household. You know, you have quite a knack for showing up just when I don't need you. And if I hadn't picked up your scent, I might have dispatched you instead."

She finished reapplying her lipstick. "It's Tutti Frutti—a quite lovely scent, don't you think?" She sniffed and let out a light guffaw. "And you couldn't have even dispatched yourself with the tactics I saw on display."

West moved closer to her. "Tactics? Don't forget, honey, about the beast in me."

"Quite. I'm sure you say that to all the girls. Your other tactics appear to have come in handy as well."

Other tactics? She couldn't possibly mean his earlier activities with Volta.

She did.

"You think you're the only one with a keen sense of smell? I hope she told you everything she knew. I also hope the raging beast in you didn't devour her in a moment of mad passion. That would have been rather tragic."

West felt a twinge of amusement. Could she possibly be a bit envious? It seemed so, though she would never admit it. "So, then it's my animal vitality that you're interested in, and what brought you here tonight? That's quite all right. I understand that you find it irresistible."

"You pronounced repulsive wrong—" She cut herself off, as a sound echoed through the room. In an instant, they both dove under the large desk at the center. West found himself on top of her, their bodies pressed together in the cramped space. Their breaths mingled as they listened intently.

The sound turned out to be nothing more than the heating system kicking on, and they both released a sigh of relief. As the moment lingered, West couldn't help but notice how natural it felt to be holding her close and was simultaneously attracted and irritated. She was a "trifling bitch," after all.

Kendra also caught herself feeling a little too cozy for a little too long. To break the moment, she made sure to jab him in the side with her elbow to remind him where things still stood.

"That's just adding insult to injury," West groaned while rubbing his ribs. "You know, I haven't forgotten how you left me for dead after saving your shapely tush in Orkney."

"I didn't," she hissed back. "The place was crawling with HIVE agents. What did you expect me to do? Explain to them that they'd have to wait to kill me because I was waiting to see if a werewolf was going to come crawling out of the dirt?"

She did have a point. He had to admit that to himself, even if begrudgingly. Damn this woman, anyhow. "All right, all right," he said. "Are we going to argue all night or look for something of use here that might possibly help with this case? And no, I'm not even going to ask how you got in here."

"Good, because I had no intention of telling you."

"Fine." West took the flashlight and swept it around the study. "Do you see anything in here that looks like it could be a safe or a hidden compartment?"

"I hadn't found anything before you came bumbling in."

"If there's no safe, then let's see about a passage of some sort. I have a feeling there's more going on here than just what is visible."

"You truly are a great detective."

West bit his tongue instead of responding to the sarcasm and continued searching. Somewhere in the walls, there had to be a panel. He turned off the lights, ignoring Kendra's protests. He relaxed and slowly transformed into LoneWolf. His highly attuned night vision and sense of smell went to work, scanning and sniffing the walls, searching for a telltale sign. There it was: a tiny line with a slight temperature difference revealed an entranceway behind the wall's faux wood panels.

An annoyed Kendra grabbed the flashlight back and pointed it at West.

"AHHH!" she shrieked, startled and still unaccustomed to the sight of LoneWolf. A furry paw quickly covered her mouth, and before she could process what was happening, he made a speedy transformation back into human form. The hairy paw became Val West's firm, rough, masculine hand, sending an unfamiliar rush through her. She had never experienced a sensation quite like it.

"Now will you please keep quiet?" he pleaded. "I don't know how you ever manage to pull off your burglaries with all the racket you make."

"For one, I don't do burglaries—well, not exactly. And for two, there's usually not a freaking bloody werewolf staring back at me."

"Duly noted. But it was for good purpose. And I found our secret passageway." A bookshelf swept aside, opening to an alcove leading to an elevator door. West gestured to Kendra. "After you."

Inside, they examined the call buttons for each floor. "Let's go with this one, dear," he said, pressing the last button, marked L. "I don't think the 'L' stands for 'Lobby.'"

West chose this moment to activate the frequency jammer. With only a window of approximately twenty minutes, they had to get in and out, and with a minimum of arguments. As the elevator began its descent, West instinctively flattened himself to the corner, in case the bottom should drop out. This wasn't his first time in a secret elevator leading to an underground lair. He couldn't help but smile as he noticed Kendra had thought the same and was wedged into the opposite corner. Satisfied the elevator held no traps, they eased out of their respective corners and watched the call buttons light up as it descended into the bowels beneath Castle Frankenstein.

When the door opened, they found the floor dark and empty. Their search by flashlight revealed an extensive laboratory, and the first area they stopped at had a curious smell. The workstation consisted of a bank of video monitors above a desk. Next to it were rows of shelving lined with camera systems and audio recording equipment. Parked under the desk was a single leather desk chair. West caught a strange scent coming from the seat, one which smelled of slightly burned buttered popcorn, petroleum jelly, and what he deduced to be crusted, stale semen.

With the clock ticking, they continued at a brisk pace. In what appeared to be an office area was a quite visible safe. West turned on the lights and pushed past the eager Kendra to the front of the safe. In his belt, he carried his trusty International Command-issued safecracking device. Before he could affix it to the lock system, the safe door sprang open.

"Sorry," Kendra said with a shrug. "I tend to get impatient."

"Yes, well..." West shot her an irritated glance while quickly shoving the safecracker back in his belt pouch. "As they say, 'time is of the essence.'"

They set about rifling through the safe's contents, turning up formulas, billing manifests, and something that looked promising: a microfilm reel. As all good spies and thieves knew, the good stuff was never on a computer, which, no matter how secure it promised to be, was always a breachable security risk. Instead, it was always on what is now considered archaic for storage or communications systems: code books, VHS recordings, eight-track audio cartridges, "Magic Eye" stereogram pictures, and, of course, microfilm.

Kendra grabbed at the reel in West's hand. "I opened the safe. I want to copy it first."

West pulled his hand away. "Patience, my dear Lady. I found it first, so let me finish my scan, and then it's all yours."

She reached for it again, but in a swift motion, he palmed it into his other hand, pulling it away just as her fingers brushed against him. When he finally tried to close his upper hand around it, he was stunned to find it empty. "Now damn it. How did you…"

"Never mind. Trade secret. Now, if *you* don't mind…" She took the film out of the canister and ran her scanning device over it, the blinking lights measuring the scan progress. Aside from the whirring of the scanner, all was silent until a loud clanking noise interrupted.

"Did you hear that?" Kendra whispered.

"Of course I did," West whispered back in a slightly louder whisper. "I have wolf's ears, remember? It sounded like a door opening. Let's take cover."

"We also have to get the hell out of here, you know. That frequency jammer of yours isn't going to last much longer."

West ran to the doorway and killed the lights. Kendra remained crouched near the safe. He tuned in his auditory senses and found the source: a creaking metal cell door had been opened.

With a slow, limping gait, the lurching footsteps drew closer. West lowered to his haunches in the open doorway and pulled back when he realized he was at eye level with the source of the footsteps. A small, hunchbacked figure with shoulder-length greasy hair, wearing a worn hooded cloak, wobbled past the door. Noticing that it was open, he shoved it shut and weeble-wobbled on his way.

West was relieved not to be seen, but what was all this, anyway? Frankenstein had a hunchback too? Before he could think about it any longer, Kendra sprang past him. She slinked out through the door with such a graceful, cat-like movement that he wondered for a moment if he wasn't the only one with animal powers. Damn the woman! There she went with the microfilm scan, and time was running out. He needed to catch up to her and get his own scan, otherwise this little adventure would end up all for naught.

After running like hell, he barely managed to catch her at the elevator and shoved his way in just as the doors were closing. "Excuse me… don't you know you're supposed to hold the elevator open for last-minute riders?"

She managed a withering smile. "As they say, 'time is of the essence.'"

The elevator started its quick ascent. "Let me see your copy of the microfilm." She held it up to show him. West didn't have time for games. He made a fast grab, and she pulled away, dropping the microfilm canister to the floor. They were still entangled in arm locks applied by each other when the elevator reached the study.

"Are you going to go for the microfilm or go for me?" Kendra asked.

"Just a minute, I'm thinking," West replied, leaning dangerously close to her.

He dropped to pick it up just as the elevator doors opened. "Too slow," she said, snatching it back from him. "Ta-ta for now," she called behind her as she disappeared into the shadows of the darkened study and presumably out a window or perhaps an air vent.

West grinned to himself. While scuffling in the elevator, he switched the canisters on the floor with his blank reel, which was the one she took from him. She'd find out soon enough. But also soon enough, the frequency jammer would fail. Time to leave the study and climb back into bed before anyone noticed.

He quietly crept out of the study, closing the door so slowly and quietly that no one could possibly have heard it. He turned, ready to pad silently up the stairs to the guest bedroom.

"Did you find the lab interesting?"

The Baron Frankenstein III's eyes were trained on West like an attack dog. "I was hoping I had a little better standing with Commander 7 and his people," he said sternly. "I should have expected this, I suppose, but

I decided to trust that you would stay in your room like a polite guest—especially when you seemed to have been so well entertained."

West didn't like the reference to his night with Volta, but also understood Frankenstein's feeling of invasion of privacy and disrespect. Offering a glass of brandy, the baron remained silent at his desk for several long, uncomfortable seconds. The warm expression was also gone, replaced by a frosty look that matched the growing chill in the air.

"Listen. I'm going to level with you. There is a very serious matter involved here—the one I spoke of that I was hoping could be resolved without any... official involvement.

"There is a situation with... how can I put this?" He paused for a moment. "With Victor Frankenstein... the First."

West narrowed his eyes. He suddenly wanted another drink. "The First?"

Frankenstein swallowed hard and took a deep breath. "Yes. As in my great-grandfather, the first Baron Victor Frankenstein, and my namesake." He pointed toward the portrait of Baron Victor Frankenstein I hanging on the wall of the study.

The baron was dressed in a Victorian-era suit, distinguished gray streaking his combed-back hair. His thin face had a harsh look, with sharp, skeletal cheekbones that seemed to slice right through the flesh. The penetrating blue eyes stared back with a gaze colder than death itself. This Baron Frankenstein's haunting image glowered over them, immortalized in the oils of the painting.

Frankenstein clasped his hands together. He looked down before continuing. "He's... not dead... exactly."

West shifted in his chair. As a werewolf, this type of thing wasn't as out of the question crazy as it would have seemed to him only a year previously. It was still crazy, just not out of the question anymore. He had a feeling the craziness had only just scratched the surface. Even now, the thought of what Frankenstein was suggesting was already enough to make his skin crawl. The atmosphere in the room was quickly turning noxious.

"You see," Frankenstein continued, "upon his initial physical death in 1879, his disembodied head was frozen in an early experimental cryogenic procedure he had developed. His head remained frozen in this state of suspended animation in a specialized glass container for decades. Several years ago, we—that is, Frankentech—developed a method to 'thaw him out,' so to speak. We thought it would be fascinating, as well as being a huge technological breakthrough, to revive him, and actually be able to speak with him, a man of such vast knowledge and scientific importance."

West didn't dispute the point of Baron Victor Frankenstein I's scientific knowledge, but thought his scientific importance was more dubious. Frankenstein was considered a monster. The fact that Victor had even considered this, let alone carried it out, showed the magnitude of how big a mistake this was.

Frankenstein stood up and paced the room. "And it was fascinating—for a time. We found out soon enough, however, that being confined to a specially designed, hermetically sealed glass container was affecting his mind. Or perhaps it was the revivification process. Either way, he became quite manipulative, and, if I may say, extremely mentally unstable. Somehow—we're not certain yet as to how—he found a way to, um… escape."

West raised an eyebrow. "Escape? A head… in a glass jar?"

Frankenstein looked away. He cleared his throat and continued. "Yes. You see, there was another specimen also preserved in a cryogenic chamber we kept in the laboratory archives. Victor I had created a… a monster made from corpses, animated by what we now know to be cosmic-ray shower lightning—a creature classified in our files as Prototype A. Victor found a way to free this murderous monstrosity and with its aid, escaped. Now, they are threatening me… and my family. I fear for my son Franklin's life."

"I see." West thought of the giant man he had tangled with in London. This had to be Frankenstein's monster. And the girl—Kendra's friend Lynda—also had to be Victor I's doing, somehow. Even in his quite compromised condition, what else could this brilliant but mad mind be capable of doing? He seemed to be doing well so far.

Frankenstein slumped back in his chair and let out a long sigh. "I'm sure you now understand the pressure this situation has put on me, as well as Igor, who is very much on edge right now."

It was a lot to absorb, and West turned it over in his mind. It didn't remove Igor from suspicion, but it did explain his less-than-courteous personality. There was no doubt he was under tremendous pressure in this bizarre state of affairs. And what of the baron? He had managed to maintain his composure, only just now completely letting down his guard with his confession.

He had let West into his confidence and no, this was not a matter for the local police or even the Bundesverfassungsschutz.* West knew this was a matter for ParaCommand, and that Commander 7 would agree.

"Baron—"

"Victor," Frankenstein insisted.

West leaned forward and looked at him very matter-of-factly. "Victor… I can help you, with the Commander's blessing, but I'll need to know more. Like the lab hidden underneath that cabin in the Orkney Islands, for instance. The one I was ambushed in."

"Yes, yes." Frankenstein sighed and put a hand to his forehead. "I'm sorry I didn't tell you about it. It was a developmental laboratory for creating synthetic body parts to be used for transplants, limb replacements, and other humanitarian applications.

"There were legality issues over research restrictions, medical ethics, and other impediments to consider. To further the project, I had access to property in the islands and had the facility built in secret. It was remote

---

*Germany's federal domestic intelligence agency-- *Editor.*

and would hopefully be undiscovered until we could achieve positive results, which could take years. How HIVE became involved, I don't know, and that also goes for the lab's destruction."

"Perhaps Igor does."

Frankenstein stood and rubbed his temples. "Yes, perhaps. But you know I disagree. There's no evidence to suggest Igor is guilty of anything other than being surly."

"I know. But if I were to find some—"

The baron looked sullen. "Then, I will believe you. Regardless, my company, my plans, and my family are in danger. I will stop this. I *will* stop this. I promise."

Frankenstein looked directly at West, his stare as cold as the grave. "You understand you will have to destroy both Victor I and the monster—and do it quickly."

West didn't like being given orders by anyone other than his commanding officer, but he did understand Frankenstein's urgency. He nodded, and the two men agreed to leave things until Commander 7 had been briefed. West agreed to himself that he would keep a sharp eye on Igor Zelensky.

...

Franklin Frankenstein awoke to a flash of lightning. At least, he thought, that was why he woke so suddenly. There was one lightning flash, then he saw another, but they were far off in the distance and no thunder followed. It was something else that had stirred him from his slumber.

Another noise, perhaps? It was a noise. There it was again. A tap, a rapping on his window. Even though his bedroom was on the first floor, the windowed portion of the wall was still at least eight feet off the ground. He thought maybe it was just a windblown tree branch tapping on the window. The only problem with that was there were no nearby trees.

Franklin's curiosity got the better of him as he slowly rose from his bed and inched toward the window. He cautiously crept forward, peeking around the edge, and was greeted by a terrifying sight: under the sharp moonlight breaking through the swirling dark clouds, the shadow of something giant, something monstrous, lurked outside. A single scarred finger reached out, tapping slowly against the glass. As he strained to see through the darkness, he froze when his gaze met a pair of dull yellow eyes staring back at him.

9: CROSSPLOT

Val West returned to an empty bed. Volta had left for her own room sometime earlier while he was off adventuring with Kendra. It was too late for sleep now, and he didn't need it. One advantage of being a lycanthrope was a high energy level which often required little to no sleep—part of the regenerative properties of his physiology.

West took the quiet time of the morning to meditate and plan his next move while he waited for the household to begin awakening. The scan of the microfilm revealed it was encrypted. He would need to get it to Borge for decryption. His ears pricked up when he heard and smelled Volta padding down the hallway.

"Miss Elettrica," West said, poking his head out the doorway. "A good morning to you."

"And to you. You seem to have gone sleepwalking last night. Did you know you suffer from this problem?"

"Actually, I was trying to find the bathroom and got lost."

She sniffed. "Something wrong with the one in the guest room?"

"Hmm." He leaned closer to her. She stood still. "It appears I did all of that wandering for nothing."

"I hope not." She broke away and continued walking.

"Volta—hold on." She paused and turned back, expressionless. She seemed oddly cold, or perhaps she was just overly preoccupied. He hoped it wasn't because he had slipped away after she fell asleep—or worse, that she could smell Kendra on him, using her seemingly supernatural feminine scenting abilities.

"Is something the matter?" West asked.

She sighed, a touch of irritation creeping into her voice. "No, nothing's wrong. I just have to pack to go to France straight away after the baron's presentation at the university."

"Wait… what presentation? As in a public appearance?"

"Yes. He's presenting a large donation at the University of Ingolstadt, his alma mater, followed by a press conference. Frankentech is making a very large donation to fund the university's new Victor Frankenstein Biological Research Center."

West didn't like this. The baron had a psychopathic disembodied head and a giant, electrically powered monster constructed from corpses threatening to kill him. A public appearance wasn't necessarily in the best interests of his safety at this time. And also, why was she going to France?

"Confidential. I'm sorry, but I have my orders," she replied in a remote and distant tone. Whoever her new superior officer was at the AISE must be on to a new lead. He didn't find it all that surprising he was being kept out of the loop following Primavera's death. Commander 7's working relationship had been with him and it was possible his successor could be pulling Volta from the case entirely.

Volta walked off without another word, and West didn't have one for her anyway. He knew their night, although pleasurable, had just been two people with high-pressure jobs relieving some stress. It had happened all the time throughout his career, and it was only now that he was getting some strange feelings about how ultimately unfulfilling it all was. As a man, he loved his scorecard marked with a large tally of women from over the years, but he secretly wondered—for the fleeting moments he allowed it—what a real relationship, one with more than a superficial purpose, would feel like.

At this time, he didn't have any extra fleeting moments to spare. If Baron Frankenstein intended to make this public presentation, West had to either try to talk him out of it or make plans to ensure his safety. Victor Frankenstein had a target on his back, and West felt an obligation to make it a hard target.

"I'm sorry, Mr. West, but that is out of the question."

West had tried his damnedest to talk Frankenstein out of this public appearance, one that was scheduled to take place the next day. The more he thought about it, the less he liked it. Just as Gino Primavera had smelled something rotten in Twatt, West smelled a gas-bloated fetid corpse of an issue here. It was one thing that Victor I and his Frankenstein Monster would have a clear opportunity to kill the baron, but so would HIVE... and Igor Zelensky, who West still had quite considerable reservations about. Since he couldn't talk the baron out of it, he would have to plan the next best thing: keeping Frankenstein safe while using this opportunity to catch Victor I and the Monster in the act—with Baron Frankenstein as the unwitting bait.

...

The next evening was an idyllic one, with clear blue skies, a gorgeous orange sunset and a calm breeze. The administration, faculty, and students alike at the University of Ingolstadt in Bavaria, Germany, buzzed with excitement. Their most successful living pupil (at least as far as they knew), the Baron Victor Frankenstein III, was about to arrive to make a fancy presentation, complete with an even fancier evening soiree, and announce he was giving them a hundred million dollars to build a new research facility.

What could go wrong?

Everything.

That was Val West's thought while perched in his stakeout position atop the building's glass skywalk, which connected the newer buildings housing the Applied Sciences division of the historic campus. A man of Baron Frankenstein's stature would have his own bodyguards, of course, but were they ready for the level of attack that West was predicting? Not in the least. He considered it less a prediction than an inevitability.

As a seasoned spy and assassin, he had planned operations like this countless times. If it was his business was to kill Frankenstein, this was an opportunity he would not miss. Not only would it be a chance to make the kill, but the confusion and panic of the crowd would help cover his tracks.

Too easy.

Elegantly dressed guests were already pouring into the demonstration hall in the central atrium below, lavishly decorated for the occasion. Outside, the media waited, flashbulbs at the ready, to capture the baron's grand entrance. West had his eye on them as well. A nearly eight-foot-tall monster was hard to disguise as a reporter, especially one carrying a glass container with the head of Victor Frankenstein I inside it. HIVE operatives, however, could easily use weapons disguised as cameras. That's why, as a concession made to West, Frankenstein had agreed to come in secretly through the side entrance.

The limousine, supposedly carrying the baron, slowly pulled up to the curb. West smiled to himself as he watched the surprisingly game and agreeable Igor Zelensky climb out of the back seat, followed by his date. And then, to the chagrin of the photographers and reporters, the door shut, and the limousine drove away. The applause coming from inside cued them to the fact that Frankenstein had made his own special entrance.

West scanned the area below, looking for something—a sign that his heightened senses could then confirm. So far, there was nothing to suggest trouble, and it would be more than fine with him if it stayed that way. With the mingling over, the presentation would soon begin. West attuned his senses, preparing for the moment he would spring into action.

A quick flickering of the lights caught his attention. A few seconds later, it happened again. Something was causing an electrical disturbance, and he didn't like the foreboding feeling that came along with it.

After more brief interruptions, the university's glittery-tuxedoed master of ceremonies took the stage. "Good evening, people and comrades of all genders," he began, his German-accented voice a blend of stress and cheerfulness. His tone took on an anxious stutter as he continued. "We are having some unfortunate electrical snafus, but since this is such a faaabulous evening, we are going to move this presentation out to our absolutely adorable outer dais in the plaza!"

While watching the attendees being herded outside, West ground his teeth, which were slowly turning into angry fangs.

This is exactly what he didn't need.

He ran along the roof of the skywalk to a ledge overlooking the plaza. On the dais, the emcee tapped on the microphone, relieved it was functioning. His introduction of the Baron Frankenstein was just beginning when a burst of static cut through the audio. "This just isn't my daaaay," he said with a whining sigh, weakly trying to laugh it off. West felt the same—only, to him, there was no joke.

The sound of distant whirring helicopter rotors grew louder... and closer. The baron was now on stage, starting to speak, but was interrupted by more crackling interference in the microphone.

As the chopper loomed closer, it appeared as a black silhouette against the burnt-orange sunset. It picked up speed and, in an instant, hovered ominously over the crowd. Above the distracted partygoers, rappelling cables unspooled down to the plaza.

Suspended from each were women clad in sleek bodysuits, accompanied by a hulking figure—a creature with a squared-off head and greenish-yellow skin, grotesque bolts protruding from its brutish forehead. In its enormous arms, it carried a cannon-sized, scoped rifle. Danger was about to descend upon this unsuspecting crowd.

West didn't need a second introduction. From his distant perch above the atrium ledge, he recognized the uninvited guest as the Frankenstein Monster, also known as Prototype A. The women suspended on the lines had to be more of the assassins like the one sent to kill Ossie Weiner—meaning, they were not only dead, but also very deadly. If monsters were crashing this party, it was time to add one more.

With a burst of adrenaline, West leaped into the air, transforming into LoneWolf. Observant attendees might have caught glimpses of his flesh becoming covered in fur, his eyes flashing red beneath a beastly brow, and his mouth snapping into a snarling set of shiny-white fangs. The black tuxedo shredded away, revealing his black spysuit, which shifted color to the LoneWolf red suit mode.

Most, however, were not that observant, as they were too preoccupied with panicking. The overwhelmed emcee was doing his desperate best to maintain order but was failing miserably, nearly trampled by the surging crowd trying to exit the plaza.

One of the invading women marched up to him. With one hand, she picked the terrified host up by the throat and flung him, sending him crashing into a nearby lamppost. The other women blocked the exits while the Monster fired off shots at the dais. The baron had taken cover but still had nowhere to run.

LoneWolf noticed this immediately and directed his dive from above toward the stage. Baron Frankenstein caught sight of him swooping down and was quite understandably terrified. With no time for explanations, he quickly grabbed Frankenstein, who responded with a wild swinging punch. For his own good, LoneWolf leveled him with a powerful headbutt.

Picking up the limp baron, LoneWolf turned himself into a lycanthropic shield as the bullet spray rippled into his back. With a high-powered rifle now his weapon of choice, it seemed the Frankenstein Monster had changed tactics from their first brutal encounter in the dark alleys of London.

The chopper continued to swirl overhead, its blades whirring, before swooping down to buzz the hysterical crowd that was just now spilling out of the exits. LoneWolf carried the unconscious Victor Frankenstein over his shoulder and charged forward, covering the prone baron as he crashed through the atrium glass and skidded into the empty building.

Spotting a storage room in the hallway, he wrenched open the locked door and deposited Frankenstein inside. For the baron's own safety, he pulled the door shut with such force that it splintered the jamb, sealing it tight. He would have to make his apologies later.

As Val West, he would have aimed to neutralize the threat and be done with it. But as LoneWolf, he wanted to fight. One of the monstrous women was still dangling from a rappelling cable, and he yanked her down. The two immediately began to do exactly what he was looking for: fight with wild, frenzied abandon. The others quickly joined in, taking the fight all across the plaza, turning it into a battleground.

The Monster turned and fired, narrowly missing LoneWolf but scoring a direct hit between the eyes of one of the women. The velocity sent her body flying backward, her skull bursting open as electrical sparks danced across her limp form.

LoneWolf sensed a strange, sudden shift. The women, now moving erratically, emitted a high-frequency hum, one that only his ultrasonic wolf hearing could detect. The noise grew louder—an electrical disturbance far more intense than the faint pulses that had signaled their arrival.

It appeared to be caused by the women's growing overexertion. Green, glowing liquid oozed from their eyes, mouths, and various other orifices. LoneWolf lunged at one, but a sudden blast of electricity shot out from the metal bolts now protruding from her temples, knocking him backward. He rolled aside, narrowly dodging another shock, scrambling for cover.

The women began twitching in strange, jerky motions. Then their bodies trembled violently. Even more violently, they started exploding. One by one, their bodies blew apart, splattering the plaza with a ghastly fountain of biological slime.

LoneWolf wiped the gore from his face and shifted his focus to the Monster. Out of ammunition, the creature tossed aside the rifle and cocked its head, sizing up the charging, savage beast. LoneWolf was eager to find out if this Frankenstein Monster was as powerful as its monstrous reputation.

The strength was certainly monster-like. LoneWolf let out an animal whine from the sheer force of the clobbering blow the Monster hit him with. While dodging another sledgehammer fist to his face, he used his momentum to slam the Monster to the ground. Both landed with a hard, crashing thud. The wail of police sirens blared as several cars arrived at the scene, unsure of what they were stumbling upon.

Not letting up, LoneWolf lunged for the Monster's throat but then stopped to regain control of his base animal instincts. He realized there was a seam across the throat—the line of a mask.

LoneWolf's first instinct was to send a smashing punch of his own at the Monster's face. As soon as it landed, he instantly recoiled, the blow sending a shock of pain through his hand. The mask covering the face may have been rubber latex, but underneath was cold, hard steel. He clawed at the mask, and through the shreds saw nothing but metal.

The dark, discolored eyes opened with a start, and the Monster sat up with inhuman force, knocking LoneWolf away. Before he could react, the vise-like grip of the creature's gloved hand squeezed around his throat. He gasped for air, unable to breathe as the iron grip tightened its crushing hold.

That was when he saw the stars.

He was momentarily dazed by the crack of a police baton crashing across the back of his head. While relieved to be freed from the monstrous chokehold, his wild, animalistic tendencies turned his fury toward the attacking officer. With eyes flashing red and glistening fangs dripping with froth, he met the officer with a ferocious growl. The policeman's face drained of color as he turned tail and ran.

LoneWolf turned back, only to be met with a monstrous boot kick, this one straight to his wolf nether region. He staggered to a standstill, reeling in pain. The imposter monster used the distraction to flee, catching the cable dangling from the lowered chopper.

Ignoring the pain in his groin (*why did this seem to not heal as quickly as his other injuries?* he wondered. *Definitely not fair*, was his conclusion), LoneWolf ran off in pursuit. The helicopter began to rise, retracting its winches. He knew he had to make this jump, or he would lose them entirely. Pushing himself as fast as he could, West felt the LoneWolf part of him turn even more primal, even more bestial than ever before. He lunged at the cable, barely catching the tail end as the helicopter ascended and surged forward.

Spotting an intruder dangling from the cable, the pilot stopped the cable reel. The helicopter shot upward, then banked sharply into a steep dive, desperately trying to shake off LoneWolf. Despite all violent aerial maneuvers by the pilot, LoneWolf clung tightly to the cable, inching his way up the swaying cable in between being swung into treetops and roof antennas.

At last, he reached the metal runner beneath the landing skid. He heaved himself onto it, gripping tightly as the speeding chopper continued its wild aerial acrobatics across the darkening Bavarian sky. Filled with a raw animal power coursing through him, he pulled up onto the landing skid.

A foot to the face greeted him, slamming into his nose and causing him to lose his grip. He had barely managed to catch the edge of the skid with one hand when he saw the foot coming again—and the face behind it.

As LoneWolf began the long fall to the ground, he knew at least now he had a name to go with the face.

Igor Zelensky could not believe his own eyes.

He had just kicked a werewolf—at least that's what he thought it was—in the face, sending it falling hundreds of feet to the ground. He hoped that had killed it. As the chopper flew off to safety, he pondered the implications. Why was a werewolf in pursuit? There had been an unconfirmed werewolf sighting in the Orkney Islands. This was no coincidence. There had to be some connection to this troublesome Val West.

Romano Orlada had claimed he killed West when he destroyed the lab and all evidence of their experiments, yet he had somehow survived. Orlada was a top man in HIVE and certainly no amateur. A thought struck him. Could it be? *Val West—a werewolf?* He sat back in his seat, lost in thought as possibilities turned over in his mind.

LoneWolf looked at the high-speed dirt he was about to eat rushing toward him. He hoped he could survive this fall, but the actual limits of what a werewolf could endure had not been fully tested, even though he seemed to keep pushing them. Sure, silver could kill—and permanently—but that was just *one* sure way. There was nothing saying that falling a few hundred feet and splattering on the ground wouldn't also do the trick. He was about to land on a nicely manicured lawn. It would make a nice grave.

He only felt the initial impact and then drifted into what he assumed was doggie heaven for a brief time. When he came to, he was surrounded by the smell of cold, damp earth. He thought maybe he was in a grave. It wasn't a grave. It was a crater created by his landing. Still in LoneWolf form, he began clawing his way up.

Had someone dropped a bomb? Maybe a toilet had fallen out of an airplane? Maybe not the toilet, but a huge frozen chunk of its contents… you know these things happened all the time. Just not in this nice, old-fashioned suburban neighborhood on the outskirts of Ingolstadt.

The neighbors poked their heads out, buzzing among themselves about what had caused the crater in Inga Scheinwerfer's backyard. Inga herself was curious. She had been taking a senior snooze in front of the television when she heard the crash and woke to a spray of dirt spattering the window.

Inga cautiously crept over to the crater, wondering if it could be a meteor. It could even be valuable. She leaned in for a closer look, then came to a dead stop. Someone was down there!

When she saw the hand emerge, she was startled, but with her good nature, she just had to help. She reached down and grabbed hold of the hand, ready to rescue this mysterious crater-dweller.

To her horror, as the figure pulled itself up, she realized that the "hand" was a fur-covered paw. And the face? A werewolf—just like the ones that mauled poor unsuspecting victims in all those late-night monster movies.

This werewolf didn't set about mauling, and instead spat out dirt and snarled, sounding suspiciously like it was yelling a string of expletives in English. Inga didn't stick around to verify—she was too busy running and shrieking down the street.

LoneWolf, still trying to figure out what had just happened, also decided that running away was the best option—in the opposite direction.

...

Too Easy.

That was what West had thought earlier about assassinating Baron Frankenstein. Only that wasn't the objective—at least, not the primary objective.

Hef Vanlin, Director of Technology at the University of Ingolstadt, had made an alarming discovery after order had been restored: the university's Quantum Collider had been stolen during the assassination attempt. The distraction had allowed HIVE operatives to swoop in and essentially walk right out with the device—a cylindrical machine the size of a bus, equipped with a battleship-sized gun barrel and a rotating array of quantum electrodes, all loaded onto semi-trailers. They had come and gone while West was busy battling exploding women and fake Frankenstein Monster assassins, all in a frantic effort to keep Victor Frankenstein safe.

Vanlin couldn't understand why anyone would even want it. It didn't work. It wasn't so much that the university had been keeping it there in secret. Although the project itself was confidential, the Collider had never been operational.

The bow-tied Professor Vanlin had explained this to all the various intelligence agencies who had shown up. "The Quantum Collider was built with Professor Weiner's specifications," he said. "But he warned it was too unpredictable, and he needed more time to work out new algorithmic equations. That's one reason why it has never been activated. The other reason is, even with Professor Weiner's reconfigured calculations, we simply don't have all the technological pieces to make it work. Some are still theoretical."

And now HIVE had it. Never activated or not, an organization like HIVE wasn't out to steal something that had no use.

West wondered where the real Frankenstein Monster—formally classified as Prototype A—was hiding. For some reason, HIVE, along with Igor Zelensky, had chosen to employ a fake for this diversion. So where was the real Monster, especially if he and the disembodied head of Victor Frankenstein I weren't here to kill Victor III?

...

The night before, Franklin had watched the thing outside his window. It lingered there, and he thought he heard it speak. No, it was another voice—calling out to him, calling him by name. He sat in the dark, unsure if the creature peering in could see him hiding in the shadows, unsure what to do. Then, just before dawn, it vanished as suddenly as it had appeared.

Now, as the darkness of night fell again, Franklin waited in dread, wondering if it would return.

He didn't have to wonder for long. The large, green-toned finger once again tapped on the window with an unsettling yet clumsy gentleness. Franklin stood transfixed before the glass, unable to look away.

Moonlight glinted off the metal stitches encircling the wrist, revealing a hand marred by deep scars. Suddenly, the tapping finger curled into a fist and smashed through the glass with a thunderous crash.

Meanwhile, high on a stone ledge along the wall of Old Castle Frankenstein sat a glass dome-shaped container, angled to overlook New Castle Frankenstein.

Inside the glass, the head of Victor Frankenstein watched, a triumphant smile slowly spreading across the face.

10: FRAU STIGLITZ'S FINISHING SCHOOL FOR GIRLS

The train to Chamonix, France, sped along through a snowy landscape of frosty white fir trees glistening in the bright spring sunshine. It chugged over winding bridges spanning great icy gorges, with glacial streams far below just beginning to awaken from their winter slumber. Val West sat comfortably in the dining car, sipping a rather good French wine after an equally good supper.

He leaned back, turning over in his mind what had brought him here and what his next moves would be. Soon, the historic Mont-Blanc Express would arrive in the world-class ski resort area of Chamonix. From there, he would catch a coach to his destination: Frau Stiglitz's Finishing School for Girls.

The circumstances of his journey stemmed from Borge cracking the code to access the files scanned from Frankenstein's laboratory safe. It hadn't been easy, and true to form, Borge complained the entire time. While they hoped to find highly classified information on Frankentech's—and by extension, HIVE's—top secret plans, they instead found only information about this school.

Digging a little deeper, Borge managed to unearth a few scant details as to who exactly Frau Stiglitz was. For someone running a distinguished school to train young women in the ways of etiquette, class, and sophistication, Stiglitz seemed rather ill-suited. The files matched her up with a Helga Fotze Stiglitz, a disgraced fifty-eight-year-old former women's prison warden from Schittburg, Germany. He'd seen a photo already and would confirm upon meeting her, but after all, how many Frau Stiglitzses could there be?

Although initially disappointed that this was the only information on the scanned microfilm, West's disappointment lifted when he was informed that, apart from Frau Stiglitz, the school was entirely populated by beautiful young women—no men were permitted. He was sure he would make it worth his time, regardless of whether any valuable intelligence was gathered.

Thanks to Borge, arrangements were made for West to pose as an education inspector, taking the place of the usual female inspector. With no thanks to Borge, however, was his cover—traveling under the alias "Wolf Whitman." West had given Borge hell for such a ridiculous name. Borge swore there was nothing he could do—all the credentials were already made and in the system. He made sure to make a note-to-self to give Borge more hell upon his return. For now, he leaned into his cover guise and was dressed in suitable Alpine attire: a smart wool suit with elbow patches, a fur-lined overcoat, and a Tyrolean hat topped off with an unnecessarily large feather.

Even though he was looking forward to what this next encounter would bring, there were still mounting problems piling up. After clawing his way up out of the crater he had left in Ingolstadt and scaring a poor elderly woman half to death, he made his way back to the university. After sneaking past security, he found the storage room where he had left Frankenstein, ripped the door off its hinges, and freed the furious baron. As he led him out, the anxious officials were relieved to see Frankenstein alive and well.

And where was Volta? She was nowhere to be found at the scene. If her cover was meant to be Victor Frankenstein's publicist and personal assistant, she was doing a lousy job of it.

West was just about to tell the baron about seeing Igor on the HIVE helicopter when local Bavarian authorities burst in with even worse news: his housekeeper, Minnie, had called them in hysterics. She had just witnessed a giant carry off young Franklin after smashing through his bedroom window.

He knitted his brow, realizing that Victor I and the Monster had alternate plans while HIVE was busy using a fake monster to orchestrate a phony assassination—a grand diversion to steal the very real Quantum Collider out the back door of the university.

It seemed to West those plans were intertwined. Just what they had in store for the boy was something he didn't want to consider. Things looked bleak for Baron Frankenstein. All of this, along with the realization that his trusted friend and business partner, Igor Zelensky, was, in actual fact, his enemy, was a lot to absorb. He felt sympathy for Frankenstein and gave him credit for his finally accepting—albeit reluctantly and likely still in denial—that Igor was working with HIVE and, quite possibly, Victor I and the Monster. Betrayal always had a sting to it, and this must have stung particularly hard for the baron.

To make the most of his time on the train, West had brought the full ParaCommand file on the Frankenstein family with him. He wasn't sure if reading the file would lead to any discoveries that could help with this operation, but it certainly added to the intrigue of who—and what—he was up against.

TOP SECRET * FOR EYES ONLY

PARACOMMAND FILE 111818
NOBLE HOUSE OF FRANKENSTEIN

SUBJECT: BARON VICTOR FRANKENSTEIN I

Victor Frankenstein I was born in June 1816 to the wealthy aristocrat Baron Alphonse Frankenstein. By birth a Genevese, the Frankenstein family was one of the most distinguished of the Swiss republic, as well as in the Odenwald mountain range of southern Hesse, Germany. Following Alphonse's death, Victor inherited the medieval castle upon ascendance to the seat of the Barony of Frankenstein.

FILE NOTES
- Educated at University of Ingolstadt in Bavaria
- Accused of necromancy after nearly two years of electromagnetism experimentation, with the sole purpose of infusing life into an inanimate body
- Genius-level intellect; assessed as mentally unstable

DOCUMENTED QUOTATION
"I will pioneer a new way, explore unknown powers, and unfold to the world the deepest mysteries of creation."
Baron Victor Frankenstein I, via statement from letters attributed to Captain Robert Walton, provided by Mrs. Margaret Walton Saville.

SUMMARY OF SUBJECT AND DESCENDANTS
The legends surrounding Baron Frankenstein and his creations are supported by fact. The creature, an artificial man Frankenstein created from corpses obtained from graves and reanimated using an early form of cosmic electro-galvanism, was reportedly seen by many credible eyewitnesses prior to the disappearance of both the baron and the Monster in 1879, speculated to have taken place in the Arctic circle—recovery efforts unknown. Both are connected to a series of mysterious unsolved murders leading up to that date.

Immediate family descendants: son, Victor Frankenstein II (1865–1931). Further descendants include grandson Hans Frankenstein (1895–1970), and great-grandson, the current Baron Frankenstein, Victor III (1965–). Victor III is rumored to be a product of genetic engineering, conceived via in vitro fertilization initiated by Hans Frankenstein in Dresden in 1943, with successful gestation and birth finally achieved on March 31, 1965. These claims are purely speculative and, as with Hans Frankenstein's purported ties to the Nazi Party, have no verifiable evidence to support them.

END OF REPORT

There was certainly a curse of Frankenstein, and the report showed no shortage of family secrets. The train lurched to a stop, and West pushed these thoughts aside for the moment, as it was time to assume the guise of the unfortunately named Wolf Whitman.

By the time he disembarked, the afternoon was well underway. As he walked across the bridge over the gurgling, green Arve River, he took in a lungful of the cool, invigorating mountain air. The fresh air cleared his thoughts as he looked around the Alpine village for the coach waiting for him. He found it parked on the edge of the town center in the form of a snowcat vehicle. Even in late April, Chamonix was still blanketed in snow, and this year's ski season would run well into May. Farther up Mont Blanc, the snow was even deeper, where the school was located in the Mont Blanc Valley, just thirty minutes from Chamonix, near the base of the Graian Alps along the French-Italian border.

The driver greeted him coldly but professionally. He seemed like a local, and one not too well-versed in English, so West warmed him up a bit by conversing in French. The conversation was pleasant enough, but superficial. West exited the vehicle under the impression this man was simply a hired service driver and, for a change of pace, was actually who he seemed to be.

His boots crunched through the patchy snow as he approached the weathered, four-story building. It was in the Swiss chalet style, with all its traditional Alpine architectural flourishes still intact. What was once an inviting hostel could now be something more hostile. Not that it was particularly foreboding, but something about it felt off despite the hopefulness of the flowers and grass just starting to poke through the melted snow patches.

The shadow of the towering Mont Blanc swept over the school, casting a cool pall over the landscape. Behind it, emerald fir trees dotted the hillside, leading up to a gently rising grassy foothill that climbed toward the snow-capped mountain slopes. On one side of the hill, a small lake shimmered, its clear mountain spring waters surrounded by moss-covered rocks, while a few remaining ice chunks still bobbed about in the chilly, crystal-clear water.

It was idyllic enough to almost make Val West forget why he was here. He couldn't help but hope he was completely wrong about this lead and that the ghoulishness of this case wouldn't infect such heavenly surroundings. His tranquil moment was harshly interrupted when he turned around.

Frau Stiglitz's file photo did not do her justice.

She was much uglier.

Her looks—oily skin stretched over one beady dark left eye, the other sporting a black eyepatch—were drawn tight by a pulled back, gray-streaked bun hairdo. This somewhat warthog-ish head sat atop a lumpy, frumpy frame. The face, which at one time may have been attractive, was not helped by the permanent scowl she wore, coupled with her ice-cold, instantly unlikeable disposition. Her voice resembled a sonic torture device, compounded by her thick German-accented, accusatory speaking tone.

"Herr Whitman? You are Wolf Whitman, ja?" It felt more like an interrogation than an introduction. West bit his tongue slightly and turned on as much charm as he could muster.

"Frau Stiglitz?" he asked, as if it could be anyone else. "I am indeed Wolf Whitman of the School Inspection Board. So delighted you could accommodate."

She sniffed at him and turned up her pug nose. "This is highly irregular. Where is Ms. Pittsfield? You must know we do not allow men here."

West paused for a breath. He didn't think it was possible to win this one over. "Frau Stiglitz. I do apologize for the inconvenience. This is my duty, and I simply must conduct this inspection, per European Council regulations. I promise to conduct myself with no less than absolute professionalism. I understand you do have students here now?"

"They are not for you. You do not interact with them, understood?"

"Forgive me, ma'am. I am simply here to do my job."

"You will do it as quickly as possible and will leave. That is how you will do your job."

"My apologies if I offended you. I—"

"You offend me by your being here."

A lone giggle was heard, and then a few more chimed in. A scent of the most sensuous aroma wafted through West's highly attuned nostrils. He turned to see a group of beautiful young women gathered on the balcony above to watch the exchange. His attention then shifted back to the foul Frau Stiglitz, who began barking at the girls in German, flapping wildly with her arms, shooing them back inside. The Frau paused to do a snort-inhale through her wide nostrils, producing a large phlegm-ball which she spat on the ground between them. West did his best to pretend he hadn't noticed.

"Frau Stiglitz, I'm afraid that Ms. Pittsfield is indisposed, and I hope we can both make this as… painless as possible."

Her demeanor suddenly shifted to one of pleasantness. Forced pleasantness, but still better than the screeching temperament with which she had greeted him. "Herr Whitman," she said through a pained smile of jagged teeth, "my apologies if I perhaps came off as brusque." She gave a slight curtsey and motioned him toward the door. "Please join us as our... honored guest."

West tipped his hat to her and followed her inside. The large entrance room was warmed by a roaring fire in the communal fireplace. It was all tastefully decorated in fine Alpine décor, festooned with vintage skis and woven snowshoes, looking very much like the classic ski lodge it once was. A grand oak staircase welcomed the way to the upper floors and lined along the stairs was a sight even more welcoming: a group of perhaps the most stunningly gorgeous women he had ever laid eyes on. All long legs, soft hair, bubble bosoms, and doe eyes, heating up the room more than the fire ever could. He thought he might have entered paradise.

Paradise was lost as Frau Stiglitz placed a bony hand on his shoulder, leading him out of the reception room and away from the young ladies. She led him to a small guest room furnished with rustic décor.

"Dinner will be served promptly at six o'clock." Her disposition had once again turned cold. She shut the door behind her, and he heard the clicking of the lock. It seemed she was taking no chances. Perhaps there was more to it than his being a rooster in the henhouse—or, more appropriately, a wolf... and on more than one level.

Six o'clock came and West was more than ready for dinner. Here, he would have a better chance to assess the situation, get a better look at the women, and perhaps glean some further information that could prove useful. The sound of the lock clicking open was followed by a knock on the door. West rose from his chair, prepared to make his grand entrance in the dining room. Instead, he met the glowering Frau Stiglitz, painfully forcing a smile on her toadish lips. She was holding a tray in front of her.

"Your dinner, Herr Whitman." Before West could quite register what was happening, she set the tray down on the floor inside the room and slammed the door, locking it again behind her. Such hospitality, West thought. If they wanted to treat him like a prisoner, then he would just have to make a prison escape.

The drop from the window was at least thirty feet, and with nothing to grip on the wall heading downward, he knew Frau Stiglitz would not expect him to attempt such a jump. The truth was, he could make that jump if he wanted. Instead, he wanted to go up.

There were two more floors above him. West dug his claws in, scaling toward the next window above. Arriving at the window, he noticed a warm light coming from inside and continued climbing. Just as he climbed past the window, his eye caught sight of a stunning young lady disrobing.

He changed direction.

The hair stood up on the back of his neck, and it wasn't just from the view of the voluptuous beauty brushing her hair in the nude before an oval-shaped mirror. No, the rising moon was swelling in size… and that wasn't the only thing.

With a resigned sigh, he turned his attention back to his mission and resumed his climb. Just a few feet higher, the fourth-floor window was dark and empty. He slipped inside, entering a dark, dust-choked room that appeared not to have been used for ages. As he padded across the floor, he held his breath, hoping no telltale creaks would give him away.

He moved cautiously down the darkened hallway, seeing and hearing nothing. Softly stepping down the staircase, he found the main floor deserted. Muffled noises drifted from a side corridor, emanating from behind a large double door—the only hint of activity in the otherwise silent building. With a gentle touch, he opened the door just wide enough to peer through the narrow crack. It appeared everyone was in there and coming in through the door directly was *not* an option.

As he continued down the hallway, he discovered a grate covering a large vent for the cool air return system. Taking great care to remove the metal cover in silence, he was soon on his way up the narrow brickwork shaft.

At the top, the shaft leveled off, and after crawling through the constricted space, he reached the vent overlooking the room below. The former lodge's ballroom had been transformed into a combination exercise room and training center, and judging by the equipment West could see, also some type of laboratory.

On exercise mats, the young women paired up for martial arts combat while others went through circuits on gymnastic equipment, performing Olympic-level feats. In another section, to West's astonishment, some girls practiced against targets. This wouldn't have normally astonished him, except one of them fired at a target with a flamethrower. The spray of flame came from her detached hand, which hung open by a hinge at the wrist.

West realized it wasn't just cold down there when another girl's impossibly pointy breasts unleashed razor-sharp knife blades striking the head of a target dummy with deadly precision, each blade fired through her blouse from her spring-loaded nipples. Frau Stiglitz stood nearby, barking out coaching instructions in her harsh German accent.

As if this wasn't enough to pique West's curiosity, he noticed he wasn't the only male on the premises. Joining Frau Stiglitz for what appeared to be a tour of the facility was the head of HIVE's European operations, the sleek, bald-headed, sunglasses-inside-wearing Romano Orlada, who had previously (and unsuccessfully) attempted to kill West on Rusk Holm. The other man beside him was someone who West now almost expected to see—Igor Zelensky.

This was a HIVE operation, and these women were more of the same who attacked Frankenstein at the University of Ingolstadt. Linking it back, West knew this also had to be where Kendra's friend Lynda became the reanimated assassin he fought on the rooftops over Piccadilly Circus.

The three of them moved into the section of the room housing the laboratory. West was losing both sight and sound, so he measured his breathing, slowly transforming himself into LoneWolf. He let out an animal growl on reflex, which echoed through the ventilation shaft.

A concerned Romano Orlada turned to Frau Stiglitz. "What the hell was that?"

"Probably just the pipes. This is a very old building."

As LoneWolf, West removed the paw cupped over his mouth, panting heavily. With the moon growing fuller, he found it increasingly difficult to rein in his animalistic tendencies. He focused his hearing and vision on Igor, Orlada, and Stiglitz, craning his neck to follow their movements.

Several girls wearing blinking electronic headbands stood frozen, receiving mental programming commands from a bank of computerized reel-to-reel tape machines. Nearby, nude women in tall glass cylinders floated in a glowing green solution. On the surgical tables next to them were what appeared to be skeletons, only metallic.

"How soon until the Brides project can go into full effect?" Orlada asked Igor.

Igor moved around the laboratory. "Look at these, Romano. Do you know what these are?" He did not wait for Orlada to answer. He motioned to the bodies floating in the cylinders and said, "These are the Brides 2.0, the Cy-Brides. With their titanium reinforced robotic skeletons, their capabilities will allow for us to achieve multi-phase objectives."

The three of them walked back out onto the main floor. With a horrifyingly shrill shriek, Frau Stiglitz shouted a call to order. The young women all fell into a lineup, standing at attention. Igor continued speaking. "Powered by the Quantum Collider, our Brides of Frankenstein will become Brides of Destruction and will be ready… soon. Phase 1 will see them seducing world leaders and bringing them under the control of HIVE."

The Frau gestured towards the girls. "Mr. Orlada, if you will notice, you will see that all the Brides wear green ribbons around their necks. This not only hides their stitching, it also provides hypnotic activation and, when needed, can also be used to implant specially programmed memories. We have already successfully tried this on a subject."

Igor pointed a finger toward Frau Stiglitz. "You need to bring in more young women. Dead or alive, we can make it work. We will need them, and we will very soon have the capability to enact all phases of this operation."

Frau Stiglitz spat a slimy gray phlegm wad onto the floor. "I shall do what I can. We have already raided the cemeteries to the point that the authorities are now on watch. It won't be easy."

"I never said it would be. Just get it done."

Her face contorted into a scowl. "I am also concerned right now about spies. In fact, we have one here right now."

Igor and Romano eyed each other with suspicion.

She shook her head in disgust. "Not either of you! It is another, maybe an agent from International Command. It is ok—we are safe. He is locked in his room right now. He came here as Education Inspector, but when I asked him where the usual inspector, Ms. Pittsfield, was, he said she was unable to come. The usual inspector's name is Ms. Crelm."

Igor gave a slight smile of relief. "Nice work, Frau, rooting him out like that. Romano, will you take care of it? I'm leaving straight away, just to make sure I'm not at all implicated. It would be… bad for business."

Orlada nodded. He took out a pair of leather gloves and prepared to go to work. He would find out, with his usual unsavory methods, who this spy was, what he knew, and then dispose of him in an icy mountain crevasse when he was done with him.

West transformed back into his human form. That was his exit cue. He needed to get back to his room and prepare for Orlada's visit. Before he began backing out of the shaft, he suddenly stopped. Something below had caught his eye.

112

Another woman, standing at attention in the same blank manner as the others, was positioned off to the side. Unlike the others, he recognized her.

It was Volta Elettrica.

11: PISTE-OFF

The Brides began shuffling out of the training center in a single-file procession. West watched from a low crouch beside the second-floor banister. He waited for Volta to pass by as they returned to their rooms in silence. What was her role in this? Was she here on assignment, having infiltrated this operation? Or was she a willing participant—perhaps a HIVE double agent, as he had once suspected, working directly for Igor Zelensky and Romano Orlada? He thought he had ruled that out the night they slept together, but her behavior since then had kept him guessing.

Or… was she one of these "Brides?"

His speculation was cut short when Volta rounded the top of the staircase. His cover already blown, he decided to approach her.

She stopped. He moved closer.

"Volta. It's Val. Val West."

No response. The lifeless eyes stared straight ahead.

"Look, I don't exactly know what you're doing here… in fact, I don't know anything about it at all, but I can help you." She turned to face him, looking through him with the same blank stare. He gazed into her empty eyes and realized she was in some type of trance—perhaps a form of hypnotic mind control. Even with the deepest levels of hypnosis, there was almost always a way to break through. He had to try.

Placing his hands on her shoulders, he looked directly into her eyes. Suddenly, a firm hand gripped his arm, interrupting them.

"Herr Whitman!" He turned to find the grimacing face of Frau Stiglitz. "This is most inappropriate!"

At this point, all the girls seemed to have been freed from their trances. They poked their heads out of their rooms and broke into a chorus of giggling.

Frau Stiglitz glared at them. "Get back into your rooms. There is nothing for you to be seeing here, ja?"

She turned back to him with a yellowed-stained, Cheshire cat smile plastered on her face. "Herr Whitman, please don't think me inhospitable—"

"The thought hadn't even occurred to me."

Frau Stiglitz seemed flustered. "Ja, of course. It is just that we do, er, have certain procedures here. Now, if you please, come with me so we may have a chat."

A trap would certainly spring somewhere. West didn't know when or where, but he knew that when it did, he would be ready to handle it. From his own spying efforts just minutes earlier, he knew they were onto him, but he still had an edge. They didn't know what he had just found out and would likely prolong the "gracious" host act, attempting to dig for more information. Soon after, the niceties would be dropped, followed by the usual interrogation-torture-death routine.

He followed Frau Stiglitz down the stairs to a long hallway. A man came out of one of the rooms, nearly bumping into them. It was Romano Orlada, and it was certainly not accidental.

"Pardon me, Frau," Orlada said in a feigned apology. "I really should watch where I am going. That was quite clumsy of me."

"It is most all right," said Frau Stiglitz. She curtsied and continued. "You are just in time to meet our other guest." She turned toward West with a menacing look poorly disguised by her fake politeness. "Mr. Orlada is our school superintendent. It is quite wonderful happenstance that you are both here at the same time."

West smiled thinly. "Yes, it certainly is."

"I'm sorry... I didn't catch your name," said, staring down West. He seemed certain he had seen him before. Perhaps he resembled someone he had killed? Which one, though? It was hard to place—they all ran together after a while. Besides, if he had killed him, he wouldn't be standing here. That was the problem. What if he hadn't actually succeeded, and this man was back? This was the typical type of silent terror that haunted people like Romano Orlada.

West stuck out his hand. "Wolf Whitman, Education Inspector. Pleasure to make your acquaintance."

Orlada met him with a firm handshake, turning it into an unofficial contest between them to see who could crush the other's hand. West gave an additional squeeze and Orlada quickly pulled away. West won.

With an insincere smile, Orlada sized him up, rubbing his bruised hand and trying to conceal the fact it was still smarting. "Are you sure I don't know you from somewhere else? You look like someone else that I knew... know."

"Sorry, old boy, but I'm most definitely Wolf Whitman."

West's calling him "old boy" grated on his nerves. With a polite but icy "yes, of course," Orlada beckoned West to have a discussion about the school while taking a tour of the facilities. Frau Stiglitz excused herself, and the two men wound their way up the back staircase. Orlada pointed out the wall decorations, offering elaborate explanations to West. It was all nonsense, as he had never even been there before and was just a way to kill time before it was time to kill.

When they reached the third floor, Orlada paused on the landing. West tensed up. Here it was. What would it be? A switchblade plunged into his guts? Or, as an appetizer, perhaps just a blast to the face with brass knuckles? Orlada would likely want to know what West knew before killing him, though he hadn't during their last encounter in the Orkney Islands.

West wasn't worried about the violent method that was coming. He knew he would survive all those things. It was that they would still hurt like hell.

Instead, Orlada motioned toward the hallway ahead. This was one of the two floors where the girls lived, though none had yet poked their curious heads out. "Mr. Whitman," he said, his smooth bald head beginning to bead up with perspiration, "let me show you one of our student rooms, and all the amenities they provide."

West exhaled slowly and followed him inside. The room was very much in the style of the guest quarters Frau Stiglitz had assigned to him, with a single bed and simple wooden furnishings. "Quite hospitable, Mr. Orlada, I must say. Very conducive to creating a stimulating environment for matriculation."

"Yes."

The door shut, and the lock clicked.

"Indeed."

The two men looked at each other for approximately half a second before they both started swinging.

Orlada picked up a wooden chair, sending it smashing across West's face. West shook it off and charged, spearing Orlada into the wall, framed pictures crashing to the floor.

In their rooms, the girls heard the loud thumps and bumps. *What was going on in there*, they wondered.

In *their* room, West and Orlada continued their clash. Orlada yanked open a kitchenette drawer and began hurling silverware. West grew alarmed as a steak knife whizzed past his head, burying itself in the wall behind him. This place was classy enough that it was highly likely this silverware was made of genuine silver. West leaped over the island countertop, driving his knuckles into Orlada's face. Orlada fumbled frantically before grabbing a silver fork and plunging it into West's right arm. An onrushing, woozy dizziness hit him.

Damn… it was genuine silver.

Everything began to fade as he stumbled backward.

Orlada staggered to his feet, his bloodied mouth twisted into a grotesque grin. He lunged at West, wielding a silver fork in each hand. Just in time, West regained his footing and delivered a kick straight to Orlada's groin. He let out a high-pitched cry, crashing into West as the forks in his outstretched hands buried themselves in the wood-paneled wall behind them.

West used the opportunity to move behind Orlada, twisting his arms back and pushing him face down onto the bed. With one arm pinning him down, West leaned forward and wrapped his still-strong left arm around Orlada's throat, pulling his head back. He let out a panicked, gurgling scream.

"Wait, wait," he pleaded. "Don't you want me to tell you my plans before you kill me?"

West leaned in and whispered, "Nope. I'm just going to kill you."

"YOU!" Orlada rasped, recognition dawning as West's arm tightened around his throat. With one brutal upward wrench, West ensured that a sickening crack was the last sound Romano Orlada would ever make.

Still reeling from the effects of the silver fork, West felt lightheaded. A blackout was coming on, and, exhausted, he fell forward onto Orlada's prone body.

Several of the young women, unable to resist their curiosity over the commotion, tiptoed out of their rooms. They found that the locked door of the normally unoccupied room had been jarred slightly open and peeked through the crack. As they pushed the door open further, they stumbled upon West, still mounted on top of Orlada's body. He stirred from unconsciousness, only to be met by girlish giggles and gasps. The door slammed shut, footsteps scurrying away.

"Unfortunately, girls," one of them sighed, "I don't think *any* of us have *anything* to worry about with *him*." The others pouted briefly before running back to their rooms, still giggling over what they thought they had just seen.

Disgusted, and with his arm still recovering, West slowly pushed himself up and dismounted Orlada's corpse. Still groggy, he opened the window to let in some much-needed air. Outside, the evening sky was darkening, storm clouds brooding over the mountaintops. He turned his gaze toward the towering Mont Blanc, its peak shrouded in shadow.

Something in the gloom caught his eye. On the snow-white slopes stood a lone, shadowy figure. A flash of lightning crossed the mountain, illuminating the object, revealing its gigantic stature.

There was no mistaking—it was the Frankenstein Monster.

Not wanting to lose the creature, he burst out of the room and grabbed a pair of the skis decorating the walls. As soon as his feet hit the patchy snow, he pushed off, gliding toward Mont Blanc. Thanks to his training with International Command, he had once been an excellent skier, though injuries had forced him to give it up. With his old wounds healed by lycanthropic regeneration, he powered his now-youthful legs through the slushy snow of the foothills, heading for the powdery slopes of Mont Blanc ahead.

Slowed by the steep incline, he transformed into LoneWolf, using the burst of animal vitality to power his way up the mountainside. In the distance, he caught sight of the Monster, still standing in the same spot. It must have seen him by now, which could mean only one thing: it was waiting.

From above, the Monster stood on skis, studying him. LoneWolf noticed a mysterious black case placed nearby. Did it contain the head of Victor Frankenstein I, the true monster puppeteering this giant henchman?

The Monster fixed his gaze directly on LoneWolf, then picked up the case and skied away. LoneWolf followed to a flat ledge, where the creature came to a stop. West transformed back and approached slowly. The Monster pointed in his direction but did not speak. Instead, a voice emanated from inside the black case he held in his hand.

"Who are you?" the voice asked, its tone an unsettling echo.

West was about to answer when he realized the Monster was not pointing at him but down the mountain. A shrill screeching pierced his keen hearing—it was the cat-strangulating voice of Frau Stiglitz, shouting from below. "This is my Finishing School… and you are finished!" She barked out a command: "Deploy the Cy-Brides!" In response, several of the young women tore up the mountainside on skis at a rapid pace.

The two stronger Cy-Brides launched stunning jumps *up* the trail, using the power of their robotic skeleton-legs. Two groups skied toward West, closing in from two sides. On the opposite side was the Monster, and the only escape route left was a rocky cliff that dropped into a deep icy crevasse—a dead end that wouldn't get him anywhere, even if he survived the fall.

West had little time to consider his options. The Cy-Brides began firing laser beams from their eye sockets. A blast shot past him, striking the icy wall behind the Monster and melting a hole through it. The Monster quickly attached the case to a bracket strapped around its chest. West ducked to avoid more laser blasts, leaping behind an ice-glazed rock for cover. As the rest of the Brides arrived to join the laser-eyed Cy-Brides, he glanced over to see the Monster skiing away down the mountainside.

He assumed the Monster had led him into some sort of trap, but staying in his present position was also not a good plan of action. He pushed off from the rock, and dropped in, chasing down the mountain in pursuit of the Monster. While he had ascended the mountain using groomed trails, he was now heading way off-piste, plunging into treacherous territory beyond any ski boundaries. The steep descent down the virgin snow of Mont Blanc was perilous, and the Brides were hot on his heels. Trees, sharp rocks, gaping gorges, and other deadly terrain loomed ahead—and far too quickly.

The Brides leaned forward to gain speed, closing in on West. He needed the technique of Val West, but at this moment he knew he needed the extra strength advantage of LoneWolf. The transformation nearly caused him to lose his footing, but he righted himself and crouched low, dodging the encroaching Brides.

A hot wind whipped past his face, bringing with it the scent of burning hair. He quickly realized it was his own facial fur, singed by the fireballs the closest Brides were shooting at him from their flipped-open hand cannons.

Two Cy-Brides jumped over him, powered by their hydraulic legs. Leaning hard, West carved a desperate turn, avoiding another barrage of fireballs.

And they had seemed like such nice girls just a short time ago.

He wasn't sure how much longer he could keep this up. The impatience that comes with being a werewolf urged him to ditch the skis and attack with wild, rabid abandon.

As he schussed down the ice-glazed slope at a breakneck pace, he realized he was going faster than he could control. It took all he had just to hold on, narrowly avoiding trees that scraped against him as he zipped past.

He made a quick zigzag around a large rock jutting out. The Bride next to him did not, plowing straight into it and exploding on impact.

Farther down the steep terrain of Mont Blanc, the Monster looked back to see the Cy-Brides gaining on him, their eye-lasers locking in on target. He power-carved into a deep turn, powder spray erupting in his wake. Without stopping, he used his powerful arms to tear a dead tree out of the ground.

Inexplicably defying physics, he hurled the tree trunk backward, clotheslining one of the Cy-Brides behind him. LoneWolf was both impressed at the display and confused—he had assumed the Monster and the Brides were in league.

To add to his confusion, another figure entered the fray—a black-clad snowboarder wearing goggles over an eye mask made of a long black sash covering his head. The black rider jumped off a cliff above, narrowly avoiding an arc of laser fire that seared the edge of his board.

The man in black pushed hard down the slope and, catching up with the Monster, took the case and continued plowing down the mountainside. LoneWolf watched him jump his snowboard over the snow-covered roofs of mid-mountain ski huts as he disappeared into the distance.

West had more immediate problems beyond skiing out of control at over a hundred miles an hour.

More Brides were on him. One clutched his arm, and he sharply cut into an S turn, the spin flinging her into a nearby tree. The high-velocity impact sent body parts flying into the air, littering the snow behind him.

The now-disembodied arm still had a hold on him, clawing and crawling toward his throat. He seized it by the hand and swung it like a club against the other Brides. The arm connected, smashing into one and sending her crashing into two others, who tumbled hard, shattering apart upon colliding violently with the mountainous snowpack.

The Monster had disappeared. Had he taken a side trail, or lost his footing trying to ski in those enlarged, block-like boots? LoneWolf didn't have time to dwell on it. The base of the mountain was approaching fast, and he had no idea how he would stop. He knew that unless he found a way to slow down, he would come to a stop very quickly and abruptly against the rocky foothills below, turning him into little more than roadkill.

To his right, he spied the small lake near the edge of the school grounds. Narrowly wiping out, he carved a sharp turn, powering himself toward the water.

Successful in his turn, now that the lake was coming up, he saw it wasn't without problems. Dead ahead was a large rocky crag, jutting out into his path, and he had no time to change direction unless he wanted to plow into the thick trees lining each side. He squatted as deep as he could, bracing himself in case this didn't work, and launched over the crag. Momentum carried him onto the surface of the lake, sending him skimming across the water.

As he waterskied toward the shore, he spotted a figure standing directly across—it was Volta. Did she know it was him? He had no choice but to take a chance on her. Together, they could escape and head over the border to Italy, where they could regroup at the AISE headquarters.

He transformed back into West, slowing his skis as he glided toward her. She was definitely a welcome sight.

What was also a sight—and an unexpected one at that—was what happened as he approached the shore. Without warning, she lifted her shirt.

He saw her headlights flash.

Then, everything went black.

12: BRIDE'S HEAD REVISITED

A raging thunderstorm battered the steep hillside of London's Highgate Cemetery, the thunderclaps rocking its over 53,000 graves. Hellacious winds bent the trees and unleashed a barrage of pelting rain on the stones and crypts of the Victorian graveyard, which was also the home to ParaCommand's subterranean base.

Storms didn't usually spook Dr. Hector Borge, but on this rather spooky night, with the laboratory lights occasionally flickering from the force of the storm pummeling the cemetery grounds above, he felt more than a little spooked as he continued his examination of the head of Lynda Callahan. He had seen many strange things during his time with ParaCommand, and even earlier, when he worked with the United States Office of Scientific Intelligence.

This was on another level. Entirely.

By mounting the head onto a remote-controlled swivel, he was able to examine it under a variety of different controls and conditions. He was taken aback when the retractable forehead bolts first pushed out of the skin during his examination of the cranium. This made her partially some type of electrical device, one that somehow utilized normal human bioelectricity in an enhanced way. It all played a role in the reanimation process, but he couldn't quite piece it all together, literally or figuratively.

The neck sutures, partially hidden by the remnants of a scorched green ribbon, showed that the head was indeed artificially attached, and the stitches themselves were small electronic circuits. Borge found all of this to be more than curious and had more curiosities for Commander 7 when he checked in via the electroform scope and speaker.

"Yes, sir… that is correct: forehead bolts. They appear to function as electrodes, routed to terminals, which are, in turn, connected to smaller implanted circuits on each side of the neck, in the Deep Cervical Nodes."

"So… like a car battery."

"In a manner of speaking, yes. You must understand, sir, this is a quite fascinating—but may I also say—quite frightening design. Ingenious in its construction, despite its current systematic flaws, it's also quite insidious in its application."

The voice of Commander 7 remained silent for a time while he mulled over these strange discoveries.

"Dr. Borge," he continued, "was there anything else of note in your examination?"

"Very much so, sir. The brain had been operated on and implanted with extremely advanced circuitry, suggesting programmable use. While this specific circuitry was necessary to reanimate the brain, a simplified version could potentially be implanted into living bodies in microchip form. The possibilities are mind-blowing, in the quite literal sense. False memories, hypnotic commands and all other sorts of capabilities would be possible—including physical modifications. That would also include the transformational variety."

Commander 7 was alarmed. HIVE, although a relatively new organization, had already demonstrated a high level of technological capability, but this was indeed on an entirely other level. This was in the realm of something only an organization as advanced as Frankentech could engineer. This all but confirmed Igor Zelensky's involvement—and worse, that meant Baron Victor Frankenstein was involved as well. However, the Victor Frankenstein he knew would never have approved of such use.

"Commander, there is more you should know about. While conducting my examination, it became apparent that the blood had also been altered. In fact, despite sharing some properties with organic blood, it appears to be some sort of synthetic blood. It was red in color initially, but took on a greenish tinge when it destabilized. This also accounted for the green hue that the skin took on at this point as well."

"What do you mean by destabilized?"

"Yes, well, for lack of a better term, it became explosive. The circuitry didn't overload first—it was the blood that destabilized, overloading the circuitry. Something in its synthesis caused it to break down, which caused a chain reaction throughout the entire reanimatic system. The blood also had another unique property: its analysis detected the presence of nano-targeted sex pheromones."

Commander 7 paused again. "I was with you until that point, doctor. Please explain."

Borge paused before punching up an animated simulation on the screen.

"If you will patch into the monitor system, sir, this display will show how the use of programmable nanites—microscopic robots—were used to amplify the female sex pheromones, and then lock in and match with a sample of the target's male sex pheromones. This could be obtained from any DNA sample from the target—skin, hair, etcetera. Once a match was locked in, well, let's just say the target would only have eyes for her."

"His eyes could perhaps even 'pop out.'"

"Yes. Just as West had described in his report of the incident of the late Miss Callahan and Professor Ossie Weiner. Although, in the literal sense, sir, that was due to her squeezing his head with the extreme strength the reanimation process had given her. The same strength which led to the overexertion of the blood, causing it to destabilize and overload the bioelectrical components."

"Yes, Dr. Borge, I do understand that. What I don't understand is why she killed Weiner if she was sent to seduce him. That doesn't make sense."

"It does," Borge replied, thinking it through while stroking his Van Dyke beard, "if the plan went awry. Something—besides the turning-green-and-melting-part—went wrong with her. Perhaps it was a brain malfunction caused by the blood destabilization."

"If he was killed unintentionally then," the Commander said, working the scenario through, "instead of persuading him by seduction to work on building a Quantum Collider for HIVE, then it would follow that they would need to steal an already built Collider."

"Precisely," Borge said. "And I don't think this is the only young lady with this particular condition. Considering the only information on the microfilm disk brought back by West led to Frau Stiglitz's Finishing School for Girls, I think we can say there are more of them."

The Commander had put enough of the pieces together and didn't like the puzzle picture that was forming. "I think it's fair to say that Agent West is in serious trouble—despite being at a school entirely populated by young women. Here I thought it was they who would be in trouble. And now that HIVE has a Quantum Collider, the troubles are compounding. The things they could do with it as just a weapon alone—"

"That's only if they find a way to make it work," Borge interjected. "And to date, no one has."

"True enough, Doctor. But with Frankentech's capabilities, I believe it could be highly probable."

Borge let out a stressed sigh. "I wish I could have given West this information, but he has not checked in. Not even with the customary tapped-in code signal from his watch."

"Have you checked the watch's pulse signals?"

"I have. There is no signal."

Commander 7 grew alarmed. There was too much at stake not to know West's status. As a super-agent—and the only werewolf in existence—he needed to know his whereabouts and whether he was alive... or dead. He would send out the usual alternative communications to reach West, with instructions for secret contact methods to connect with ParaCommand.

The Commander would send out a series of numbers to be broadcast over shortwave radio frequencies. He would also arrange for radio and television commercials to air in the Chamonix market, containing hidden coded messages. A trained agent like West could find many ways to send a message back safely using a code translator, either with a code book or by memory.

"Dr. Borge."

"Yes, sir?"

"We need to locate agent LoneWolf, Priority-1 status. You know what to do. Call in our reserve agent."

"I will do my best, sir. As you know, contact is not always possible, and tracking is, by design, not likely either."

"You'll have to use everything at your disposal to make it happen. We can't wait for contact to be made to us or rely on the occasional unscheduled and unauthorized visit. Let me know when contact is made, and I will call in for a mission briefing. That is all."

"Yes, sir," Borge replied as Commander 7's waveform and speaker cut out, leaving only a fading static as it powered down.

The stress was getting to Borge, and he suspected he might be developing an ulcer. He went to his mini-fridge and chugged a glass of beet juice, then another—the closest he ever came to what could be called drinking heavily.

Not only did he need to locate Val West, but he also had an even more challenging task: finding ParaCommand's one-and-only reserve agent, one who could only be found when wanting to be found:

Lady Kendra Kenton.

13: TO THE VICTOR

Where was Val West? He didn't know either. All he knew was that his head was pounding. Beyond that, it was dark—too dark for even his enhanced animal eyesight to make out any details. He racked his still-swimming brain, searching for a memory of how he ended up here—wherever "here" was.

He groaned and rubbed his aching head. Slowly, the fuzziness began to fade, and it all began to come back clearly. The last thing he remembered was everything going to black after being flashed by Volta Elettrica. It seemed she was no longer an acting double agent but had fallen completely under the control of Frau Stiglitz and HIVE.

Though his vision was still blurry, his sharp sense of hearing was fine, and it picked up the sound of heavy, lumbering footsteps approaching. All he could do was brace himself for what would come next.

The heavy steel door creaked open with a groan. Light poured in, silhouetting a tall, menacing figure, its massive shoulders barely fitting in the doorway. *That's just tremendous*, thought West—the Frankenstein Monster was his prison guard. Despite what he saw on the death trip down the side of Mont Blanc, he and the head of Victor Frankenstein I were still somehow connected with HIVE or at least working according to their own agenda.

With his eyesight now adjusting, he could see he was in a crumbling stone dungeon cell. The shadowed monster came forward and, with its iron grip, yanked him up by the shoulders. West thought this a suitable time to change into LoneWolf. There was no need for him to close his eyes, as they involuntarily scrunched together from the pain of having his arms pinned to his sides as the Monster carried him out. He took a deep breath to start the transformation.

Nothing.

He breathed deeper and tried again. Still nothing. He then came to horrifying realization he was not wearing the wolfskin belt. If he didn't get it back, the next time he would be able to turn into a werewolf—and involuntarily at that—would be the coming full moon.

If he lived that long.

With his arms tightly pinned, he had no choice but to go along for the ride. As he was carried out of the cell, the dim lighting revealed the rocky stone walls of a passageway. He also could now see his captor and it was *not* the Frankenstein Monster—at least not Prototype A. This was another monster. Exactly what he needed.

The creature's face was obscured by a metal mask, seemingly grafted or stitched onto its skin. A grimacing slit served as its mouth, covered by a wired grating, while a thick metal forehead hooded dark eyeholes that shadowed mismatched, watery, pale yellow bloodshot eyes. Bolts protruded from the upper temples like antennae—or, more fittingly, horns. Long, stringy black hair framed the steel face mask, which was reinforced with clamps bolted into its head. The monster wore a black and green bodysuit, and the powerful hands, clad in thick black gloves, kept West tightly in their grip.

Upon entering a laboratory, this monster slammed West down into a hard metal chair. The lab was filled with unusual scientific equipment, a bizarre fusion of the arcane and the advanced. Spinning wheels covered in lights chugged away, powering rows of oversized glass bulbs that zapped with electrical pulses. Racks of test tubes and vials filled with colorful liquids and powders lined the workspace, alongside an array of switches, control panels, and bubbling beakers, while modern computer systems blinked and beeped away.

Most disconcerting were the rows of jars in assorted sizes, each containing brains, hearts, and other human body parts. A pair of discolored, detached eyeballs floated in a bubbling, green-colored solution, seeming to turn and stare at West by their own accord.

From this position, he thought an escape seemed quite possible. However, before he could formulate a plan, he was distracted by the sight of a diminutive hunchback waddling into the room. It was the same one (after all, besides Dr. Borge, they weren't a common sight) he had encountered when he and Kendra were prowling the laboratory beneath New Castle Frankenstein. Still, both the dungeon and this room were far from new construction. They must be back in Germany, within the underground structure of Old Castle Frankenstein connected to the other, newer laboratory in the castle east.

Heavy chains were draped over the hunchback's hump. He leered at West with a broken-toothed grin, stroking his pointed beard while cackling maniacally at a joke that was apparently lost on West, who found no humor in any of this.

West soon found the source of the hunchback's delight when the imp picked up a whip and began to flog him. However, this was no ordinary whip—it was electrified. The shocks crashed like thunder in his ears, and he reflexively writhed. He nearly toppled backward in his chair, only to be jerked upright by a swift cuff to the back of his head from the Monster.

The hunchback hooted and danced with glee while he thrashed away. One after another, the shocks jolted through West's body, causing him to vomit uncontrollably. Once he was deemed to be sufficiently subdued, the hunchback finally took off the chains he was carrying and bound West to the steel chair. So much for an escape.

Things were going about as badly as they could for West. He heard a mocking greeting and lifted his weary head to find the gloating face of Igor Zelensky. The first thought that raced through his dazed mind was, should he break free, his first act would be to bury his fist in Igor's smarmy grin. His next thought was to at least curse him out good, which he did. The reply was a stinging lash to the face with the electric whip by the giggling hunchback.

Then everything went black again.

A splash of cold, filthy water roused West awake, a rude reminder that this wasn't just a nightmare spawned by a bad Alpine dinner. It was all too real, and the mischievous, drooling grin of the rat-faced hunchback welcomed him back to consciousness. The tiny fingers reached closer and began poking him in the face.

"That's enough Morpho."

Igor Zelensky patted him on his hump and the little man lurched away to stand beside the Monster, who remained still and at attention, his only sound a wheezing, machine-like breathing coming through his mask. Heaven (or more appropriately, hell) only knew what was behind the mask, and the more West thought about it, the less he wanted to know.

"So, what's next then, Igor? More torture? Or maybe cut out my organs to use in whatever kind of experiments you're doing down here?"

A slight smirk appeared on Igor's face. "That decision, my friend, is up to my boss to make."

"Who's that?" West asked angrily. "If you mean your HIVE boss, Romano Orlada, he's lying dead somewhere in Chamonix."

"No," Igor replied. He walked up to West and leaned down to stare straight into his face. "I don't mean the late, and certainly not lamented by me, Romano Orlada. He was never my boss, and I never took orders from him, despite what he may have thought."

West twisted in his chains. There was no give. Still, he had to try. His officially issued lock picks were stashed in his suit, if only he could reach them. So far, not so good. Perhaps, if he was left alone—free from the watchful eyes of the Monster and Morpho the hunchback, he could contort himself enough to reach a lock pick. They had searched him thoroughly and found his belt, but had they discovered the picks and other diversion devices hidden in his spysuit?

"Igor," West asked, "when am I going to meet your boss? I want to speak to him directly. I have information he will be interested in."

A voice spoke from behind him. "I highly doubt that."

West thought he recognized the voice. He definitely recognized the slicked-back blonde hair and distinctive blue-eyed face now glaring at him from behind tinted aviator shades:

Baron Victor Frankenstein III.

The laughter of the others echoed off the stone walls, creating a maddening chorus. Wondering if he might be going mad himself, West stared at the ground and only one thought came to him.

Just f------ tremendous.

Frankenstein studied West with the look of a surgeon inspecting an unsightly new growth. His fingers tapped rhythmically as his mental gears turned. Morpho did a hyperactive jig, drooling like an overexcited dog.

"Calm down now, Morpho," Frankenstein said, his tone almost gentle. He turned to West with a shrug. "You see, Morpho gets aroused by violence."

Without looking back, he sent a cracking backhand across the hunchback's face. Morpho licked the blood from his split-open lip with a demented squeal of ecstasy.

"All right, now stop it, before you soil yourself." Frankenstein turned his attention back to West. "You must forgive Morpho. He suffers from deviancy."

"You're one to talk," West said. From across the room, Igor shot him a glare with his beady eyes.

Frankenstein grinned. "You are very spirited, Mr. West. I like that. Or is it Mr. Whitman? You know, you really should know the name of the regular school inspector if you want to fool someone as meticulous as Frau Stiglitz."

West had to give credit where credit was due. That was a crucial mistake, and one made very early on. It turned out the cover name "Wolf Whitman" was the least stupid thing about this botched undercover operation.

Frankenstein casually strolled over to the imposing seven-foot figure obediently guarding the doorway. "Now that you've met Morpho—albeit informally—allow me to formally introduce you to Xorror. He was built right here, one of my little side projects. Morpho handles the cemetery detail and occasionally finds me some exceptionally good parts." Morpho grunted at being recognized. "Anyway," Frankenstein continued, "He's been dubbed *Xorror*. He's a bit of a horror, but he does have a certain X factor, don't you think?"

"A charmer, for sure," West replied dryly. Xorror turned his head robotically, cocking it to the side as he stared with his dead-yet-alive eyes. He slowly crept closer, standing over West in an uncomfortable silence. Memories flooded back of their first meeting—the fake assassination attempt on Victor Frankenstein. West also vividly recalled the rather unpleasant feeling of his fist striking the solid metal face under the rubber monster mask.

"Xorror was made out of 'a few good men,'" the baron explained. "You see, he is also a prototype, but more advanced than Prototype A. He is a prototype supersoldier, and many soldiers died for this chance to live again, to be... more than the sum of their parts."

Frankenstein picked up one of the jars of body parts lining the shelves. He removed the lid and pulled out a slime-covered bloody eyeball, dangling it by the roots. "I just love to plunge my hands right in and build these creatures with my own hands. To finger the eyeball, to thrust life into the gallbladder..."

He paused, the thrill of talking about his true passion causing a shiver to move through his body. "Frankentech has been a phenomenally successful enterprise, to say the least. But the real success is in building a new life—taking dead parts which are of no use but to the worm and reanimating them as a new man… a super-man. Or even super-women. You've met them—true beauties made of sugar and spice, and much, much more, as you've found out.

"With this work, the original reanimation thesis can still be proven to be correct. The biggest failure was that first attempt, the wretch known as Prototype A. He is not an Ubermensch—a *superman*. He is a hideous monstrosity, a disgusting, unpitiable freak, one who has been nothing but ungrateful to his creator for his own creation. It is rather like spitting on God."

"So is trying to play him," said West, who received a strike across the face from Xorror in reply. The hit rattled his head and after shaking it off, West had more to add. "If you're so fond of great-grandfather-head-in-a-jar, then why the problems between the two of you? You seem like you'd be well-suited to be working together."

"Alas… philosophical differences. However, there can be no community between him and me. We are enemies. And you have done a lousy job of destroying both him and Prototype A for me. I'm sure Igor and his associates can do better."

"Victor I and the Monster also kidnapped your son. I notice you haven't mentioned him at all."

"Yes. An unfortunate and unforeseen circumstance. I'm certain HIVE will eliminate the head and the miserable demon, and we will retrieve the boy."

Frankenstein was all cold, clinical, urbane menace. West had been deceived by the false veneer of polite warmth the baron had managed to project. Clearly, it must have been quite a painful effort for a sociopath like Frankenstein to keep up such an act. The baron turned away, striding across the laboratory to a large glass cylinder containing a fleshy glob floating within it.

"While you're here, I'd like to show you some of my other creations—new works I hope you'll appreciate. This one is part of 'Project Blobule'—a completely new flesh cell now growing on its own. He will grow into a fully formed Nu-Man. That's what I call them, and in case you are wondering, Frankentech already has the patent on the process and the name. *Nu-Man, Nu-Men*, are a registered trademark of Frankentech, all rights reserved."

He let out a lusty sigh and looked upward. "Think of it: an army of these creatures at the command of a nation... or HIVE."

West restlessly rocked back in his chair, but Xorror's iron grip clamped down, holding him firmly in place. Morpho hopped back and forth, flicking his tongue in sadistic anticipation.

"So, you're just another flunky for HIVE, like Igor?"

Frankenstein shot back with venom, "That is rubbish, and you know it!" After a moment, he regained his composure, continuing in a calm and measured tone. "HIVE is not my concern—only the completion of my experiments. If it wasn't HIVE, it would have been anyone else with the desire to give their military the advantage of such a technology and provide the deal needed to complete my vision. It could have been the Russians, the Chinese, the Arabians... it matters not; they are only a means to an end, to be used in the name of science."

West looked at Igor, wondering whether he shared Frankenstein's views on HIVE. Igor simply stared off into the distance, his silence revealing nothing.

"HIVE did get me a Quantum Collider though," the baron added, "so they are on my good side. For now."

"You know, Frankenstein, Commander 7 spoke very highly of your character. Obviously, he was wrong and usually someone of his stature and experience isn't wrong about these things. He said you had even helped him."

"Ah, yes. Commander 7. What a curious case. Once a top-level secret service agent for Her Majesty, now a spymaster whose mind is all he has to offer. I can help him, you know. He just needs to come around to my way of thinking, and with what I have to offer him, I bet I can make that happen."

"You obviously don't know him as well as you think you do. He'd say 'Balls to you! And balls again!' Then he'd tell you to go straight to hell and shove it up your—"

Frankenstein's eyes hardened, then a sliver of a smile crept onto his lips. "Don't be so sure. Just as every man has his price, every invalid can be seduced by the thought of being a vital man again. Perhaps you understand this better than most, considering your own… condition. Perhaps you could be seduced by this opportunity yourself."

Frankenstein walked over to a safe embedded in the rock wall. After turning the combination, he opened it and held up the wolfskin belt. "Mr. West, tell me… are you secretly a wrestling champion on the side? Otherwise, what a strange fashion choice for someone who is usually so nattily dressed."

He walked back over to West and held the belt up in front of his face.

West fidgeted.

Xorror grunted.

Morpho salivated.

Igor yawned.

"You know, I have been most interested in the various reports of werewolves. Not just werewolf sightings, but one that may even be in the employ of a secret service organization. Does this sound familiar to you? And no, I'm not referring to the intelligence reports circulating with the wild rumors that Otto Skorzeny was not only alive, but also a gold-peddling Nazi werewolf building a werewolf army in Transylvania—until a mountain fell on him. I'm talking about reality here. Not ludicrous disinformation."

"Yes, that definitely all smells like a load of bullshit to me."

Frankenstein nodded to Xorror. The brute struck West with another heavy swat to the face.

"Just to make sure you didn't have any implanted tracking devices, we did a body scan on you, and quite interestingly, you have an unknown blood type. How strange, don't you think?"

"No. It keeps the Red Cross off my back."

"I don't appreciate the humor. But now, if you really are a werewolf... oh, the things I could do! Can you imagine a werewolf brain in Xorror? Or creating entirely new beings with shape-shifting capabilities. The thought is, quite frankly, beyond exhilarating."

He continued to dangle the wolfskin belt in front of West, just out of reach. "I bet you'd like this back. And not just to keep your trousers up."

West reached toward the belt. "Well, if you don't mind..."

"I do mind. Xorror, Morpho—"

Xorror gripped West's arm, wrenching it high before slamming his fingers down against the cold metal of the chair, over and over. With each crack of bone meeting hard steel, West thought he might go into shock, but then Morpho provided a shock of a different type, coiling the electrified whipcord tightly around West's neck. The overload of vicious brutality sent Morpho into a frenzy, causing him to soil himself in bliss.

Finally, the baron raised a hand, signaling for them to stop. Reluctantly, Xorror and Morpho stepped back, leaving West dangling over the edge of the chair, his body twitching, every nerve ending screaming from having been thoroughly assaulted.

"Morpho," said Frankenstein, tossing the belt at him. "Keep this safe. I find it remarkably interesting and would like to further examine it later. Igor—"

Igor stood up, ready for instruction.

"Please make travel arrangements for Mr. West." Frankenstein walked over to the slumped figure of West and grasped his face, forcing it toward him. Frankenstein noticed West's eyes had rolled back in his head and he delivered a stiff slap to make sure he understood him.

"I really would love to have my own werewolf to experiment on. I have other business to attend to, so for now, we'll send you to the island.

It's rather funny—you and the unfortunate Miss Elettrica were fumbling about, trying to find out more about 'the island' and nearly caused an intelligence leak at the Orkney installation. That's where we built the Brides, and it caused us great irritation to have to move them to Frau Stiglitz's before they were fully ready. Thankfully, we implanted the information we wanted you to know in Volta's now-programmable brain. Implanted counterintelligence. Way ahead of anything your people have.

"Now, you're going to *my* island, Frankenstein Island, and you'll wish you had not found out anything at all. And, once our present operation is in motion, we'll start a new experiment… on you."

Frankenstein turned on his heel and walked toward the door. On his way out, he snapped his fingers in command.

The last thing West felt was Xorror's hand crashing down on the back of his head like a ton of bricks.

14: LADY'S NIGHT

"Sufferin' Cats! A bloomin' humpback!"

Inspector Denis Hooey of Scotland Yard was not having any of it. The tall, lanky policeman, sporting a dignified, clipped mustache and distinguished salt-and-pepper hair, stood unmoving in his quite elegant (for an inspector's salary) tan overcoat and black bowler hat. He fiddled with his pipe (from a very reputable tobacconist, of course) before deciding to give up trying to light it, as the drizzling rain refused to cooperate.

But by God, this little fellow before him would, whether he liked it or not. The inspector had spent over twenty years on the force and was certainly no one's fool.

Dr. Hector Borge begged to differ. He really didn't have time to dillydally with the good inspector. For days, he had been searching in vain for Val West. He also had been searching, equally in vain, for Para-Command's lone reserve agent, Lady Kendra Kenton. The only difference is she was typically missing and untraceable by choice. West's comlink watch still had no signal, which meant it was likely completely dead.

West himself might not be so completely dead, depending on how he was killed, so there was a strange comfort in that. Borge wasn't quite so convinced West was in jeopardy, anyway. Sending him off to a school populated by impressionable young women meant he most likely had started a harem by now and lost track of what day (or week) it was. It was the wolf's blood in him. That was what Borge wanted to believe, and whatever West had gotten himself into, he hoped it wasn't too rough going.

He looked down at the mud puddle forming at his feet. Lit by streetlamps, he could clearly see the reflection of Inspector Hooey and the prisoner he had shackled to his arm—Lady Kendra Kenton. Following Kendra's trail, or lack thereof, was a frustrating task, one that Borge wasn't sure was possible, until what seemed like a lucky break—for him, that is. For her, not so much.

Inspector Denis Hooey was delighted. He had pursued Lady Kenton for several years. Her aristocratic status was not enough for him to look the other way, even though her reputation was one of stealing from those who had it coming to help right the score for those who didn't. The law was the law, and he was going to teach her a valuable lesson, with some well-deserved jail time attached. He was just a little miffed that it wouldn't be in his jail.

Days earlier, Borge had started his search. After nearly giving up several times, his computer spat out the latest arrest reports, causing him to nearly fall out of his chair when Kendra's name was listed. Upon arriving at Scotland Yard that evening, he found she was neither booked into a cell nor up for release on bail. Instead, he found her outside, standing next to the New Scotland Yard sign and handcuffed to Inspector Hooey.

"Hold up, little fellow," Inspector Hooey said, raising his hand. "This is a police matter, and this woman is in custody. Go on about your business."

Borge did not know the man, but felt confident he could gain her release by using official channels. For now, he wanted to know what she had done this time to get herself into this current predicament. The law never appreciated her unique talents as much as intelligence agencies, where the line between legal and illegal was as murky as the shadowy world they operated in.

"You're her doctor, you say? And a humpback?"

"Hunchback. Or kyphosis, to be more accurate."

Hooey raised an eyebrow and shook his head. "Right. Well, I caught her snooping about the Frankentech London building. Probably casing it for another robbery job." He glared at her. "That's right, innit?"

She went to jab him with her shackled arm, but stopped herself.

"Your father would be ashamed of you, stealing, sneaking about like some kind of bloody spy. That's no life for someone from a noble family."

She had to chuckle at that one, but still wanted to elbow him in the groin, even if it added extra time to her sentence.

"Anyway," he continued, "I caught her there thanks to a very conscientious citizen who rang me with an anonymous tip."

A quite convenient, anonymous tip is what came to Borge's mind. To hopefully help the proceedings with the somewhat dim Inspector Hooey, Borge produced a few of his credentials: Medical Physician's license, Doctor of Metaphysical Sciences, and Doctorate in Applied Technological Sciences.

"All right, all right, so you're a doctor… hopefully, her psychiatrist. But let me tell you, Dr. Borge, she is not above the law. I am holding her for extradition to Geneva on a burglary charge at Baron Victor Frankenstein's Chateau de Chillon. Seems she has a bit of history with targeting Frankenstein. I know a clear-cut pattern when I see it, and this case is rock-solid and closed before it even needs to be opened. That, is a fact."

Ignoring it was, in actuality, an opinion, Borge bit his tongue. Kendra fidgeted, trying to move away from Hooey as much as possible while handcuffed together wrist to wrist. She knew she could get out of the cuffs, bop Inspector Hooey on the head, and be on their way. Borge saw the look in her eyes and knew this was what she was thinking. He gave her a look in return, telling her to hold off.

Borge began to speak. "Inspector, we are—"

Hooey cut him off. "Hold up. What's this now? You're a bleedin' Dutchman as well? I would know that accent anywhere. I've spent some time in Helsinki, I'll have you know."

"Yes... um, well, you see, Inspector, we are in a hurry." He handed a business card to Hooey. "If you could call this number, I'm sure you'll see everything can be sorted out as more-or-less a misunderstanding."

Hooey let out a loud guffaw. "Misunderstanding, my eye." Despite his doubts, he examined the card. "There's just a phone number on here. Who is it that I'm calling? I don't like tricks being played, not that the likes of you could outsmart me, anyway. Maybe I ought to run you in, too, 'doctor.' Bah!"

Keeping a leery eye on Borge, he prodded Kendra toward a police telephone box mounted on the light pole near the curb. Expecting nothing but a load of tosh, he dialed the number with a smirk on his face. He then quickly stood up straight, his expression taking on a much different tone.

"Yes, sir. I mean, I didn't know, sir. Yes, sir, right away, sir."

He hung up the phone and turned to Borge. Inspector Hooey had just had a brief conversation with Commander 7, who told him in no uncertain terms he was to free Lady Kenton.

"It pains me to have to do this," he said. "She's still a right ruddy thief and a menace. I've got a file—a big file—going on her, you'd do well to know."

"If it helps, Inspector," Borge added, "it is not the Genevese police coming. They are HIVE agents."

"HIVE? What are they, bloomin' bees? What do you mean, 'The Hives?'"

"They are a secret international syndicate."

Hooey only offered a blank look.

Kendra rolled her eyes and said tersely, "The baddies."

Hooey understood it in those terms, and after fumbling with his key, freed her from the handcuff.

"Now listen," Borge said, holding out another card. "There's a very high likelihood of trouble once these fake Swiss police arrive. Call and ask for Major Flanagan of International Command. Tell her to send agents to intercept them."

Inspector Hooey reached down and took the card from Borge. He read it intently, then scratched his head under his bowler hat. "Say, what goes on here? This is a blinkin' lampshade store!"

Finished with this conversation, Borge turned to leave. "Call the number—they can shed more light on the situation."

Kendra planted a kiss on Hooey's cheek and thanked him for his understanding. He grumbled a response and watched her drive off in Borge's car, scot-free. While continuing to mutter under his breath, he suddenly realized she had cuffed him to the light pole.

…and somehow made off with the key.

Squealing tires tore down the street, and she was quite amused at the sight of Hooey cursing her out in the rearview mirror.

As Kendra sped down the A4200 through central London, she considered how grateful she was for escaping what could have turned into a very sticky situation with HIVE agents. However, she wasn't necessarily all that keen on tracking down Val West. Deep down, she finally had to admit to herself that she found him attractive. Maybe it was pure animal magnetism, but she also couldn't reconcile the fact that he was also a bona fide monster, just like the one that had killed her beloved father. It was a difficult thing to overlook and was far more than a simple character flaw.

"This is quite a nice ride you have here, Hector," she said, approving of his choice of the souped-up cherry red 1978 MG Midget 1500.

"Why thank you. It is nice, but it's no ThunderBird. I'm afraid West did such a number on it when the two of you were in the Orkneys that it will be quite a while before I can get its molecular structure to hold its vibrational subatomic separational shift. Speaking of West, I can tell you have some reticence in helping to find him. Is it because he stiffed you by switching the microfilm copies at Castle Frankenstein?"

She had almost gotten that off her mind. No, she hadn't, but had been trying to tell herself she had, and that it didn't still make her blood boil. Even so, fair play is fair play, and he got her using an old school sleight-of-hand trick she should have spotted. She considered the idea that maybe she was being too hard on him, but then closed her eyes momentarily to flush the idea from her mind. For a few uncomfortable minutes, only the sounds of the rain spattering the windshield and the rhythmic back-and-forth of the wiper blades did the talking.

Finally, Kendra broke the silence.

"Not that I'm actually concerned, of course, but do you think West is okay?"

Borge thought for a moment. "Val West is probably the most resourceful agent I have ever worked with. Even though the signs would suggest otherwise, I like to think he is all right."

The faintest whisper of a smile fell over her face. "You think a lot of him, don't you?"

"I do. We have our squabbles, but he always comes through and is true to his word. He is a very honorable man, and that is an increasingly rare quality in this day and age. You know, your father thought a lot of him, too."

Kendra winced. "And that's my big problem with West. Not that he was respected by my father, but that one of his kind killed him."

"That wasn't West's fault. Commander 7 sent him on a mission and the nature of that mission unfortunately involved another werewolf's retaliation. Sir Cedric was part of the mission, and proud to be part of it. He knew the risks, as with all missions, and if nothing else, he went out on his feet, fighting to the very end. He died like a man, in battle with a monster."

She considered her next words carefully. "And now, West is the last werewolf in existence. But he could bite others, just as he had been bitten. That means other werewolves—the kind who don't have control of themselves—could, in turn, kill others. I can't let someone else lose a father or anyone else close to them because this one monster still lives."

Borge was staring out the window, watching the streetlamps of London streak by as she drove far faster than she should. "Lone-Wolf…Val… truly is the last of his kind, because I have removed his werewolf venom-producing glands, so now neither his bite nor scratch will be able to infect anyone else." He turned to Kendra and saw a look of surprise and relief on her face. Maybe it was both. Maybe it was even a slight look of hopefulness.

"I do hope you understand," he continued, "that he never wanted this. From the moment we found him, all he wanted was to be cured. He said he wanted to live and die as a man and felt even though his condition comes with many physical benefits, it still made him a monster. He didn't want that. I think a part of him still feels that way. You know, he had a chance to be cured—"

Kendra's ears perked up, and she turned toward Borge.

"Yes, it's true. He needed to bring me the werewolf that bit him so I could use its DNA mutagens to reverse-engineer the genetic modifications caused by the bite infection. But by destroying the creature instead, he saved the world—and countless lives—from its wrath. West was also prepared to destroy himself, if that's what it took to stop this monster, using a lethal dose of silver poison. In the end, it didn't come to that—but he was only a second away before I lent a timely assist."

Kendra seemed visibly moved. Borge thought her eyes even looked a little misty, something she never would have admitted.

But she admitted it to herself.

There was still so much to dislike about that man… or was there? Kendra thought about what she did like: he was tanned, dashing, darkly handsome and attractively disreputable. She thought he rather resembled a clean-shaven version of the classic film star Errol Flynn, and the white streak in the front of his hair was quite distinguished... like the youthful version of a silver fox. Yet, he was not actually as youthful as he appeared. And he was certainly not a fox, but a wolf—a werewolf, a monster, and there was nothing to like about that.

Or was there?

Borge sat in silence, leaving her to wrestle with her conflicting thoughts. As they motored down Swain's Lane and approached the wall surrounding Highgate Cemetery, he pressed a button on the dashboard, activating the hidden street entrance.

Soon they would be briefed by Commander 7 on the new mission—one he was now certain Kendra would not refuse: to find Val West.

15: MAROONED

The low-flying plane's cargo doors opened, and with a swift kick to the rear, Val West faceplanted onto the hard sand. After spitting out several mouthfuls of dirt, he watched the plane climb in altitude until it disappeared into the distance. That left him in his present situation—marooned on a small desert island somewhere in the middle of the Pacific Ocean.

A cloudless sky left him at the sun's mercy and it showed none, beating down on him with sweltering heat. After coughing up several more lungfuls of dust and dirt, he tore off the tattered remains of his spysuit, and fashioned it into a loincloth. He felt especially naked without the wolfskin belt around his waist. Ever since it had come into his possession, he had always worn it and counted on it to control his transformations and his consciousness as a werewolf. He really could use it about now.

What he needed even more was to strike the thought from his head. He didn't have the belt, and he'd have to find a way out of this with what he did have. His throat was as parched as the burning sand beneath his blistered feet. Before he could think of anything else, he needed to find fresh water—and fast.

Towering cliffs surrounded the beach, encircling the island like prison walls—and for all intents and purposes, that's exactly what they were. That meant he would have to climb and, in effect, break *into* the prison. His eyes stung from blinding hot sweat as he slowly scaled the most promising route, trying to find hand and footholds on the searing rock face. Black flies swarmed him, biting at his skin mercilessly, but he dared not swat at them, knowing a single misstep would send him plummeting off the rocky cliffside.

He arrived at the rim and looked over it to see a thick blanket of trees and vegetation, which meant there had to be fresh water somewhere. What else lurked in the green hellscape ahead? What kind of wildlife inhabited the island? After finding water, he would need to find food, and then there was the other question: how deserted, exactly, was this island?

Was he alone?

He took a shortcut down by leaping onto the top of a palm tree and sliding down the trunk. Dense foliage covered everything like a thick green fog, the jungle ahead even thicker and darker. He had no choice but to keep moving, praying he'd find an above-ground water source soon. The heat from the sun intensified, as did his choking thirst. Spying a rock formation, he grabbed a handful of pebbles—an old survival trick to stave off thirst—and stuffed them in his mouth. For now, they'd have to do.

The heavy, muggy air made every breath a struggle. Clouds of ravenous mosquitoes feasted on his flesh as he pushed to break through the tangled underbrush. Several times he felt dizziness induced by heat and exhaustion creeping in, and he fought hard against it, even as each step became more difficult than the last. To collapse here would be fatal. He would be devoured by the swarming insects, along with the legions of fire ants crawling the jungle floor, or perhaps swallowed up by the strange plant life that seemed to have an even stranger life of its own, long before he woke—if he woke at all.

He pressed on, his body wracked with dry heaves. Then, a glimmer of hope began to shine in his mind like a beacon. His heightened animal senses detected what he knew was the scent of water. Or at least he hoped it was. Could this be an olfactory mirage of some sort?

Ignoring the razor-sharp leaves and thorn-covered bushes slicing into his skin, he abandoned all caution and ran toward the source of the scent. There it was, dead ahead: a shimmering blue pool of clear water, fed by a small waterfall on the far bank. West would have salivated at the sight if he could have produced enough saliva to do so. Stumbling over himself to get to the pool, his mind was already tasting the cool, fresh, life-giving water—a mirage come true.

He came to an abrupt stop at the water's edge, crashing face-first into the dirt. Something had coiled tightly around his leg, squeezing harder… constricting him. Now, lying helpless on the ground, he heard it. He should have heard it while racing toward the water, but he was too focused on quenching his choking thirst. It was the unmistakable sound of slithering. It now came through loud and clear as he struggled to roll onto his back to confront his unseen attacker.

With all his strength, he threw himself into the turn and quickly sat up, only to find a flicking tongue darting toward his face. It was unquestionably a snake's tongue, but this was a snake unlike any he had ever encountered. Yellow, reptilian slit-eyes were set deep within a humanoid face, its skin a vibrant green, covered in glistening scales. The snake creature locked eyes with him, its long tongue flicking rapidly.

West shook his head. Now it was this. When all he wanted was a damn drink of water.

He finally got his wish. The snake-person rose from its crouch, revealing humanoid legs and torso, the powerful tail still wrapped around West's leg. At least he hoped it was its tail.

The mystery appendage tightened, and the snake-thing spun, whipping West into the water. He had no time for a gulp, however, as he held his breath during a long plummet to the bottom. His tired lungs strained, struggling to keep what little breath he managed to hold on his way down.

He kicked off the rocky bottom, hoping to surface before his next big gulp would be all water—and with it, a watery death.

With a desperate gasp, he broke the surface and thought he had never taken a breath so sweet.

The moment was spoiled by the realization he was surrounded on the shore by a circle of spear-wielding… well, he didn't know exactly *what* they were.

West surveyed the motley group, and a bizarrely colorful group of weirdos they were. The snake-thing stood at the front, its forked tongue flicking in and out of its fanged mouth, saliva dripping. Beside it was a hulking, ape-like creature with some kind of strange mechanical device strapped to its head. Or was it implanted? From here on in, he would question *everything* he was seeing. It stared back at him, unblinking, with glowing, silvery eyes.

Adding more glow, and even more bizarreness, was a skeleton crouched in a fierce fighting stance, jawbone clattering, sharpened spear at the ready. Its bones glowed with an unsettling phosphorescent red, casting a pulsing, eerie light even in the scorching daylight.

Off to the side stood a pitiful figure, a sad-faced misshapen creature who didn't quite seem to have his heart in it. He, too, held a spear, though he kept it low and close to him. A closer look revealed this was no creature but a man, with some undetermined deformities—his most grotesque feature being an exposed half-skull. He kept one hand busy swatting at a constant swarm of flies, desperately trying to keep them from burrowing into his exposed brain tissue.

Whether this was a hallucination or not, West decided either way he had waited long enough, and had already endured enough to get his long-awaited damn drink of water.

The spears edged closer.

"Hold on," West said, addressing the entire group. "I'm going to need a minute." He began furiously lapping up water as the strange creatures looked at each other, unsure of what to do next. The skeleton tapped its metatarsals on the rocky lip of the pool, waiting impatiently for West to finish his well-deserved drink.

The lapping stopped. West took one last big gulp of air and one last glance at the figures on the shore, and then suddenly dove back under the water. A barrage of spears followed behind him as he swam underwater with all his speed, pushing to reach the far shore. Just as he broke the surface, the now-familiar snake appendage caught him in mid-leap, coiling tightly around his body. West was spun in a dizzying whirl before crashing down hard onto the jagged rocks lining the far shore, the impact knocking the breath out of him.

With a weary groan, he did his best to shake it off and tried to get to his feet. His vision was tinted with red, the red glow of the skeleton standing over him. West was in no mood to be trifled with by what he considered a "bag of bones" and what he assumed to be the least threatening of the lot.

His assumption was wrong.

Shockingly wrong, it turned out.

The skeleton caught his swinging uppercut with its own bony fingers. Its skeletal hand glowed an even brighter luminescent shade of crimson, sending a crippling electric shock through West, spiraling him into the by-now merciful darkness of unconsciousness.

The skeleton backed away, its glowing red bones dimming to a soft light. The others picked up a bamboo pole they had brought with them and set about tying West's feet and wrists to it. Led by the skeleton, the mysterious monstrosities carried their captured quarry off, disappearing into the wild jungle bush.

Deep within this bush, several charred concrete structures stuck out from the tropical foliage like unsightly blemishes. The buildings made up what was a small village, and in its center sat a large communal table constructed of bamboo and thatch. Seated at the table was a humanoid creature with a fly's head and wings, buzzing away. It saw the marching hunters approaching and hovered closer.

"Bzzzzz! Whaaat eeeze theeees?" the fly-creature asked, rubbing his human-sized fly claws together.

"Never you mind," the skeleton replied in a harsh, metallic voice, its irritation causing its bones to glow brighter. The fly-creature's eyes (all of them) widened in excitement, and it drifted over toward the skeleton, helplessly drawn to the bright glow.

"Get away, Tony," the skeleton hissed through clattering teeth. "Or I'll zap you for good this time."

The fly-creature—Tony, as it seemed—buzzed away over to the sad-faced man-creature and stuck out a long fly tongue, which wriggled forth toward the exposed brain. His gloomy expression turned to rage, and he belted the fly with a veiny green fist.

"Geeeeeezzzzz, Karl. Doooo you have to beeee so haaaaaarsh? Zzzzz, Zzzzsksst. Zzzerrrrr."

"I get quite enough from the damn flies already," he said in a gruff voice. "Keep your tongue out of my brain, got it?"

The ape-thing grew impatient. It thumped its chest. "We eat! We eat!" making its demands through an implanted voice box.

"Zzzzzyyyessssss," Tony agreed. "Weeee eaaaatttsssszzzzzzz!"

The snake-thing flicked its tongue in anticipation.

EAT! EAT! EAT! EAT! EAT! EAT! EAT! EAT! EAT! went the chant, growing ever louder.

"NO!" a deep voice bellowed.

A towering woman, bulging with muscles, and muscles bulging on top of those muscles, stepped forward. Her skin was a sickening shade of pale green, veined with corded dark emerald varicose lines, further marred by a collection of scars and stitches. The grimacing face was supported by a strong masculine jaw, with urinous yellow eyes encircled by hollow dark craters. On her head of scraggly, matted dark hair sat a bejeweled gold tiara. Across a teeny, G-String bikini, she wore a beauty pageant sash in white, with sparkling gold print (to match her tiara) emblazoned with the title, "Miss Fit."

The others froze in her presence. Only Tony Fly spoke up.

"Weeeeezzzz not eaaattzzzz?"

Miss Fit glowered at him, flexing both arms downward as the ripples moved through her massive musculature like ocean waves.

"No. I have received word from on high that he is *not* to be eaten."

The creatures all pouted with sad looks, except the one known as Karl, who seemed pleased.

"But," she added, "The Powers did not say he could not be *beaten*."

By now West had awoken from his slumber and wished he would have stayed unconscious. He groaned at the thought of yet another beating coming his way. Couldn't any of these people be sociable?

Miss Fit held up a hand. "He shall be beaten for not being one of the chosen misfits, and he will be beaten until he is deemed worthy." She pointed to one of the concrete buildings. "To the jail with him—put him in the irons."

"Wait," West said. "You mean we're not going to eat after all?"

Another shock from the skeleton sent him back to black before he could think about his own hunger or contemplate his fate.

Waking up on a crumbling concrete floor, West rubbed his aching neck and back, and—before he got to the rest of the lengthy list of aches and pains—looked up to see he was being watched through the steel bars of his cell. It was the sad-looking man-creature, this time alone.

"Psssst," he called out in a hushed tone, "Are you awake?"

West rubbed his temples. "Unfortunately, yes, that seems to be the case. Is it time for another beating already?"

"I'm not here to beat you. I didn't want anything to do with any of your other beatings either."

"Oh, I see. Just going straight for eating me then and skip all the formalities?"

"No, you don't understand. I'm not one of them… well, not really. Move over to the window on the other side. I'll come around and talk to you where we can't be seen."

West eased himself up off the floor and looked around at his current lodgings. It was an all-concrete room, coated with remnants of creosote, from a fire that had ravaged it at one time. The front wall entirely concrete block with a steel barred gate door. No furnishings. No food. No water. No toilet, other than the soiled spot in one corner, which looked like it had been designated as one. The walls were all barren concrete slabs, except for the tiny, barred window on the back wall, which West moved his aching body toward.

He was met by the man-creature, who had climbed a small palm tree outside the window and was hiding in its fronds.

"Well, now," said West. "You seem to be a little more civilized than your fellow islanders. If that's the case, then perhaps you wouldn't mind giving me some information. Let's start with who you are."

He smiled. "I would be happy to. My name is Karl. Karl Van Hammer—onetime graduate student and research scientist, now a full-time misfit."

"Let me guess: you worked for Frankentech."

"Good guess. Before I was just another misshapen mutation cast away here, anyway. I worked directly under Igor Zelensky, as Dr. Frankenstein—the baron—was often away on business or with his family at their estate in the U.S. At first, the work was very good. With Frankentech's varied tech products and research, I got to spend time on all kinds of projects, and I genuinely loved my work."

West nodded. "Then something went south. I'm assuming our friend Igor had something to do with it."

"Another good guess, but it wasn't just him. It started with him, though. With Dr. Frankenstein gone so often, Igor soon had me doing other things. Things he claimed were okay because they were engaged in development for world governments, although confidentially, of course. Soon enough, he made me his 'arms dealer,' which meant I had to procure limbs, as well as organs and bones and all kinds of grisly things for these other experiments he and the strangely changed Dr. Frankenstein were now working on."

"Why was it such a strange change?"

"Because the baron had always spoken against those types of experiments—the kind the family had been infamous for, starting with his great-grandfather, the original Victor Frankenstein. Anyway, I couldn't do it anymore. I was there to work in the Applied Sciences division—research and development—not be a graverobber. I told Igor I wished to resign, and in response, he and Dr. Frankenstein made me their next experiment. They wanted to find out if they could make an exposed brain functional. They did—injecting me with God only knows what. It turned my skin this ghoulish green, made my hair fall out, and twisted my flesh, making me just another one of Frankenstein's monsters."

It was a sad story, and West knew Karl was no monster. He was determined to do whatever it took to bring the true monster to justice—permanent justice.

"Has anyone ever successfully escaped from here?" West asked.

"Alas, no… unless you count the sweet release of death. This is a no-fly zone, arranged by Frankenstein with the United States government, and only Frankentech aircraft can fly through. Years ago, this island was used by a research scientist expanding on the work of Victor Frankenstein I for the U.S. government. The doctor created all manner of ghastly grotesques: animal/human hybrid mutations known as 'the Beast Folk,' as well as human/plant mutations known as 'Fruitations.'"

"Interesting. And here I thought that was just how stupid people pronounced the word 'fruition.'"

Karl chuckled softly. It had been so long since he'd felt any joy that he hadn't been sure he still could. He continued. "Yes, well, some of the

Beast Folk and Fruitations are still alive and live here in Misfit Village. These concrete buildings are the burned-out husks of the compound. At some point, everything went all to hell, and the hybrids killed the doctor and burned everything down. They overran the island until Igor Zelensky purchased it to use as a top secret dumping ground for all of Frankentech's illegal failed experiments. Most of the original inhabitants were killed and eaten by the hungry misfits."

"And you all consider yourselves to be misfits?"

Karl's expression turned back into one of resigned, sad acceptance. "If the shoe fits… We were all given that name by our leader, Miss Fit. We are all her misfits. And since Frankenstein sees it that way, it is a perfect fit, if you will pardon the expression."

"This… Miss Fit. Who is she?"

Karl lowered his voice to a terrified whisper as he spoke of her. "Miss Fit is the supreme queen of Frankenstein Island. I knew of her from my time at the Frankentech labs. She was a rejected prototype Bride, after the injected protoplasmic Blobule formula caused her musculature to grow out of control. No longer beautiful, she was rejected for the Brides Project, and was cast off here.

"Of all the misfits, she is the strongest of us all, perhaps even stronger than the Robo-Apes, who all moved over to the other side of the island—that is, except for Ape-X. Miss Fit has also declared herself the Supreme Beauty Queen. We all must vote her the annual pageant winner, or she will rip our heads off with her bare hands. You've met most of the others, but without introductions. Besides her and Ape-X, there's also Tony Fly, who is a 'flybrid,' and Red Skeleton—he's a temperamental phosphorescent electro-skeleton powered by a magnetic heart. Oh, and of course, you know Snake Boy, who is Miss Fit's minion, her favorite."

West paced around the drab cell. This was a hell of a situation to be in. And one to be thinking awfully hard about how to get out of. "What do you think about secretly building a boat or raft?"

157

"Unfortunately, we are hundreds of miles from the shipping lanes," Karl said with a defeated frown. "No one comes by here. No one leaves here. But you and I can be friends."

"I appreciate that, Karl—and we are friends now." Karl beamed at this. "This Miss Fit—she said that she talked with the Powers. Is that Frankenstein? Or Igor? She must be communicating with them in some way—perhaps with a transmitter."

"I know of no such thing. None of us would ever dare sneak into her quarters to find out."

West mulled over the idea. If he could get his hands on this transmitter—if it even existed—he could somehow get a coded signal to Para-Command. Until he found a way out of his cell or could convince Karl, he had nothing but time to kill.

"When you told me about Miss Fit, you mentioned you knew about the Brides Project. When you were at Frankentech, did you know about a professor they were working with named Ossie Weiner?"

"Oh yes! I was part of that project... for a time, at least. While trying to perfect an augmented regulator, the biomechanics team at Frankentech more-or-less accidentally invented something they called the Fabula Device. Interesting as it was, it had no practical use for Frankentech, but they realized it could be the key to successfully powering a Quantum Collider.

"They contacted Dr. Weiner, and while he was greatly intrigued by the Fabula Device, he refused to build a Collider for Frankenstein. Weiner had calculated that even though it would power the Collider, a disturbance with the crystals would cause it to collapse in on itself, sucking it into an interdimensional black hole. It was too risky to do at that time, even with—or I should say, *especially* with the Fabula Device."

Karl let out a yelp and disappeared from view. West craned his neck to look through the window at the ground below.

Gone.

The cage door rattled, and he turned around to see Miss Fit carrying Karl by the scruff of his neck. She hurled him inside and slammed the door shut again. Karl had hit the wall hard and painfully slid down to the floor, trembling.

"I trust you had a good story-time." She sneered at West and held up the key, swinging it back and forth to taunt him. "You want out, yes? Both you and your new friend? You will soon get your wish.

"You are both being sent for a ride into… THE DANGER ZONE!"

16: YELLOW JACKETS REQUIRED

On the blue Mediterranean, a small speedboat ferried out a fiend named Igor Zelensky toward a luxury yacht anchored in Italy's Gulf of Spezia. The vessel, called *Alvarium*, had sailed in from the Black Sea to host a meeting of HIVE's senior management team. Known as the Yellow Jackets for the golden blazers they wore to signify their status, the management consisted of bankers and other criminal types, each handpicked by HIVE's upper echelon.

The air was fresh and salted with wisps of sea spray. It was a good day for Igor to be fitted for a new jacket of his own, tailored in yellow hopsack wool—one he felt he had deservedly earned. He was set to address the group, who would determine his future with HIVE and, more specifically, his promotion within its ranks. Although this was a big moment for him, his unwavering loyalty to the cause made his induction feel like a mere formality, one with no dispute.

As the business partner and close friend of the late Baron Hans Frankenstein, and later mentor to his son, the young Victor, Igor had seen their differing approaches and knew which one he preferred. Mentored in the ways of ruthless effectiveness by Hans, he had later forced himself to bite his tongue at the follies of Victor's youthful idealism. He supposed at one time in his own youth, he also had held those same ideals. But Hans Frankenstein had taught him early on that power and greed were natural ambitions of the great—qualities to be embraced, not suppressed. And while Igor's greed and lust for power drove him, he had been dismayed that this philosophy did not appeal to the young Victor.

Under Victor and Igor's leadership, the late Hans Frankenstein's company, Frankentech, grew into a global force. Yet, Igor had always bristled at the less-than-profitable ventures Victor wanted the company to pursue, at the expense of far more lucrative developments like bioweapons and using the secret "Frankenstein Formulas" to create super-soldiers and other military applications for the highest bidder—or bidders.

Why not sell to both sides? They would be fighting it out, anyway, in whatever military conflict they were involved in. Why not let them fight it out with the best? Meaning, of course, Frankentech products.

While he couldn't do it exactly under the Frankentech banner, what Victor didn't know wouldn't hurt him. That was what special, carefully buried subsidiaries were for.

The opportunities of late with HIVE, along with Victor's change of mind, had finally aligned with his visions of grandeur. It was not all smooth sailing, though. They now had a Quantum Collider, which was key, but there were other issues. Spy agencies were on them—most recently the Italians, along with International Command. There was also interest from the CIA prior to that. Even if their agent snooping around the Orkneys hadn't been killed by the Nuckelavee, they could have been bought off easily. The other agencies could not.

The baron had thought perhaps it wasn't International Command proper investigating, but rather a carefully buried subdivision of their own—the one employing this Val West, a werewolf, as preposterous as it sounded. Igor knew it wasn't preposterous at all. He had seen it with his own eyes from the helicopter.

Once West had been captured, Frankenstein discovered that he possessed an unknown blood type. Then there was that strange wolfskin belt, adorned with antique golden plates engraved with wolf imagery. They had interrogated him and sent him off to the island, and presumably the trail he was blazing toward them would end there.

Igor was also certain HIVE would be very interested in having West be *their* werewolf agent. Frankenstein could perform the necessary brain modifications to make that happen.

To top it all off, Romano Orlada, the head director of HIVE Europe, was dead—killed by West in Chamonix. That was a nice favor, unknowingly done for him by West, giving him a clear path to succession. He was on his way to the top and he could almost taste it as he entered the yacht's boardroom.

Gathered around the polished oak table were the other members of HIVE Senior Management, all men in powerful positions spanning the globe. At the head of the table stood Herr Ziegfield, the most senior of the directors. "Mr. Zelensky," Ziegfield said, in his commanding tone. "Thank you for joining us."

Each of them wore their golden blazers as officially recognized Yellow Jackets—the mark of HIVE's elite. As Igor entered, they stood to acknowledge his arrival.

He walked through the thick cloud of expensive cigar smoke which filled the room and took his seat, trying not to reveal any nervous anticipation. The other directors eyed him up with expressionless, unreadable faces.

The representative of HIVE Asia, Director Huángfēng, asked the first question. "Mr. Zelensky. Before we get to the other matters at hand, I have received reports on the series of deaths of HIVE agents, and it would appear the cause is one of Baron Frankenstein's monsters. What explanation do you have for this?"

Igor could sense the tension, but remained calm. This was an opportunity.

"Director Huángfēng, please understand that this was *not* authorized by me. This was Baron Frankenstein's doing. It was his fault this creature, the one called 'Prototype A,' was allowed to get loose and escape. I told him to destroy it, along with his head he insisted on keeping alive. I was acting in HIVE's best interests. He was not."

The answer seemed to satisfy Director Huángfēng, but Director Vespa of Corsica leaned forward with a follow-up. "What steps are you taking to resolve this issue?"

Igor replied smoothly, "Well, for one, after securing the Quantum Collider—using a plan I would remind you I devised—we set up the Monster, Prototype A, to look as if he was behind it. I also arranged for Frankenstein to convince the investigating intelligence agent that the Monster needed to be eliminated."

"And this has not been accomplished?"

"Not yet," Igor admitted. "Unfortunately. But it will be, and for our purposes, it does not matter at this point. All they have for leverage is the abducted son of Frankenstein, and they can have him for all I care. We have what truly matters—the Collider. We have the real leverage… the real power… the real stroke."

The others looked at each other to confer and nodded in silence.

Vespa wasn't entirely satisfied and continued to press. "And what of the Brides Project? We have invested a lot of time and effort into this, and Baron Frankenstein's genius has been invaluable in achieving its success."

"This is true," Igor answered, maintaining his calm demeanor. "And now the Brides—and the Cy-Brides—are nearly ready for deployment. Frankenstein's soldiers are also close to being combat-ready. According to him, the Collider's power is the final piece needed to stabilize them. Then they are ours… HIVE's."

"Mr. Zelensky." It was Director Prince Galen of Moldavia who spoke this time, leaning forward, his eyes scanning the room. "Now that we have the Quantum Collider, along with Frankentech's technology to make it operational, allow me to suggest we don't necessarily need the

Baron Frankenstein—once the Brides and his soldiers are fully functional."

He paused, waiting for objections. None came. He then added, "Going forward, all we really need is Frankentech… under the leadership of Igor Zelensky."

The other directors fell silent, then, one by one, they nodded in agreement before buzzing amongst themselves.

Director Ziegfield called them to order. "With the unfortunate demise of Romano Orlada, we do need a new head of HIVE Europe. I think Mr. Zelensky's accomplishment of obtaining the Quantum Collider and his taking control of Frankentech, which will allow us to put it to a more universal use, qualifies him to not only become an esteemed fellow member of the Yellow Jackets of HIVE, but also to take Director Orlada's place as the new Board Director and Senior Vice President of HIVE Europe. I make the motion to nominate his appointment, pending approval from the Queen."

The motion was supported and carried unanimously by the board.

"Now, please rise, Director-Elect Zelensky."

Igor rose, and a bright golden Yellow Jacket was held open for him by Director Ziegfield. Beaming with pride, Igor bowed as the others applauded.

He addressed the group. "A new day has dawned for HIVE. A new era, as *the* true superpower of the earth, with the Quantum Collider being the superweapon to usher in this new era."

The applause continued, followed by an endless flow of champagne, caviar, and the finest cigars.

The fool. Igor's thoughts drifted to Victor Frankenstein. He could also have been here, at this very table, if not for his foolish obsession with building creatures out of the dead, creating monstrous abominations he alone considered masterpieces. He was like an artist, and to Igor, artists were always flakes, always fools, even if they happened to possess scientific genius-level intellects.

Igor had thought his partnership with Frankenstein would be one of equality. After all, there was more than enough for both of them.

It was not to be. Igor had always played second fiddle, and now he was the master violinist, and on his way to being the conductor of the whole damn symphony. The green flesh of Frankenstein's creations could never match the green of the jealous envy coursing through Igor Zelensky. He had come to bitterly despise Frankenstein's unwavering dedication to his work, especially when it came at the expense of capitalizing on power and profit.

He now realized that, though the Baron was a genius—and an evil one at that—most importantly, he was truly a madman. Igor wasn't evil. He was merely greedy and certainly not mad.

Frankenstein, however, was cut from an entirely different cloth. He would come around to HIVE's way of thinking.

Or else.

17: THE DANGER ZONE

"What the hell is the Danger Zone? I think it goes without saying that it doesn't sound good at all."

Karl Van Hammer looked at Val West with shock and fear in his eyes. "It is a death sentence. No one has ever survived the Danger Zone."

West wasn't sure what day it was, but he could feel the moon's growing power. It was in its Waxing Gibbous phase, and in a few more days, would be full. That would change things drastically. Even more drastically, without the wolfskin belt—what would he do as a completely uncontrolled, unstoppable savage beast? True, he might be killed in the Danger Zone, but his death would be short-lived once the lunar rays found him.

Heavy yoke collars, linked to rusted steel cables, were fastened around each of their necks. They were dragged away by Ape-X, with Red Skeleton at the rear, ready to send a shocking blast of electricity through the cables should West or Karl step out of line. Or, if it amused him, which it did several times along the way.

After each stinging shock, Red would cackle through his chattering teeth. Miss Fit led the procession, which came to a halt at the start of a rough trail carved into the dense jungle foliage. A crude sign made of weathered wood was nailed to a palm tree at the entrance, and painted in red—or perhaps it was blood—were the scrawled words, "DANGER ZONE."

Miss Fit was salivating with anticipation. She turned her piercing yellow eyes toward West. "Do you know where you are?"

"In the jungle?"

Miss Fit kicked him in the groin. Hard.

West doubled over in pain. Red Skeleton shocked him back upright.

"NO! You're in the Danger Zone, baby," she screeched, "And you're gonna die!"

The misfits all took up spears, poking them at West and Karl. The yokes were released, and they were prodded down the trail. West thought the Danger Zone might be a welcome reprieve.

The overgrown trail barely even qualified as a path through the thick, untrimmed bush. The duo, stripped of all but loincloths, walked along it gingerly. They were on high alert, awaiting the first danger to come, knowing they were in a place called "The Danger Zone," after all.

Nothing… so far. Other than the rough ground beneath, and the blistering heat, it could have been a pleasant jungle stroll. West looked back, noticing the darkness of the bush had already obscured the entrance point. They were on their own now.

"Danger Zone, my ass," an irritated West commented. "If this is their idea of danger, then they don't know the meaning of the word."

A worried Karl raised a finger and shushed him. He spoke in a quiet, nervous whisper. "Did you hear that?"

West tuned in his hearing. There was a slight rustle in the trees above, followed by what he thought sounded like a high-pitched…giggle? Or was it a snort? No, it was more of a squeal.

The squealing grew louder into a boarish chorus. West heard the distinct sound of the creak of a nock—an arrow nock. He knew what was coming next and grabbed Karl by the arm, the two of them bolting down the trail. A flurry of tiny arrows rained down from the treetops, and one was heading straight for Karl's forehead.

West leaped, diving toward him. They rolled into the underbrush, the arrow zipping past.

"That was close," Karl gasped. "Thank you, my friend. I hope I can do the same for you at some point."

"Don't mention it," West replied, looking for some form of cover. He spotted a rotting palm log and raised it over them as a shield. Another volley of arrows came down from the trees, pincushioning the top of the log. West yanked one of the small arrows from the trunk and inspected the tip. "Poisoned, no less."

"Yes… it's the Pigmies. They live up in the treetops. More of the old islanders, the hybrids," Karl explained. "They are dwarf warriors mutated from swine DNA."

West began clawing at the underside of the log, hollowing out a portion of the punky wood. "As nice as this little 'hambush' is, we can't stay here. We're going to have to take a chance and hope we can run faster than they can jump from treetop to treetop. Get yourself into position and on my signal, we're going to stand up and run under this, together."

The squeals, mixed with threatening grunts and oinks, surrounded them as more arrows thudded into the carcass of the tree trunk, sending splinters flying. West gave the signal, and they broke for it—arrow tips tore through the spongy wood, narrowly grazing their heads. He poked his head out; blue sky broke through the thick canopy ahead—a clearing!

"Come on, Karl, push!" An arrow grazed the back of Karl's leg, almost breaking the skin.

West lifted the trunk higher, higher than Karl could reach, but once the little man could see the blue sky, he ran even faster to keep up. As soon as they reached the clearing, West dropped, propping the arrow-covered tree trunk behind them as a shield.

The arrows had stopped. West paused to catch his breath. "So, that was a little dangerous."

Karl only offered a nod of agreement. Cautiously, they left the shelter of the tree trunk and found themselves in an open clearing leading to a ravine up ahead. Not wanting to venture back into the trees with Pigmies snorting about, they opted to go down into the ravine. West took an arrow in each hand to at least have some sort of weapon.

The ravine was about twenty feet deep, mostly rock stubbled with scattered shrubbery tangled in dead vines, but it was long, stretching far beyond what they could see. The scorching sun bore down on them, and West wished he had taken the tree trunk to use as shade. He scanned the rocky walls of the ravine as they walked, wondering where—and when—the next form of hell would spring forth.

Karl stopped for a moment and split open a coconut he had found. They both eagerly ate the coconut and drank its juice. West thought about his last meal—a dirty plate with some unidentified slop on it, shoved under the cell bars. It had smelled like rat to him, but he had held his nostrils shut and ate it anyway.

West stepped ahead, then abruptly stopped, throwing his arm back to stop Karl. A sudden blast of fire belched out from the ravine. He looked up at the top of the ravine wall and caught the flash of sunlight glinting off the tips of spears, then noticed the bamboo structures loaded with razor-sharp lances, pointing down at them, ready to fire. They hurried on, dodging flame blasts and the death rain of spears firing from above.

Karl called out from behind. When West turned around, Karl was dangling by his fingertips from the edge of a concealed pit trap. He lunged forward to catch Karl's hand before he lost his grip, catching a glimpse of the deadly wooden spikes waiting at the bottom.

A buzzing sound cut through the chaos, and West found himself walking straight into Tony Fly. "ZZZZzzzzzzzZZZZ," was Tony's greeting as he hovered around them. West tossed one of the poison arrows he had brought with him to Karl, then raised another at Tony Fly.

"Buzz off, you son-of-a-bitch."

"ZZZZZZZZZ, come flyyyyyy wiiiith meeeeeeee!" Tony excitedly rubbed his claw-hands together, then grabbed West by the back of his loincloth strap, swiftly propelling them both over the ravine. West struggled to twist himself toward Tony but was unable to get his bearings as they careened through the air in spinning turns.

Tony Fly banked a hard left. West used the gravity to shift his weight, delivering a left-handed swat to Tony's many eyes. The human-sized Dipteral mandibles snapped at West and after a disorienting dive, he nearly lost his arrow.

Not nearly enough for Tony Fly's sake.

With a fierce thrust, West buried the arrow into Tony's neck, yellow slime spewing out of the vein. The fly shot skyward like a rocket, zooming out of control. West grabbed at a wing, tearing it off Tony's back. Far below, the wing fell to the ground beside Karl. A feeling of dread filled him as he watched West riding the berserk Tony Fly across the sky, certain he was about to be on his own.

With only one wing remaining, and the poison setting in, Tony dropped into a spiraling nosedive. As the ground rushed up, West bailed, tumbling hard across the ravine floor. Behind him, Tony crashed proboscis-first into the earth, triggering a flame-blaster upon impact that instantly incinerated him.

A worried Karl hurried over to check on West, praying he had somehow managed to survive this death flight. To his relief, West rolled over with a groan.

West glanced back at the smoldering remains. "He must not have heard this is a no-fly zone."

Karl let out a groan of his own.

Apart from the occasional spiked projectile and unpredictable fire blast, the rest of the journey through the ravine was rather uneventful. At last, they came to its end. A new nervousness crept in as they imagined what new dangers might be lying in wait.

West stopped them at the edge. Treacherous quicksand stretched to the end of the ravine, blocking the path to what appeared to be a lush valley beyond.

"Well," said West. "We're not going through this way. And no way for us to cross it." He scanned the perimeter and noticed a narrow rocky lip along the edge of the quicksand. On the far side was a rock bluff with the shadow of a cave mouth. It seemed there was a way to climb up past the cave, and West's hopes lifted, though he wasn't entirely sure why. Even if they made it, what new horror would greet them? No, he had to stay positive. He had to keep going.

Tiptoeing over the sharp rocks, they slowly inched their way along the edge. Reaching the opening of the dark cave, they stopped to look in.

"Let's keep moving," West said. "Whatever's in there, I'm sure we don't want any part of it."

Karl nodded in agreement, and they proceeded cautiously along the narrow ledge that stretched across the cave's mouth.

ZAP! An electrically charged bolt shot out, ricocheting off the jagged rock at the cliff's edge.

"What the hell is this now?" West yelled, his voice bouncing off the rocky walls of the ravine. Above, on the other side, stood Red Skeleton, creating ball-lightning in his bony hands. He hurled the charged orbs toward them, the energy crackling as each ball struck the surrounding rocks.

West turned to Karl. "I guess we're going in, anyway." They dashed into the cave, lightning balls crashing and blasting behind them.

The dark cavern was less than welcoming, its walls dripping with moldy sweat, the air itself an assault as the foul stench of death stung their nostrils. West and Karl were of the opinion that this wasn't necessarily an improvement over the situation outside, but they kept trudging deeper into the cave tunnels. Despite the stench, West welcomed the moment to collect his thoughts without being under attack.

Here he was, stranded on a desert isle populated by grotesque experimental misfits that seemingly lived to inflict punishment and torture—there were certainly some psychological issues behind that. Now, he was trapped in this death course known as the Danger Zone. Even if he successfully made it out alive, he still had the misfits to deal with, not to mention this rotten hellhole of an island he had to escape. It all seemed hopelessly bleak to him, despite the many challenges he had managed to survive unscathed in the past.

A rattling scream from Karl interrupted his moment of reverie. The cave had led them into a chamber with a dead end. His scream came as a wall of bamboo bars slammed down behind them, blocking their only way out.

Along with his growing anger, West felt a growing animalistic rage rush through him, the approaching full moon infusing his cells. His lips curled back as he ran his tongue across his sharpening teeth. Enraged by yet another trap, even here in the depths of this dank cave, he unleashed a series of strikes and kicks at the bars. The bamboo splintered, but still stood intact.

"It's steel-reinforced bamboo!" He grunted in dismay, frustration mounting. Karl yelped again as the sound of stone scraping against stone echoed through the cave.

The yelp was well founded. The cave's stone ceiling was lowering—never a good sign—rusty metal spikes extended out through the rock, sharp and ready to strike, growing closer each second.

Sweat poured off West. Was this it? Could this really be the end? After all he had been through? Goddamnit, no!

On a side wall, a dust-covered ship's wheel stuck out of the rock, connected to a chain pulley system. He followed the chain upward. It appeared to be part of the contraption lowering the ceiling. West gripped the wheel and wrenched it with all his strength, but it wouldn't budge—rusted tight.

Time was running out.

West cranked the wheel again, struggling hard to break it loose as the spikes inched closer. A fierce glow burned in his eyes as his lengthening fangs dug into his lip, a trickle of crimson rolling down his chin.

Karl saw the bared fangs and the glowing red eyes, and for a moment, he was almost more alarmed by this than by the impending doom from above. "W-W-What are you?" he stammered, knowing West was too busy to answer, and half relieved he couldn't.

There was no time to answer. There was no time at all.

The spikes grazed their skin, and with one final, mighty effort, West broke the rust off the wheel and got it to turn. As he had hoped, it was connected to the ceiling mechanism, and his furious turning of the wheel stopped the movement, retracting the ceiling.

While turning the wheel, West noticed the chain pulley underneath it, disappearing into holes in the rock floor they stood on. Turning the wheel had stopped the ceiling trap. What was this other chain doing?

They got their answer as the ceiling stones clicked into place. Under pressure, the chain snapped and fell from its pulley. Suddenly, the floor swung open beneath them, plunging them into a dark cavern filled with icy water.

"Karl! Are you all right?"

Karl bobbed up. "Damn them," he said, spitting out a mouthful of foul water. "A trap to stop another trap. Not exactly fair play. But yes, I am quite all right."

He suddenly disappeared under the water. Something had pulled him down. Something big.

West dove under, using his heightened night vision to cut through the murky depths, and found Karl struggling with a monstrous figure he recognized all too well—the skinless half-humanoid, half-horse, all-terrifying visage of a Nuckelavee, a botched first attempt by Frankentech lab dumped here on this cursed island. A broken shackle hung from its neck, having been released by the turning of the ship's wheel. Its single, blinking eye glared back at West.

Karl thrashed in the creature's grip, panicking. His fingers desperately grasped for his only defense—the poison-tipped Pigmy arrow West had given him. With all his strength, he thrust the arrow into the horse-like head of the Nuckelavee. It bucked wildly, letting out a gargled whinny of pain.

However, the beast wasn't finished yet. The large lamprey-like mouth widened, its razor-sharp rows of teeth whirring. It chomped down ferociously, devouring the upper half of Karl's body. The remaining pieces floated and bobbed in the blood-filled murk.

The Nuckelavee turned its lone eye to West and lunged. With the poison starting to take effect, its frenzied attack only intensified. It struck at West and grabbed him by the throat with its long arms, pinning him against the sharp rocks below.

With no other choice, and running out of air, West saw the only thing that could possibly save him: one of Karl's severed legs floating nearby, a jagged piece of broken-off femur jutting out. He grasped frantically, reaching out to catch it as it floated away. His fingers finally closed around the ankle, gripping it tightly. With perhaps the last of his strength, West drove the sharp, broken bone end into the Nuckelavee's single eye, burying it deep into its brain.

Death came instantly, and the creature let out a final, deafening screech as it collapsed, its grip loosening. His lungs screaming, West surged upward, racing for a life-saving gasp of air.

For a precious few seconds, he lay floating in the pool, exhausted from the trials of the Danger Zone and saddened by the loss of Karl, his one friend in this godforsaken place.

Above the pool, a section of the cavern wall rolled to the side, letting in a flood of bright sunlight. West looked up wearily, wondering what this could be, feeling his spirit cracking at the thought. Silhouetted figures came into view, lowering a rope. He considered refusing it, but he also couldn't stay here. He had to take his chances. Maybe he did have some spirit left.

When he finally reached the outside, he was less than overjoyed to discover his rescuers were the misfits. Miss Fit herself stood before the bloodied and battered Val West.

"You have survived the Danger Zone," she said in her horridly masculine screech. "You are a worthy foe. But you are not one of us, and for that, you shall be sentenced to your fate."

Exhausted, West finally collapsed and was carelessly dragged down the rocky path to the beach. When he awoke, it was to the soothing sound of crashing waves. For a moment, he thought maybe he was in heaven—until he opened his eyes to the sight of Miss Fit.

"Here is your reward and your sentence, outsider," she snorted.

West realized he had been bound with rope to an old ship's mast, his arms stretched out to the crosspieces. He struggled against the coarse rope biting into his skin as the other misfits—Ape-X, Red Skeleton, and Snake Boy, lifted the mast.

They stopped when West was at Miss Fit's height. She stepped forward and pulled out two large, rusty spike nails. With a grin twisted in perverse delight, she picked up a giant mallet and drove each of them through West's wrists, burying them deep into the wood beneath.

West gritted his teeth from the unbearable pain, cursing under his breath as he conjured up a few precious drops of saliva to spit at her. At Miss Fit's order, the misfits raised the mast upright and dropped it into a deep hole in the sand.

"You will find I am not entirely without mercy," Miss Fit said. "You will have an excellent ocean view. It will also be in full view of the sweltering sun." She laughed a hideous laugh, sneering at him with black lips. "This is what you get for not being a freak of nature like us."

"Tremendous… come see me in a few days."

Miss Fit called for a spear. She turned it around, raised it up, and cuffed him across the face with its handle.

"We will, and without your invitation. Soon, it will be our Festival of the Full Moon on Monday. You will be our honored guest."

"I can't wait."

Miss Fit eyed him curiously. She thought it looked like he had just winked.

The misfits returned to the village, and he was left alone with only his pain for company, his time to be spent waiting.

Waiting for the moon.

18: BALLOONED

The scent of the misty, dew-covered wilderness tickled his senses as he bounded through the tall field grasses, gliding effortlessly, naturally, bathed in the sweet light of the full moon. He paused to bay at it, in tribute, as pure animal worship. The smell of rabbit triggered his appetite. One was nearby and he would have it. Joyfully, he loped off on the balls of his feet into the shadows, the thrill of chasing his prey coursing through his very being, his primal soul, the coppery, earthy taste of rabbit blood already on his lips in anticipation.

Blood on his lips. Gore on his claws. The taste of torn flesh on his tongue. To run, to hunt—this was all there was, and all there needed to be.

"Val, can you hear me?"

The soft sound of a familiar voice gently stirred Val West. He was still half-asleep, but he knew the voice. It was the voice of Lady Kendra Kenton. There was no rush to wake. Earlier, he had been tormented by a horrifying nightmare of monstrous mutants and deadly games on an island of terror. That was all behind him now, a horrid dream to be forgotten. He listened to her voice, sweet like a song, and was glad he had come back—back to her, the woman he wasn't sure he had truly felt for until now.

Now he knew, without a doubt. He was ready to awaken from this blissful slumber, ready to take her and…

He was jolted away from this heavenly dream, back to the nightmarish hell of being nailed to a rotting ship's mast on Frankenstein Island. The sun blasted straight into his eyes as it rose over the mast at high noon. Soon, his burned, blistered skin would again be battered by the unrelenting heat of the sun, the whipping winds, the blasting sands of the beach, the merciless biting of the blackflies and the pecking of the swirling scavengers treating him like a piece of carrion carcass. Only he wasn't dead.

Not yet anyway.

West was uncertain how long it had been. Had it been two, or was it three days? One of the misfits had come and poured water down his throat yesterday—or maybe it was the day before—to ensure he stayed alive as long as possible. Time was completely lost to him. Every hour was a never-ending feverish delirium wracked by terrible hallucinatory visions. Only rarely did he manage to find some relief in his brief, scattered moments of merciful sleep.

Should he come through this, he would see to Kendra. He knew how she felt about his condition. He could convince her otherwise. He might even be able to convince her not to use her silver bullet on him.

Then, perhaps… they would go out for an evening, just the two of them.

It was a wonderful, sparkling thought, one that made him nearly weep. These thoughts, as fleeting as they were amidst the horror, kept him going. The moon would be full in days. How many, he did not know, but he watched each evening as it moved across the sky, growing bigger, growing brighter, looking down at him from above the ocean, telling him the time was coming soon.

Each night through his agony, through the feverishness of his infected wounds, he could feel the change coming, growing wilder and wilder inside him, the feeling beating in his chest like a primeval drum. It would take the full moon's power to send the needed WLF ray energy to fully trigger his transformation, and until then he must hang on, mentally. Physically crucified, he had no other choice but to hang on.

He would not be broken. Not by Miss Fit. Not by her misfits. Not by anyone.

Day Four: Nightfall.

Val West had been dreaming for so long he wasn't sure if he was awake or asleep anymore. If he had been lucid enough, he might have noticed the feeling of the last gasps of life leaving his body. Just as it had on previous nights, the fat orange moon appeared from behind the far cliffs of the island. Only on this night, it was fatter than it had been.

It was as fat and round and as *full* as it could grow.

The sound of drums beating through the jungle carried on the breeze down to the lonely beach. Beating the drums was a procession of misfits, led by the exalted one, Miss Fit, the first rays of moonlight glinting off her bejeweled tiara. The parade wound down the cliffside trail to the beach, where several bonfires were lit. There, the gruesome gang of Miss Fit, Red Skeleton, Ape-X, and Snake Boy gathered, now joined by other assorted oddities and ends.

They would light their torches and wave them, for it was the Festival of the Full Moon on Monday. In such a desolate, misery-ridden place, this was their monthly celebration, and they would dance all through the night around the great flames of their death-fires.

Pounding drums and dancing, the misfits paraded around the mast Val West hung from. He was no longer conscious and did not see the glimmering shine rising over the ocean, blue moonlight illuminating the gently rolling waves lapping at the beach. The bonfires crackled, chanting filled the air, and the imposing Miss Fit presided over the festivities, her golden eyes gleaming.

Another pair of eyes turned a reddish yellow.

Val West's eyes snapped open. His head was still drooping, but the eyes returned to life at the moon's first shining rays. Bathed in the warm orange glow of the bonfire on one side and the cold blue of the moon on the other, the lifeless body began to quiver.

Miss Fit noticed, raising a hand to silence the drums and for all to be silent. Alongside the other misfits, she watched in morbid curiosity as Val West's body began its inhuman metamorphosis. The body trembled, the face contorted, ears sharpened to points, and his nose elongated into a beastly snout. Fur sprouted rapidly over the bruised and blistered bare skin while feral fangs jutted over his lower lip, frothing with a rabid foam. As his head lifted, he glared at the misfits with burning red eyes, his fangs gnashing in fury. Hands that were now claws chafed against the thick nails pinning his wrists to the wooden mast.

Now fully transformed into LoneWolf, he let out a long howl. A chill cut through all of their bones, especially those of Red Skeleton, whose bones clattered uncontrollably.

To the misfits' shock, the beast tore its wrists free from the embedded nails, shredding the ropes that confined him to the post. With an unearthly growl, he leaped down onto the sandy beach before them.

All were silent.

Miss Fit stared at the beast snarling at them in the firelight. She turned to the others. "He is truly worthy. He is one of us."

Under the pale blue light of the moon, the misfits all raised their torches, beat their drums loudly and began chanting, "We accept you."

"One of us!" Miss Fit gushed lustily.

LoneWolf cocked his head, listening, but not understanding the bizarre display before him. However, somewhere in the far reaches of his primal mind, a mind where West was not present, not conscious, he somehow remembered. He knew, on a base level, the way they had treated him, just as any animal remembers those who have cruelly mistreated them.

The Danger Zone. The pain.
The death of Karl. The torture.
The crucifixion. The destruction.
The breaking... of his mind.
His body.
His soul.

As these images flashed through his animal mind, he instinctually reacted in the most primitive, savagely animal way possible.

Before the misfits could react, LoneWolf was already upon them, his claws slashing, his fangs biting through flesh. The lead misfits—Snake Boy, Red Skeleton, and Miss Fit—backed away in terror. Ape-X tried to stand his ground, but was immediately ripped apart, a shower of shredded simian entrails splattering the remaining survivors.

LoneWolf launched himself through the air, a projectile of apocalyptic vengeance. Snake Boy hissed at him, his tongue flicking furiously until LoneWolf snatched it, tearing it out by the roots. Claws slashed across Snake Boy's face, slicing it into bloodied chunks.

Red Skeleton pulsed his magnetic heart, glowing a hot red as he charged himself to full power. The bright light caught LoneWolf's attention, which is not at all what Red wanted. Staring down the skeleton through the wall of flames from the out-of-control bonfire, his unleashed savagery drove him to attack the shiny, glowing object. He soared over the inferno, claws outstretched, rage burning in his eyes. The skeleton's eye sockets popped in terror at the sight of the rampaging beast dead ahead.

Quickly clasping his hand bones together, Red focused all his pulsing energy into a crackling ball of lightning. With only one shot at this, he unleashed a mighty energy bolt, pouring every ounce of his power into it.

If he'd had tear ducts, he would have cried.

LoneWolf pivoted mid-air, narrowly avoiding the blast as it struck the cliffside instead. The depleted Red Skeleton heaved a bone-rattling sigh of resignation, which was to become a death rattle. LoneWolf's leap connected with a thunderous impact, an explosion of shattered bone fragments littering the beach, each a tiny red ember glowing briefly before fading into darkness.

Miss Fit stood paralyzed, enraged disbelief washing over her. This was the last thing she had expected. How dare this freak, this uninvited misfit, ruin her Full Moon festival? The others lay dead in various states of dismemberment, the gore pooling into crimson reflections that danced in the flames. She screeched in a low, primal register, her voice echoing off the surrounding cliffs. LoneWolf looked up from the carcass he had been feasting on and howled back at her, ready for more combat.

The two monsters faced each other on the blood-spattered beach, oblivious to the round, dark shape slowly moving in front of the moon, growing larger as it approached. Miss Fit flexed her bulbous muscles, roaring with wrath. LoneWolf bared his fangs and answered with a ferocious growl. Snorting like an incensed bull, she charged across the sand. A torch lying on the ground still blazed away. He picked it up, raising it high, swinging it in a powerful arc.

Miss Fit barreled toward him, sand flying beneath her powerful feet. LoneWolf released the torch, the flames spiraling toward her head. Her screeching reached a terrifying pitch as it connected, and she realized her hair was ablaze. In a mad panic, she stumbled toward the water, plunging into the waves.

LoneWolf surveyed the surrounding carnage, threw his head back, and unleashed a long howl of triumph.

The shadowy shape was no longer in front of the moon. Now, a giant shadow fell across the baying LoneWolf, a shadow belonging to nearly eight feet of trouble. The werewolf looked up to see a face framed by a squared-off head, green-yellow skin, and a thick protruding brow—the grim visage of none other than Prototype A, the Frankenstein Monster.

LoneWolf snarled at the towering intruder. The Monster wrapped his enormous, vise-like hands around LoneWolf's neck, powerfully lifting him off the ground as he thrashed wildly, snapping his fangs in defiance. The Monster lumbered across the beach with slow but powerful strides toward the darkness of the ocean.

With a sudden, well-placed kick, LoneWolf broke free of the Monster's powerful grip. The two squared off, the tension mounting as to which would strike first, until both monsters lunged at each other, pummeling each other backward across the beach. LoneWolf seized the Monster's arm, whipping him toward the furious blaze of the bonfires. The Monster froze in fear at the sight of the flames, raising an arm to shield his face as he staggered away from the raging fire. Not wasting the opportunity, LoneWolf leaped onto the Monster's back, sticking him with his sharp, talon-like claws.

Both monsters came to a dead stop at the sight of Miss Fit.

Slowly emerging from the water, Miss Fit stumbled back onto the beach, her scalp covered in grotesque, bubbling burns. She stopped in her giant-sized tracks when she set her eyes on the Frankenstein Monster.

Oh, hot damn, she thought, quite literally. Heated up by more than just her burns, she decided this was going to be her man. She preened and strutted along the shore, running her veined, green-skinned hands along her musclebound giantess legs, eyeing her new conquest. With a slow, sultry shimmy, she danced to a strip tease under the light of the moon, suggestively tugging at her bikini straps with long, fungus-green fingernails.

The Monster and LoneWolf exchanged looks, partly of confusion, partly of disgust, the utterly bizarre display bringing their battle to a standstill. Miss Fit sashayed closer, running one of those filthy nails up the Monster's thigh, her intentions clear.

LoneWolf had seen enough. In a fit of fury, he lunged at her, his fangs tearing a gaping chunk out of her neck. A geyser of green blood erupted, spraying the air as she screeched in shock. The screeching stopped suddenly as the rabid and maniacal LoneWolf had bitten through the metal sutures connecting her head to her body, tearing it completely off. With a hiss of animalistic rage, he hurled her severed head across the beach, where it splashed into the crashing surf with a toilet water *plop*.

Using the distraction to his advantage, the Monster leveled LoneWolf with a giant fist to the face. The force of the blow sent shockwaves through the werewolf, disorienting him. The Monster grabbed him by the scruff of the neck and continued toward his original destination—down the beach, where, hidden in the shadows alongside the rolling ocean waves, a metal-barred, roofed cage awaited.

With a grunt, the Monster tossed the limp werewolf into the cage and slammed the door shut with a heavy clang, locking it tight. A spotlight shone down from above, and he signaled to it with a wave. He made his way to the top of the cage and clung to a cable leading to a hot air balloon drifting silently above in the night sky.

In the balloon's cramped rectangular basket, the masked man in black—the same one Val West had encountered on Mont Blanc—turned up the burner, raising the balloon and the cage beneath it. The Monster climbed up into the basket and sat down next to the man, taking a well-earned breather. Watching nearby, from the glass-domed capsule he was confined to, was the smiling face of the head of Victor Frankenstein I.

"Excellent work, Adam. Stage One is now complete. We now have our second superweapon. Next… we go to war."

The balloon rose high above the night sky, the crash of the thunderous waves far below now a soft lull. Off in the distance, the fires of Frankenstein Island raged an angry red. Above, the full moon cast a radiant bright blue, lighting their course across the dark ocean.

The journey was a bumpy one, however, as the balloon's cargo had regained consciousness and was not at all happy with confinement to a cage.

19: BRING ME THE HEAD OF VICTOR FRANKENSTEIN

The balloon was certainly not the fastest way to reach Frankenstein Island, but with it being in a no-fly zone, it was the only option to travel undetected. It had been a slow journey, moving only as fast as the winds could carry its crew of the Frankenstein Monster, the masked man in black, and their captain—none other than the disembodied head of Victor Frankenstein I.

With several hours before they would arrive at the small airstrip where a chartered plane awaited, the man in black settled into the basket, leaning back and rubbing his eyes beneath the mask that concealed the upper half of his face. He looked down at the ocean, mesmerized by its glistening surface, which sparkled like gemstones under the brilliant crystal moonlight. Blinking stars dotted the black sky, with the Southern Cross shining brightly above.

He had a lot on his mind and reflected on all that had happened in recent days. His thoughts drifted to how, just a short time ago, it was all so different—when his main focus revolved around video games, sports, and especially girls, along with the exciting new thrill of young love that came with their discovery.

When he was still just a teenage boy named Franklin Frankenstein.

He had been understandably scared when he first heard the rapping on his window that night. When he saw the bolted-together, hulking creature standing outside looking in, he became even more understandably terrified.

It was hearing the voice that truly unsettled him.

The voice called to him in a tone that resembled his father's, yet had a strange, echoing, almost ghostly quality that transfixed him. He thought it all had to be a dream. It *had* to be… until the giant hand crashed through his window.

Confident in his newfound strength, he took up a fighting stance, but the gun aimed at him by the monstrous hand was a different story. Panic set in as he stood frozen, helplessly watching the finger squeeze the trigger.

A cloud of gas sprayed from the gun barrel, and everything spun, growing distant as blackness enveloped him. From what he had pieced together afterward, he knew the Monster had carried him off, the shrieks of the family housekeeper, Minnie, echoing through the castle and on down into the valley.

When he awoke, he found himself in a ramshackle hut built inside an icy cave high up on Mont Blanc in Chamonix. As his eyes adjusted, he saw the giant looming over him, clad in a thick, well-worn sheepskin vest that looked as if he had made it himself after devouring the rest of the sheep. The decaying burlap clothing and giant-soled boots appeared to have been crudely stitched together in a time long past—and indeed, they had been.

Franklin instinctively sprang up to attack. The Monster stood calmly and took his strikes, offering no counterattack, as he was also largely unaffected. He pointed to a nearby log, and spoke to Franklin in a stilted, slightly rasped, slightly lisped, primitive voice.

"You… boy—you sit."

Despite his instincts urging him to flee, Franklin found himself sitting down. The Monster reached for a black carrying bag and placed it on a flat rock pedestal. He opened the bag, removing a large glass-domed cylinder. A shock went through Franklin when he saw it contained a disembodied head. He received a second shock when it began to speak.

"Franklin. I know this is difficult, but try not to be alarmed."

"Difficult" was an understatement, to say the least. The head spoke in the same tinny, echoing voice he had heard calling to him from outside his window—the one that sounded like a ghostly version of his father's. The face was instantly recognizable, as he had seen the portrait countless times before. It belonged to the infamous Baron Victor Frankenstein I.

The head studied him with its piercing blue eyes. Its skin was deathly pale, the sharp cheekbones threatening to poke through the thin, stretched flesh, and the gray-streaked hair remained, looking as though the painting had come to life. Franklin supposed maybe it had. Unlike the portrait, the white-gray flesh was marked by a dark line of stitching across the top of the forehead.

Once again, the head spoke in its eerie ringing echo. "There are many things I could say to you, but I know you would not be willing to listen. So, I will start with this, which will, doubtless, incite your curiosity. Then you can decide."

The head looked directly into Franklin's eyes.

"Aunt Harriet's bust."

Franklin's stomach twisted. He knew exactly what this statement meant. When he was nine, he and his father were playing a game of catch with a baseball in the drawing room at the family home, FrankenCrest. One of his mother's prized heirlooms was a bust sculpture of her old, departed Aunt Harriet—a bust which also contained old, departed Aunt Harriet's cremated ashes. Leaping to catch the ball after an errant pitch by his father, Franklin tumbled into the bust. It fell to the ground, smashing into pieces. To make matters even worse, a stiff breeze blowing through the windows swept away Aunt Harriet's last remains.

Franklin broke down in tears, knowing how upset his mother would be. His father reassured Franklin he was not to blame. It was his idea for them to play catch in the drawing room, and he would make sure mother would never know. He had run interference, arranging to have the bust secretly repaired, filled with substitute ashes, and replaced without her ever knowing. This had been their secret—a private memory shared only between father and son.

And the head of Victor Frankenstein I knew this secret.

In this moment of realization, Franklin Frankenstein recognized a chilling truth. He knew it deep within his heart, as dreadful as it was. There was no doubt. A son knows these things.

He was speaking to his father.

Over a crackling fire in an icy cave on Mont Blanc, the head of Victor Frankenstein I—who was, unequivocally, the legitimate Baron Victor Frankenstein III—told his tale to the young Franklin. As the story unfolded, a thirst for vengeance—as strong, if not stronger, than his father's—grew inside Franklin.

With his chilly, reverberating voice, Victor related his story.

"Several years ago, I came upon a most remarkable discovery. My father—your grandfather, Hans Frankenstein—had a less-than-stellar reputation for his alleged experimentations during World War II. Years later, he had me to count as one of them, growing me from a fetus in a test tube as part of an experiment he had started during the war. This has never been proven, but it doesn't need to be. I have his documents, along with a tome titled, *Secreta Vitae et Mortis*—Latin for 'The Secrets of Life and Death'—a compendium of experimental research notes compiled by my grandfather, Victor II, and his father, Baron Victor Frankenstein the First.

"Victor II passed down a secret to his son, Hans. Before his death in 1970, the sealed instructions he intended to leave for me were lost, hidden in an undisclosed location. It was the detection of unusual radioactivity beneath the east wing of Old Castle Frankenstein that led to the discovery of this secret: a lab housing a small nuclear reactor that powered a cryogenic facility. Inside the vault, frozen in suspended animation, was the specimen marked 'Prototype A'—also known as the Frankenstein Monster of legend—and the preserved, disembodied head of Baron Victor Frankenstein I, retrieved after their disappearance in the Arctic.

"The book held detailed instructions on how to revive them successfully. The process was not yet possible when my father died, but I realized the innovations I had helped create through Frankentech could make it possible *now*.

"Of course, I was excited. Who wouldn't want a chance to speak with their own long-deceased great-grandfather? Especially one with the scientific genius mind of Victor I, albeit a controversial one. And the Monster—what a marvel of science he was. What an achievement it would be, to restore him to life once again. The experiment files showed he had been taken out of cryostasis once before, by Hans Frankenstein. With the technology available to him, he had been unable to revive him successfully, but had, quite grotesquely, made some modifications, such as the steel lower jaw and teeth.

"Plans were made to bring Victor I out of cryostasis. The process was carried out by a small team, in secret: just me, Igor, and our assistant Karl. The procedure was a success, and with the implanting of a larynx device, we were ready to speak to Great-Grandfather. With his peculiar condition, he needed to remain contained in the protective glass dome, the one you now see before you.

"Igor and I spent many hours conversing and learning from him. After I would retire to bed, it turned out he and Igor would converse for many more hours about many other things—making plans, it would turn out.

"Soon after, his demeanor changed. He said he was falling ill, degenerating, and he knew why: he needed a blood transfusion and it needed to be a genetic match—meaning me. This was an easy choice to make in order to save him. I agreed, and Igor would perform the procedure.

"While on the surgical table, not long after Igor inserted the IV line into my arm, I knew something was amiss. I felt faint, and far beyond the usual expected lightheadedness. Soon after, I fell unconscious, and the true nightmare began.

"Only after waking, and seeing my own face staring back at me from the other side of the glass, did I fully grasp the horror of what had happened. Victor I and Igor had conspired, using Victor's expert instruction, to transplant his brain into my body—a genetic match. Then, as a perverse experiment, they placed my brain into his disembodied head, 'for study,' as he so coldly put it. He then proceeded to take over my family, my company... my life."

At this point in the story, tears filled Franklin's eyes as a wave of sorrow washed over him. Yet, it was bittersweet in its own way. He had been certain that his father no longer loved him, convinced he had lost the bond they once shared. Now, he felt joy in knowing that his father still genuinely loved him—and always had, but it was overshadowed by the bitter knowledge that his father had been nearly destroyed by Frankenstein and Igor. A fiery need for vengeance burned brightly inside him.

Even in his current state, Victor was still able to weep, and he did. Franklin stood up and moved closer, the closest the father and son would ever get to an embrace again. Victor smiled through his darkened tears at Franklin and told him he was growing up to be a fine man... a strong man. He took a deep, wheezing breath and continued his story.

"After weeks, then months, of being a lab experiment, I decided to make plans of my own. I was connected into the computerized monitoring system, and I learned how to manipulate it. In doing so, I discovered the system for the cryo-chamber and was able to thaw and revive Prototype A. When he awoke, he made quite a mess smashing through the cryo-chamber vault doors, and when he stood before me, he didn't recognize me as Victor III, but as Victor I. Thankfully, I was successful in convincing him to not smash me to bits. Instead, he took me, in this glass bubble, and smashed his way out of the lab.

"At that point, all I wanted—no, needed—was revenge. I discovered Igor had been working with the international organization known as HIVE. He had been trying to oust me from my own company, but then he found an even better method—to oust me from my own body!

"We followed them, spying on our own behalf. We traveled to London, where we encountered other agents already on the trail. Then we followed all the way to Orkney, back to New Castle Frankenstein to get you, and finally here to Chamonix, where Victor I, Igor and HIVE are plotting something. I don't know exactly what it is, but they wanted a Quantum Collider and found a way to get one. Anyway, we tracked an agent here to Mont Blanc. Initially, we thought he was with HIVE, but then came to find he was not. And I think it's quite safe to say there is more to this 'School for Girls' than meets the eye."

Jarred from his thoughts by an abrupt lurch from the wild cargo below, Franklin stood up and checked their present course. The balloon drifted steadily over the Pacific, still heading toward its destination.

Once again losing himself in thought, he recalled how there definitely was more than met the eye at the school, especially when it came to the stunning young women populating it. And how, as he prepared that evening, an ominous spring lightning storm brewed over the peaks of Mont Blanc. After dressing entirely in black, he had donned a black bandanna he fashioned into an eye mask. As he waxed the board he had stolen from a nearby ski lodge, he realized that all the time spent snowboarding on the slopes since he was a youngster was about to pay off.

He was ready.

But how was it he felt so ready?

It was while spying through binoculars, watching the school in the valley below to see what this secret agent would do—or more accurately, what he would do once his weak ruse was discovered—that his father told him another secret:

Franklin was also a Frankenstein creation.

To give him a genetic advantage, Victor had given his mother treatments while Franklin was in utero to help their baby develop to the highest human potential. The ethics of this decision can be debated, but the intent was noble.

What happened next was anything but.

With full access to Victor III's files, Frankenstein discovered the modifications made to Franklin. He decided to accelerate Franklin's advanced DNA with his own treatments, dramatically enhancing his strength, stamina, and overall athletic performance to superhuman levels. However, it was not done in the same altruistic spirit that had guided Victor.

Frankenstein wanted Franklin's body. As in, he literally wanted it… for himself. Franklin's supercharged young body was being prepared to be the next destination for Frankenstein's brain.

Over his dead body—not mine, was Franklin's position. He had already been afraid and confused enough by what was happening to his body and how his "father" had been treating him. He didn't know he had been experimented on. Puberty was difficult enough, and Franklin was dealing with it ten times over.

He knew the baron was disappointed in his strength tests, but he had deliberately held back—he didn't want to reveal his true abilities. He had wanted his father to love him, regardless of whether he could pass those tests.

Now that he had discovered the truth and had not only his actual father back but also the love that had never been lost, he intended to make the most of the time they had, while they still had it. Though death would inevitably soon come to claim his father, he would do his damnedest to ensure that until then, they would never be separated again.

The balloon's basket rocked violently back and forth. The werewolf was rattling the cage again. The Frankenstein Monster—Prototype A—was annoyed. Leaning over the edge, he shouted angrily at the beast before settling back to watch the first glimpses of dawn break over the horizon, red streaks tinting the gently lapping waves below. This werewolf was disturbing not only his peace, but also his concentration.

Victor had been teaching him how to speak, and while clunky, he found his thoughts and expressions gradually becoming more articulate, as they once had been before the frozen death. How different this Victor Frankenstein was from the one who had created him.

Dubbed "Prototype A," he was not only the first creature created by Victor Frankenstein I but also the intended Adam of this new species. "I ought to be his Adam," he had thought countless times. Instead, he was a fallen angel—dubbed unworthy, to be rejected and called a miserable demon by his creator, and a monster by all those he encountered.

No Eve would be made for him, despite the promises made by Frankenstein over a century ago. The heavy weight of terrible loneliness and sadness ached within him—through his bones, through his artificial heart, through his real soul—the soul given to him by the true God, not by Frankenstein, the soulless creator masquerading as a god.

"Avenge not yourselves… for it is written, Vengeance is mine; I will repay, saith the Lord."

This is from the Book of Romans, Chapter 12, Verse 19. Prototype A had been learning to read with the copy of the Bible Victor had given him. Although he believed the words, he knew he would have to disobey, at least this once. As an instrument of vengeance, he would declare everlasting war against he who had created him and sent him forth to a life of misery. He would serve the repayment of vengeance on this false Lord, Victor Frankenstein—not only for himself but also for the boy and for the father he had found in Victor III—the man who called him Adam.

As a man, he would be called Adam. Maybe someday, he mused, he would be that man. For now, though, he was Prototype A, and he would be that which he needed to be.

A Monster.

The magnificence of a sunrise high above the ocean still moved Victor III, even as he watched from behind glass, trapped in a head that was not his own. He recalled how that view once made him feel—when he was still a man. And "was a man," was how he thought of it. He truly had been emasculated, and he realized the seething hate and insatiable lust for revenge filling him now also made him a monster, rotting him from the inside out. The only redemption from the darkness he found was in bringing light to the creature, Adam, and, of course, to his own son, Franklin.

All three had been betrayed by the monstrous Victor I, and all three would not stop until justice had been carried out. Yet, the betrayal ran beyond just Victor I. There was also Igor, a man Victor had trusted implicitly since childhood. Cracks began to appear in their relationship when Victor suspected Igor had involved Frankentech in business dealings with the international syndicate known as HIVE. Igor denied any involvement, pleading ignorance—a feigned ignorance, as it turned out.

Soon they would arrive at their destination: a small island airstrip where Victor had chartered a cargo plane from a local pilot. From there, they would plan the takedown of Frankenstein. And now, Victor had a secret weapon to add to his arsenal: a werewolf.

At their first encounter, Victor hadn't been sure who Val West was working for. Once he determined West was not a HIVE agent, he realized they were working toward similar ends, no matter the organization he was allied with. As a globally recognized tech giant, he had interacted with enough world government organizations to understand their inner workings—the strange, shadowy world of espionage, the bluffs and double bluffs, the complex game of human chess known as "The Great Game." Nothing, and no one, was what it seemed, and that went double for this Agent West.

When Victor saw him on the slopes of Mont Blanc, the realization that he was not exactly... human, was an unexpected turn. What kind of organization would employ a werewolf as a secret agent? Sure, there had been stories circulating in the intelligence community of a werewolf super-agent clad in red, and the tabloids had all run with it being a CIA lab creation. If there was one thing Victor knew, it was lab creations, and this wasn't one—at least not one of his.

He had forbidden Frankentech from engaging in the type of experiments that had tarnished his family's reputation and had spent his entire life working not only to change that image, but also to use his resources and technological capabilities to improve the world. Now, his great-grandfather and his former best friend were doing everything they could to destroy all he had built.

It was unlikely his brain could survive another transplant, and even if it could, the procedure remained an unwritten secret known only to Victor I. He would be trapped like this. His life was in ruins, and all he could do now was make it right for his son and his suffering wife, Monique. This devil, who had stolen his body and his life, had also taken her. Franklin had told him of how she cried her nights away, wondering what had happened to the man she loved. If she knew the awful truth, she would drown further in her sorrows.

The balloon descended as they approached the site of the airstrip. Prototype A groaned, knowing he would soon have to wrestle with the cage to bring their werewolf cargo with them. Day was breaking, and when it did, Val West would become a man again and they could talk. That is, if they could get him to listen.

And then, more importantly... to join them.

20: THE LORD AND THE NEW CREATURES

"Welcome back, LoneWolf."

The speaker box voice of Commander 7 greeted Val West warmly as he entered ParaCommand headquarters, hidden deep beneath London's Highgate Cemetery. The Commander, monitoring the scene through the mounted security camera system, was surprised by West's return. He was even more surprised by his guests: a young man dressed entirely in black, his upper face obscured by a mask, and a hulking creature with a flattened head adorned with electrode bolts. The monstrous figure carried a glass bubble-shaped dome containing what appeared to be a human head.

"I see you've brought visitors." He was very much hoping for a good explanation for this.

To Commander 7's further surprise, he was startled to hear a voice coming from the head's mouth. "Commander, good to hear your voice again. It's just unfortunate it has to be under these grim circumstances."

"Mr. West," the Commander said in a stern, authoritative tone, "please report."

Val West recounted everything that had transpired since leaving for Frau Stiglitz's Finishing School for Girls. Many of his questions about his rescue from the island had been answered during the flight from the

Pacific back to London, though the journey had been rough going at first.

As expected, West hadn't wanted to hear what Victor had to say. Fully healed after his transformation, he felt re-energized and grateful for his rescue but remained confused about the motives of his rescuers. It had taken a leap of faith from both sides before West finally, cautiously, stepped out of the open cage door. Rather than the expected attack, he instead found the extended hands of Franklin, Prototype A, and, symbolically, Baron Victor Frankenstein III.

Victor's hollow voice rang out through the glass, explaining how they tracked West and had the Monster follow him during his travels. By hacking into the Frankentech computer files, they finally managed to locate him on Frankenstein Island.

After relaying all this to Commander 7, he was convinced this was indeed the true Baron Frankenstein, a man he had known and felt indebted to. The dead blue eyes in the head of Victor Frankenstein I reflected a weary sadness, mirroring the feelings of the living brain inside— Victor III's brain.

"Commander, I thank you and Mr. West for your help. It is also tragically ironic that you and I should both find ourselves in a similar state now."

The Commander offered no reply.

Victor turned his sadness into a warm smile. "I must say, I am very impressed with your facility here. I also wish I could meet your Dr. Borge."

"Thank you, Victor. I'm afraid Dr. Borge is still out searching for Agent LoneWolf. I have been unable to make contact with him. The signal indicates a high-level electromagnetic presence, so I assume he and my other agent are in a location using a jamming frequency."

"The doctor's work is most impressive, and I pray he is not in any danger. You know, I had no idea for a quite a long time who this intriguing LoneWolf was working for, but I should have known you would be the one to have a werewolf secret agent under your command."

"You should have known," the Commander said, "but as a good spymaster, it is also my business to make sure nobody does."

"Touché."

Seated next to Franklin and Prototype A, West was deep in thought. Suddenly, he realized…

"What did you mean by 'other agent', sir?"

"I mean," the Commander explained, "he is with our reserve agent, Lady Kendra Kenton."

West threw up his hands. "Well, now that's just tremendous *and* splendid. Why didn't you tell me she was officially part of ParaCommand from the start? Has she been working on this case the whole time, too?"

"Agent LoneWolf, don't forget yourself." If West could have seen the Commander's face, he would have slunk back across the room. "She was not assigned to this case, officially. And if you hadn't disappeared, she still wouldn't be. But she is now.

"Is that clear?"

West was annoyed, but he also couldn't shake the way he had started to feel about her while nailed to a mast and dying.

That was real.

True, she did rub him the wrong way, but he thought perhaps, in time, they would end up rubbing each other the right way. He also prayed that she and Borge weren't caught up in some deadly danger… or worse.

Commander 7 again spoke. "Before we decide our plan of action for this—Operation Frankenstein—we will need to find out as much as we can about what lies in wait. Victor, what can you tell me about Frankenstein and HIVE's plans, in particular with the Quantum Collider? That is what concerns me most right now."

"As it should, Commander," Victor explained. "A Quantum Collider on its own is essentially useless, as it cannot be activated without substantial destabilization, thus not allowing for the generation of quantum particle energy. However, thanks to information obtained by Val on Frankenstein Island, we now know that the Fabula crystal device developed by Frankentech appears, as it would seem, to have solved this problem.

"The very real threat here is that being a Quantum Collider, it can make use of the quantum function—that is, connecting two points simultaneously. Meaning, as a directed energy weapon, it could fire at a target from its location and connect instantaneously, causing mass destruction from right where it sits... which is at Castle Frankenstein, despite what any law enforcement intelligence reports may be suggesting to the contrary. If my assumptions are correct, the Collider could be ready for use within days of integrating the Fabula Device."

West began pacing with nervous energy, some of it stemming from the lingering effects of the full moon, which would rise in a few hours. "Which means we have no time to lose."

"Correct," Victor replied. "They will need to test it first, of course. But once they find out it works, and if the Fabula Device is stable, then HIVE could put it into operation. The geopolitical implications of a group like this having such a powerful device are staggering."

"Hold on a moment," West said. "You said 'if the Fabula Device is stable.' Karl mentioned this as well, on the island. What do you mean by 'if?'"

"Exactly that. I sat in on its development, and while it theoretically works as a stabilizing power converter for the Collider, it is by no means stable itself. And should the Collider overload, not only will it level everything for miles in its blast radius, God only knows what other horrors it could unleash.

Franklin shuddered. "So... that's not good."

"BAD!" the Monster added, waving a giant-sized arm for emphasis.

"Very bad," Victor clarified. "It would be apocalyptic. We need to get in there and very carefully remove the crystals from the Fabula Device to depower the Collider. However, tuning the crystal frequency outside its strict parameters could cause the whole thing to collapse in on itself, creating an implosion in the immediate surrounding space-time—essentially a reverse black hole of dark energy. It could suck you into its vortex, and who knows where you would end up? Perhaps another dimension, or in space, or as a collection of scattered atomic dust."

"We all agree that this is bad," said West. "What's equally bad—if not worse—is if HIVE employs the Collider as a directed energy weapon. So, there's not a lot of good happening here."

"This is true," Victor acknowledged. "And we don't know what Victor I has planned for its use."

West shot them a worried look.

"That's how it goes from bad to worse."

...

"Would you just look at Blobulus? How fast they grow!" Frankenstein beamed at his latest creation, part of what he called Project Blobule. The new formula, which he named Nuflesh, had stunning potential. The small blob of Nuflesh he started growing in the capsule was already taking on a humanoid form.

He had begun developing the process in the nineteenth century, but with the limitations of contemporary science, he had been unable to stabilize it. Upon his return, he found that twenty-first-century advancements couldn't stabilize it either—until he discovered the research on the Quantum Collider. These quantum theories filled in the gaps of what was missing in his work to reanimate the dead body parts used in his creation, much like the one he was working on at the moment.

Igor entered the laboratory, followed by the waddling, deviant hunchback Morpho. Frankenstein, covered in gore, had his hands deep inside a cadaver, pulling out parts for another handmade creation. He closely examined a bloody spleen while crowing over Blobulus's progress.

"Baron," Igor said, ignoring the blob creature bobbing in the large cylindrical tube, "about these tests with the Collider."

"Yes, yes. I know our friends from HIVE have their own designs on the Collider, but my work is imperative. You understand I have waited a very long time for this, and if not for me, HIVE would not even have this opportunity."

Igor furrowed his brow. "So, you do not pledge allegiance to HIVE, then?"

Frankenstein did not look up from his work. He expertly sawed through the cadaver's flesh into the bone, deftly ducking aside to avoid the spray from a bursting artery. Gently reaching into the chest cavity, he removed the heart, studying it thoughtfully, captivated by its intricate veins and infinite possibilities. With careful precision, he deposited it into a tank radiating a strange green glow.

He gazed upon the splayed-open corpse before him. What was he looking for? There was something inside, but it wasn't inside this body. It was something inside of him—a restless need for validation, for recognition.

He had to have it.

He would get it.

Lost in the far depths of his thoughts, he absently recalled that Igor had asked him a question… about HIVE. Again, always with these trivial matters when he was busy.

"Oh, heavens no," he replied, dismissing the idea. "I have my research to focus on. I have no further need for them now that they have provided me with a Quantum Collider.

"This," Frankenstein said, pointing at the roughly reassembled puzzle of body parts on the table next to him, "*This* is my work. This is what I pledge my allegiance to."

Igor turned away and walked over to the capsule, contemplating as he examined Blobulus. Morpho twitched nervously, like an impatient pet waiting for instructions.

"Now, Igor," Frankenstein said, pulling off his bloodied gloves. "I want you to pay attention—this is particularly important. I have completed my calculations, and without question, the Collider will indeed stabilize the Nuflesh process, including the blood and entire circulatory system. This means we can advance the Brides project—and the soldiers as well.

"Igor… are you paying attention?"

He was not. He turned to Frankenstein. "Yes, of course."

"Good," Frankenstein continued, pointing to a simulation on the computer screen. "This is *the* breakthrough we have been waiting for. The Collider will be able to generate the proper bio-energy fields to infuse and animate my creations with an enhanced quantum human energy field—essentially, if you will, a synthetic soul.

"With this new process of synthetic biological quantum galvanism, I can create a new population and finally be recognized as a master scientist—as well as God to my New Creatures. Picture it, Igor: a new species that will bless me as its creator and source. They will all owe their existence to me."

Igor merely nodded, expressionless.

A thrilling energy ran through Frankenstein, giving him a shiver. Here it was: true vindication of his scientific theories, now a reality after all these years. He deserved to be recognized as a scientific genius on the level of—no, above—Newton, Darwin, Da Vinci, Moreau, Einstein. He would be rightfully proclaimed the greatest.

If only his doubting father could have witnessed this—his absolute triumph. An army awaited, populated by his Nu-Men, supersoldiers of limitless quantity. Alongside them were his beautiful Brides, irresistible and unstoppable, each one a perfect fusion of seduction and weaponized capabilities. Through them, he would reshape the world in his own image.

"Morpho," he called impatiently. "Fetch me a bottle of champagne and two glasses." Moments later, the hunchback hobbled over with an expensive bottle of bubbly. Frankenstein barely glanced at him as he waited to be served, then dismissively waved him away.

He raised his glass to Igor. "A toast. To Homo Superior, my Nu-Men... the New Creatures. And to me, their Lord."

His "Lordship" tossed back the champagne and then immediately went back to his work with the cadaver. Igor stood by the doorway, staring down at his glass without taking a sip. He too was preoccupied with his own work, planning for his own future—as the head of HIVE Europe and, perhaps more importantly... the leader of Frankentech.

These New Creatures would be better serving the HIVE nation, *the* new world power. It would be a new world that would once again leave Frankenstein behind if he didn't reconsider his allegiances.

If he wouldn't come to heel, he would be crushed underfoot.

21: STITCHING THE PIECES TOGETHER

Volta Elettrica had overheard every word Frankenstein said, leaving her in cold terror. She had been wondering what was happening to her, especially since her time at Frau Stiglitz's School. Not only had she felt out of sorts, there also seemed to be missing time she couldn't account for. She knew she was taking an awful risk by sneaking down to the lab, but she also knew Frankenstein had done *something* to her, and she needed answers.

Now that she knew more—much more than she expected—she would have to report in. Try as she might, focusing and concentrating, she found she could no longer remember her own contact at the Italian Secret Service. That greatly troubled her, and rightly so. So much of her mind was tangled in a strange, murky brain fog.

She did remember the handsome agent, Val West. She couldn't exactly recall why, but something about him had made a big impression. Somehow, she had to find a way to reach him.

As she snuck off, back toward the elevator, Igor Zelensky watched her movements through the slightly cracked open door of the laboratory.

...

Come nightfall, once again, the moon would be full, and West was still without his wolfskin belt. That meant, once again, he would transform into an out-of-control, rabid werewolf. He still had no idea how to prepare for that, and with Borge out of contact, there would be no backup options to control the beast—and more importantly, keep him from ripping apart anyone they didn't want torn to shreds.

Before setting off on this dangerous assignment, West took some time in the ParaCommand training center to see what young Franklin was capable of, with the Monster joining in. *Damn, this kid is fast... and powerful*, he thought to himself as they went through the paces of a standard Agents Academy workout. Prototype A was even more powerful and nearly impervious to harm, standing there stoically as they threw everything they had at him.

After a few rounds of one-on-one sparring, West was impressed, but not enough to bring Franklin into the coming fray at Castle Frankenstein. Victor would need to come—and would insist on it—to deal with the Quantum Collider. Of course, the one-man brute squad, Prototype A, would accompany them. But the boy was just that—a boy, even with his enhanced speed, strength, and agility. West hoped Victor would not insist on bringing him along. The safest place for Franklin was to stay at ParaCommand until they returned... if they returned.

To prepare, West brought them into the arsenal to weaponize for the battle ahead. He donned a new LoneWolf spysuit, and in its holster he added a newly sighted-in .45 caliber H&K Mark 23 semi-automatic pistol.

Franklin's eyes were glued to an outfit on a stand behind a glass case. It was a specialized molecular spysuit, in a variation of the regular ParaCommand color scheme of black with red highlights, and featured the addition of a protective eye mask equipped with optical scanning devices.

West explained its bird-like design derived from an experimental test Borge was working on. "It's kind of stitched together from pieces and parts."

A rare smile crossed Victor's gray lips. "Aren't we all?"

The Monster grunted.

"Yes, well, no offense meant," Victor added quickly.

Franklin's eyes remained fixed on the suit.

West knew what Franklin wanted and tried to dissuade him. "Kid, you're pretty tough, all right. But you're not ready for that... and you're staying here."

Franklin's eyes now flashed with rage. He had already survived deadly scrapes and managed just fine on the death trip down Mont Blanc. He would go to Castle Frankenstein whether Val West allowed it or not. This was his family, and as he glanced over at the head housing his father's brain, he knew time was running out.

The head of Victor Frankenstein I was showing signs of degradation. The dark rings around the sunken eyes were growing darker. A blackening pus pooled in the tear ducts. The pale skin was developing tiny, rapidly spreading green lesions. His breathing, assisted by the mechanisms in the base of the glass dome, grew more labored.

"Mr. West," the tinny voice spoke, wheezing with each word, "I respectfully suggest you give Franklin another go, testing him as if in true combat. You will find him more than capable, if unrefined."

"And he will be coming with us."

West winced. The hard but somber eyes in the glass bubble pleaded as much as they demanded. "You can see that my end is drawing near. This head was meant only to survive in a delicate, controlled environment. I will have as much time with my boy as I can, while I still have it."

It was hard for West to argue. He wished he had known his own father. He had not, with the secret service effectively raising him. Soon, Franklin would be without a father. The boy would need guidance, which West could start offering now. He reluctantly nodded and motioned for Franklin to follow him back into the training center.

"You're a little rough around the edges," West said, in between dodging Franklin's rapid punches, "but you can more than hold your own." Franklin responded by tossing him across the room. Slowly, painfully, West peeled himself off the wall. "Technique is very important," he gasped, catching his breath, "but in a pinch, if you stick with that, kid, you'll be all right."

West was more impressed than ever. This kid had the skills, but what he lacked was experience—and that was about to change.

Back in the arsenal room, they were greeted by Victor, whose weary eyes glowed with pride. "You see how good he is? You will promise to train him?"

Franklin leaned down, their eyes meeting through the glass dome. "I'm ready now, Father."

West turned to face them both and shook his head. "No, you're not."

He crossed the floor to the glass case containing the avian-designed suit and its face-fitting eye mask, sizing them up. He motioned for Franklin to join him.

"Not until you have this. The suit will molecularly adjust, within reason, to fit you."

West looked Prototype A up and down. "Sorry, we don't have anything running 'Absurdly Big and Tall.'"

He received a long, low, rumbling groan in reply.

Franklin placed his hand on the glass, staring at the suit in awe. This was really happening. Despite the seriousness of their circumstances, he couldn't help but feel a thrill, and a chill, running through his body. West eyed the suit's odd design, with its bird-like lines and scalloped body armor resembling engraved feathers, and was thankful Borge would no longer be able to talk him into wearing it. "It looks a bit like the Maltese Falcon."

"More like... a raven," was Franklin's interpretation.

West could see the boy was smitten with the suit and the opportunity it gave to make him a teenaged "superhero."

"Okay then, kid… 'Raven.'"

"Yes," Franklin said, beaming. "I will become Kid Raven—the scourge of Victor I and Igor."

West was amused at Franklin's youthful enthusiasm and apparent fandom of Edgar Allan Poe. With his great strength, it was easy to forget he was just a fifteen-year-old boy. He was also quite possibly the most successful Frankenstein creation. Underneath the bravado, however, was the real truth. He was hurting.

Even though he had been reunited with his real father, time was quickly running out. Maybe Victor could survive for a time in his present condition, but even the slightest damage to the protective glass dome would be fatal.

There was also one other thing: it seemed Victor wasn't intending to survive. Once he had stopped Frankenstein, his mission, his time here, was over. It would be up to Franklin to carry on his name and memory.

Commander 7 and Victor had arranged transportation. They would be flying into the Frankfurt Airport, and then head for the Odenwald Mountains.

There, they would begin their assault on Castle Frankenstein.

...

The search for Val West had been a fruitless one for Dr. Hector Borge and Lady Kendra Kenton. Although it had not borne any fruit, it wasn't entirely uneventful. At Frau Stiglitz's Finishing School for Girls, they found the place deserted—except for a lime-colored double-decker bus that suddenly burst out of a barn, nearly flattening Borge in the process as it screeched away down the road. Fortunately, Kendra had seen it coming and dove at him, knocking him out of its path. Unfortunately, they were unable to catch up to the bus as it sped down the mountainside and out of Chamonix, destination unknown.

Now they found themselves in southern Hesse, Germany, dining on a late lunch at the Jagdschloss Kranichstein in downtown Darmstadt. They both would have liked to say the trail led them here, but there was no trail. It was as if West had disappeared across the ocean. Their meal was a quiet one, each lost in their thoughts, mentally preparing for what lay ahead.

Borge figured they might as well indulge in the local cuisine, especially if this was to be his last meal. He ravenously dug into the crispy Kartoffelpuffer, paired with a lightly sautéed Affenschwanz, and a sweet, syrupy Dörrpflaumenkompott, all washed down with a pint of rather potent Köstritzer Schwarzbierbrauerei Schwarzbier. He hoped he would still have room for a slice of Arschgeweihkuchen, lavishly topped with luscious Himbeergeschmack and just a slight drizzle of Mandelblättchen—after all, it was in season.

They had already encountered a taste of danger in their search, and their next stop would be the final one—at least with what they had to go on—and it could turn out to be the most dangerous, for a number of reasons. This location was one which had been avoided, due to mounting political pressure and complaints to official channels from Frankentech, who deemed it an affront to even suggest any HIVE ties. In the meantime, the Commander was also doing his utmost to keep the investigation going, treading as delicately as possible.

Kendra felt more than a bit listless. She couldn't pin down how—or what—she felt about Val West. That had been true since before their first meeting. Both she and Borge were considering, without saying the thought aloud, that West might be dead.

Her stomach turned, and she knew it was her spiraling thoughts causing it, not the German cooking—she had barely touched her Königsberger Klops and Fliederbeersuppe. Even the pints of locally brewed Donaudampfschifffahrtsgesellschaftskapitänsweizenbier she was downing could not drown out the relentless tide of worry over West's fate.

As the sun sank lower, its rays streamed through the windows, bathing the Jagdschloss Kranichstein in a warm golden glow. Borge and Kendra sat in silence, contemplating the situation over the last forkfuls of a sumptuous Zwetschgenknoedel, wondering if they were truly ready for the next phase: investigating New Castle Frankenstein.

...

Volta had spent hours agonizing over what to do next. The horrifying realization that she couldn't remember her superior at the Agenzia Informazioni e Sicurezza Esterna filled her with panic. What had been done to her to erase that part of her mind? What else had been done? She struggled to recall her time at Frau Stiglitz's School and couldn't get it to add up with what little memory she had of it.

There were also conflicting, fragmented memories crashing down from before then. She had given Gino Primavera and Val West the information about the Orkney Islands, but now she recalled how, upon finding the file, she could tell it had been planted for her to discover. Yet she had sent them into a trap, and something had made her do it—something, or *someone*, that was taking over her thoughts, her mind. Dueling memories, some real, some implanted, swirled around in her brain.

And then there was Val West—she had not seen or heard from him since they had slept together that night at New Castle Frankenstein.

That night...

She had awoken from a dream—or at least she thought she had. She had found herself alone, in his bed. Or had she?

It felt like a dream, a nightmare she couldn't shake awake from.

A nightmare where she ran out of the darkened bedroom, out of the castle and into the stormy night. The wind howled and clawed at her flowing white nightgown as she fled down the dark winding path away from the monstrous spectre of the castle. Voices echoing through her head tormented her, the commands taking control. One voice was louder, slithering inside her thoughts. It was so familiar, yet she couldn't place it. Yes, she could. Igor. Somehow, he was invading her mind.

And then... she awoke again, back in her own bed, as if none of it had happened. But had it?

Had any of it been real? Or was it all part of this haunting dream?

One thing she knew for sure: her night with Val West had to be real. She still felt sore two days later, and that wasn't all in her mind. But the rest? She couldn't be as certain. Unless her memory was playing tricks on her, she thought she had seen him at Frau Stiglitz's School. Had she been used against him there as well? Was he alive? The questions spun in her mind, leaving her feeling hopeless.

For now, she would hide herself away on the castle grounds, working to come up with a plan while desperately trying to remain free of Frankenstein and Igor.

But for now, she had only one question, one that could undo all of her plans:

Could she trust herself?

22: BELT BRAWL

Through the binoculars, New Castle Frankenstein appeared harmless enough. It was as ugly as modern architecture could get, but apart from its harsh, angular glass design, nothing about it seemed particularly ominous. It was what lurked underneath that Borge and Kendra were concerned with.

That was ominous.

Also ominous was Borge's inability to make contact with Commander 7. After arriving at their stakeout position, he had tried calling with his three-way wrist communicator and also by broadcasting a coded tone via shortwave. There must be some form of interference coming from the castle, blocking his communication attempts. He hadn't thought to bring any alternate methods, as these were almost always more than reliable.

Almost always.

He fiddled with the controls, making another attempt, grateful for a moment to rest his stubby legs after their long hike. They had started at the southern outskirts of Darmstadt and then disappeared into the darkness of the Palatinate Forest. The trek through the dense woodland carpeting the Odenwald mountain range was slow and arduous as they scrambled over jagged rocks and through clusters of twisted, tangled branches. By deliberately staying off-trail, the two-and-a-half-kilometer climb felt at least double the length.

Old Castle Frankenstein was still closed, even for the tourist season—closed by order of landowner Baron Victor Frankenstein. When construction began on the new castle, the baron "uncharacteristically" repossessed the donated grounds surrounding the historic site. This new building served as a front for his secret laboratory constructions beneath both castles. He had his plans and wanted no interlopers on or near the grounds.

Two such interlopers, Dr. Hector Borge and Lady Kendra Kenton, had skirted the edge of the tree line along the eastern side. Now completely on their own, unable to contact the Commander, they sat in the dark shadow cast by the old castle ruins, scouting the area. Apart from the castle, there was a multilevel garage structure and several smaller buildings. One tiny building was of particular interest: Kendra had watched it rise from beneath the ground.

"There!" She zoomed in with her binoculars and nudged Borge. "Do you see it?"

"Yes, I see it." Borge was peering through his own binoculars, slightly irritated, as he was perfectly capable of spotting it on his own.

"It must be another entrance to the underground lab. We may not have to break into the castle after all."

"Hmm, yes." Borge was getting nervous. He had never been active in the field before. Searching for West was one thing, but this current situation would undoubtedly lead to action. As that possibility loomed closer, he felt an icy panic creeping up his spine. Without question, he was quite terrified. "Can we wait until after dark? It's too risky at the moment." Kendra nodded in agreement, and he breathed a long, slow sigh of relief.

"We'll wait until twilight." She checked her chronometer. "That gives us about thirty minutes."

For some reason, this reprieve only made Borge more anxious. Perhaps it was the thought of a five-foot, two-inch hunchback taking on large, armed goons—or worse, monsters—that had him feeling hesitant. He had another suggestion. "How about tomorrow instead?"

She surveyed the scene more intently. "How about now?" She grabbed his arm, pulling him along toward the nearest outbuilding, dashing from tree to tree for cover. Borge immediately regretted ever bringing up the suggestion.

One large oak tree was all that stood between them and the first building, fifty meters ahead. As they reached the tree trunk, a shape suddenly popped out from the shadows, startling them. It was a shape that was just as startled herself, the shapely form of Volta Elettrica.

"Oh, it's you," Kendra said coolly.

Volta looked confused. "Do I know you?"

"No, but I know of you."

"Do you know a man named Val West?" Volta asked, a glimmer of hope in her eyes.

Kendra scowled, her eyes narrowing. "Yes, but apparently not as well as you do."

A twinge of slight jealousy could be detected, but Borge wisely chose not to mention it. He cleared his throat cautiously. "Ladies, can we argue about this somewhere else?"

Kendra turned her glare away from Volta and pointed toward the building. "What's in there?"

"It's just unused stables. I can get us in… let's go." Volta started to run, but Kendra yanked her back, spinning her around.

"Just hold on, sister. Why should we trust you? What are you doing skulking about, anyway? Aren't you Frankenstein's secretary?"

Volta planted her hands on her hips, her expression one of growing, intense dislike. "Why should I trust you? And what exactly are you two doing, 'skulking about'? And no, I'm not a secretary. For your information, I'm AISE."

Kendra conceded that Volta had made a number of fair points, shrugged, then followed her inside.

The stables were dark and empty, filled only with the scent of hay and old wood—a perfect hideout until they made a dash for the underground entrance. Volta stood before them, her voice trembling as she explained, the best she could, what was happening and what was happening to her. Kendra didn't want to buy the story, but she had to admit it rang true with everything else going on. Reluctantly, she decided to put aside her issues with Volta and trust her… for now.

"You know, we're searching for West ourselves," Borge added. "He's been missing. We were hoping we would find him here—and, well, alive, ideally."

"No!" Volta found herself yelling out in anguish. "He can't be dead… I… I need him."

Kendra bit her lip. She was about to say something anyway, when Borge not-so-subtly kicked her in the shin.

Suddenly, the loud mechanical grind of machinery interrupted their conversation/argument, sending them scurrying into the shadows. The noise came from a freight elevator rising nearby. When it stopped, the little hunchback Morpho toddled out, flipping on a light switch. There went their cover. Although Morpho didn't notice the intruders tucked away in the corner, Borge saw him—and his eyes widened at the sight of Morpho proudly wearing the wolfskin belt around his little waist.

Kendra saw it too and was itching to leap into action. Firmly placing his hand on her shoulder, Borge held her back. "This one is mine," he whispered, feeling braver than maybe he ever had. He did have at least a five-inch height advantage.

Borge sprang out at the startled Morpho, with both of them staring each other down in a standoff. A moment later, it was on, and the two began scrapping in a flurry of flying hay and swinging fists. "You give hunchbacks a bad name!" Borge shouted while pummeling Morpho with wild punches. Morpho squealed for Xorror to come help him. Within seconds, the giant, metal-masked henchmonster shambled from the elevator, lurching toward them. Borge connected with a knockout punch to Morpho's jaw, scrambling to snatch the belt off him before the creeping monstrosity closed in.

Xorror's massive hand clamped around the back of Borge's neck, effortlessly lifting him off the ground. Borge struggled, determined to get the belt around his waist instead of wriggling free. *Come on, just one more snap*. He focused his nubby fingers on the fastener as the crushing pressure of the giant hand tightened around his throat. A spinning darkness spiraled in his eyes.

Kendra and Volta prepared to jump in, but just as they did, Borge surprised them once more. The belt clicked into place, tightening around his waist. "Don't worry, girls... I created a backup user for the belt... and it's me!" Borge squeezed his eyes shut, and to everyone's astonishment, transformed into a pint-sized hunchbacked werewolf.

Xorror released his grip and stepped back, tilting his head in bewilderment. With a fierce growl, Borge-wolf lunged, snapping his fangs and slashing his razor-sharp claws at the stunned giant. Kendra and Volta quickly joined the fray, and together, the trio launched an all-out assault on the monster.

Kendra whirled into a spinning kick, connecting with the back of Xorror's head. Volta went for a stiff boot to the groin, which she instantly regretted, as, like his face, this was also covered in thick metal.

While reeling from the pain in her foot, Volta suddenly froze in place. A sharp, piercing frequency ejaculated in her ear. Deep in the bowels of the subterranean laboratory, Igor had been listening through an implanted microphone, accessible through Volta's ear. This, along with implanting false intelligence reports, was among the many vile experiments performed on her.

Now even more curious about this belt, he activated his control program, sending its commands straight into Volta's cerebral cortex. He wanted the belt, and she was going to get it for him. Volta's eyes flashed white as the commands registered in her bio-hacked brain. She slowly turned toward Borge-wolf, who was still fiercely battling the perplexed Xorror.

The Igor-controlled Volta crept up behind Borge and yanked the belt from his waist. Stunned, he stumbled back, disoriented by the abrupt physical shift of changing from wolf, back to man. Before he could regain his balance, Volta's other arm shot forward, delivering a stiff judo chop to the back of his neck, sending him crashing to the ground.

An unimpressed Kendra let out a sigh. "This is why I have trust issues." Without warning, she lunged at Volta, who quickly tossed the belt to Xorror. The hulking monster strapped it on, but to no effect; it was calibrated only for Val West and the now-unconscious backup, Dr. Hector Borge. Xorror tapped the belt's gold wolfs-head faceplate, but still nothing happened. With a dismissive shrug, he decided to keep it on as a trophy.

Kendra and Volta circled each other, poised for action, each waiting for the perfect moment to strike.

Igor could hardly contain his excitement. Viewing this all through Volta's eyes on his camera monitor, he decided it was now time to test out all of her specialized modifications. His eager fingers excitedly raced over the control panel until they found the programming button for full activation.

Suddenly, Volta stopped moving. Her eyes ignited with a fiery red glow. Kendra watched this with a growing dread and decided it was wise to retreat momentarily, uncertain of what was coming next. One thing was certain: many more modifications had been made to Volta than she had realized.

She was now a full-fledged Bride of Frankenstein.

Sparks of energy clustered around Volta's ruby eyes, followed by an eruption of charged laser beam blasts. Kendra decided not to question it at this point and simply did her best to dodge the deadly laser fire. But she was starting to question her situation.

Well, Kendra, all this is right barmy now, isn't it? How in the hell did you get yourself into this? Things used to be much easier—when the laser beams you were dodging were from security alarm systems in high-level heists.

All this strangeness lately... more like outright bonkers... This is all Val West's fault.

As she executed a life-or-death acrobatic-martial arts-gymnastics routine throughout the stables, her inner monologue continued to convince her it really was all West's fault—giant monsters, mutated sea creatures, bloody eye-laser light shows, and, most of all... WEREWOLVES. If he wasn't dead already, she would have to kill him. So far, she hadn't made a single misstep, but that was at least half—if not more—due to sheer luck. Eventually, luck—good or bad—always runs out. Like now, for instance...

A stray blast caught her in the arm, incinerating part of the sleeve of her sleek catsuit.

"Bitch! This is one of my favorite outfits!"

This was now war.

Her simmering anger finally boiled over and she charged at Volta. Igor quickly switched tactics, deploying the Frankentech-patented Knocker Gas™ from Volta's at-attention artificially perky breasts. A thick, suffocating cloud sprayed from both nipples, enveloping the room, choking Kendra as she struggled to breathe. Panic set in as she scanned her surroundings, realizing she was caught in a deadly trap.

There was nowhere to turn. With Volta firing lasers and incapacitating breast gasses on one side and the metallic-faced menace of the monster Xorror on the other, Kendra thought maybe her luck as an adventuress had finally run out. She had a revolver with the one silver bullet she had been saving, but against these two, it seemed unlikely to do more than slow them down. Still, if she could reach it in time, it was a slim chance, and a slightly better option than sending that one bullet into her own temple.

Volta's eyes flared once more with fiery red photons, a sight that sent the increasingly bewildered Xorror fleeing down the elevator, abandoning the unconscious Morpho. Kendra squeezed her eyes shut, bracing herself to meet her doom. When she finally opened them, the gas was dissipating, and Volta lay face down on the floor.

The door had exploded off its hinges with a violent crash, sending Volta sprawling to the ground as splintered wood flew across the room. Lurching through the remnants of the wall was the imposing figure of the Frankenstein Monster, carrying Victor's head in its glass dome. Behind him came the masked, supersuit-clad Kid Raven, Franklin Frankenstein. Kendra's breath caught in her throat—this was all enough to alarm her even more, having no idea who they were beyond their questionable, albeit misrepresented, reputations.

Then, through the debris and mayhem, Val West entered, and she finally was able to take a breath. Or maybe she was just taken breathless. She didn't know, either. They locked eyes for a moment before she rushed over, nearly tripping over the still-motionless Volta.

"Val," she exclaimed, throwing her arms around him, her voice a mix of joy and disbelief. "Thank God you're alive... thank God you're here!"

"So, Frankenstein has been operating on your brain, too?" Although West was taken aback, he was appreciative of her uncharacteristic behavior and even more uncharacteristic moment of sarcasm-free sincerity. Kendra responded with one of her customary sharp elbows to his ribs. He winced from the jab, but no longer had any worries she wasn't herself.

The groggy Dr. Borge joined them, rubbing the knot left on the back of his neck from the judo chop.

"Now that we're all here," West said, "let's not get too far ahead of ourselves. We don't have much time before nightfall and moonrise. I was hoping to get the belt back, but with it wrapped around Xorror's waist, we'll have to go this route instead." From his belt bag, he pulled out a cable linkup and something that caught everyone's interest—especially Franklin's: a device that appeared to be a video game controller.

West felt around the back of his head. There it was—the jack that Borge had drilled into his head to connect him to the NeuraComlink, a satellite-based communication device exclusively used by Para-Command. He plugged the cable into the linkup jack as Borge prepared the control unit. On their previous mission* Borge had used this device to control West's movements as LoneWolf. But now, with West possessing the wolfskin belt and able to maintain his conscious mind in werewolf form, the control unit was no longer necessary.

All was ready. Borge powered on the connection to the NeuraComlink. He would soon be back to controlling LoneWolf again and he felt a sense of confidence come over him, knowing he literally had a superweapon at his fingertips.

Nothing.

With the twilight giving way to the growing glow of a moonlit night, Borge desperately worked to establish the connection. It was no use. The NeuraComlink would not connect. Maybe it was the frequency blockers around the castle, although that normally wouldn't affect a device like the NeuraComlink. Maybe the batteries were just dead. Maybe it was this or maybe it was that. None of it mattered now.

A grim realization came to West as he steeled his nerves and spoke as calmly as he could. "Unfortunately, it looks like I will only be with you for a short time." He glanced uneasily out the large window near them. Soon, the moon would rise, its powerful rays transforming him into a beast beyond control.

He turned to Kendra. "You still got that silver bullet?"

She placed her hand over the small revolver in her garter with its lone silver bullet. She nodded.

"You're going to need to use it. Once I turn into the wild LoneWolf, you will all be in deadly danger. Borge will have to extract the silver later and try to revive me."

---

*comprehensively chronicled in *Bite of the Wolf*- Editor.

Borge's voice trembled with dread. "West… I can't… I won't… guarantee that. The silver could cause permanent death or irreparable damage. There's no way of knowing. You simply can't do this!"

"What *is* guaranteed," said West, "is that I *will* go berserk and kill everything in my path, making me another threat you don't need to deal with. You all will have to handle it from here. Without the wolfskin belt, there is no other alternative. There's nothing here to contain me. You have to do what is necessary to stop Frankenstein, and that includes stopping me."

He looked over at Franklin, who stared at the floor with a downtrodden expression. "You've got this, kid. And Borge… I have faith in you. See you on the operating table."

"Dammit," Borge muttered in frustration, "I had the belt… just couldn't hold on to it."

Kendra felt a choking sensation rise within her, one she only rarely knew. She shook her head.

"No."

West looked straight into her eyes. God, they were wonderful. That was all he wanted to be thinking about when he looked into them. Instead, he did his best to go cold. "You have to. Swear to me that if we don't get the wolfskin belt back by the time the moon rises, you will fire that bullet."

Kendra hesitated, turning her face away.

"I swear I will do it," she said, her words a broken whisper.

The first dim rays of the moon crept through the window, casting their light over the solemn faces.

Kendra took a deep breath. She had found another reason to hate werewolves, one she had never considered.

She also found her mascara was running.

23: HERE COME THE BRIDES

An earth-quaking rumble shook the stables, rattling them to their foundations. Borge rushed to the far window and saw two giant-sized antennas rising up through the castle grounds. The trembling was followed by a deafening hum that sent tremors rippling through the earth.

Borge's face turned ashen. "Frankenstein is starting activation procedures for the Quantum Collider." He recognized this type of antenna system. It would be used to collect cosmic energies from the ionosphere, channeling the energy into the Fabula Device, which, in turn, would use its crystals to feed the Collider.

The tremors came to a sudden stop. Val West was still trembling, but for a different reason. He could feel the rising intensity of the full moon pulsing through his body, knowing the transformation into a rabid, killer beast was just a few racing heartbeats away. Each beat ticked like a berserker time bomb, ready to destroy everything in its path.

Kendra watched him go through the convulsions and contortions with a mixture of horror and extreme sympathy. West snapped his head toward her, his eyes reddened and glowing, his mouth now filled with more fangs than teeth. He growled, "Shoot!"

She was trembling almost as much as he was.

At one time, she was actually looking forward to doing this. Now the thought sickened her. With shaky hands, she raised the revolver and pointed it at West.

"STEADY!" he roared, his voice rapidly losing its humanity.

She pulled the hammer back, her heart sinking as she felt it click.

CRAAASH!

Xorror burst through the wall, charging straight at them. Either Prototype A or Kid Raven could have handled him, but Kendra took the opportunity to make a split-second decision. Quickly switching her aim, she fired the silver bullet straight into Xorror's eye. The monster staggered back, instinctively raising a hand to cover the mask's eye hole. Dark slime spurted from the socket, streaming down the steel face mask.

Kid Raven rushed forward, yanking the wolfskin belt off Xorror and tossing it to Kendra. The wounded monster swung with a backhanded strike, sending Kid Raven crashing into the wall. In response, Prototype A threw a crushing concrete fist at Xorror, denting the metal face. The two Frankenstein Monsters squared off, locking up in a power struggle of monstrous dominance.

West, in the midst of lycanthropic transformation, snarled and clawed at Kendra as she frantically tried to fasten the belt around his waist with one hand while pushing him off with the other. She could feel the hot breath and sharp, gnashing fangs coming closer, scraping against her upper arm. Doing her damnedest to withstand the gnawing pain, she put everything into snapping the last buckle tight.

Just one more....

A fang point pressed hard against her throat. She had to snap this into place before the next snapping was her neck in the powerful jaws of the wild beast.

Got it! As the last snap clicked, she dove into a roll. The rampaging beast froze, his demeanor instantly changing. LoneWolf grabbed hold of his head, taking a moment to regain control.

Kendra looked at her now-shredded other sleeve, red fang imprints still visible on the bare skin of her arm. "You beast. This is one of my favorite outfits!"

LoneWolf turned toward her with what she could have sworn was a fanged grin.

She got to her feet, brushed herself off, then further examined the damaged sleeve. "Bad dog."

Across the stables, Prototype A was airplane-spinning the wounded Xorror, adding both further insult *and* injury before tossing the monstrosity down the open elevator shaft. Satisfied, Prototype A dusted off his hands and lumbered over to check on Kid Raven, whose inexperienced pride was more bruised than anything else. Picking up the glass dome containing Victor, he followed the others to investigate the giant antennas towering over the grounds.

Six levels below, Frankenstein marveled at the sight of the Quantum Collider.

Resembling the similar-in-concept Large Hadron Collider, at its base was a large circle made of ionic energy rings and various synchrotrons, controlled by a sprawling supercomputer filling an entire wall. At the center spun a massive sphere covered with magnetic shields and columbite spokes. A long titanium barrel rose from the top, ready to channel the focused quantum energy through an array of crystals.

This device would send powerful, mysterious quantum particles into Frankenstein's creations. Nearby, a dozen capsules filled with his Nu-Men—supersoldiers created through various means—were momentarily at rest. Suspended in their cocoons of crystal glass, they awaited the moment of their new birth. HIVE was also awaiting the Collider's use as a directed energy weapon… a death ray capable of striking any target on command.

LoneWolf knew their arrival had been well announced, making a sneak attack impossible. The only question was how to reach the Collider without getting killed—such as being blasted to infinity by the Collider's giant gun barrel, among other threats. Frankenstein's armed security forces would be coming for them soon, if they weren't on their way already.

Almost as if in answer, the screech of tires snapped their attention toward the front gate. A lime-green double-decker bus—the same one that had nearly flattened Borge in Chamonix—plowed through the gate, barreling straight toward them. LoneWolf snarled in fury at the sight of Frau Stiglitz's sphincteric face glaring from behind the wheel.

The bus swerved wildly before skidding to a sudden stop. Frau Stiglitz jabbed a finger in their direction and began barking orders in her thick German accent. The bus was overflowing with the beautiful beasts known as the Brides. One by one, they began filing out of the bus, eye-lasers, Knocker Gases™, and flamethrower hands in hand.

LoneWolf gave a growling command to move.

They dashed off, with Kid Raven doubling back to grab Prototype A, pulling him—and his enraptured gaze—away from the busload of busty Brides.

At the ear-splittingly screeched command of "Fire," the Brides unleashed a relentless barrage of bullets and laser blasts.

LoneWolf weighed the options, and none of them looked good. They couldn't make it back to the stables, and the nearest cover—a few scattered trees—wouldn't hold for long. Kendra grabbed his arm, pointing to the small building she and Borge had seen rise from underground. The deadly onslaught of gunfire and lasers blasted toward them, each shot striking ever closer.

When they reached the building, it was, of course, locked.

Prototype A growled in frustration with an inarticulate "Grrrrr," and tore the metal door open, nearly ripping it off its hinges. A laser blast struck the doorframe, inches from where Kid Raven stood. He gulped nervously, realizing how close it had come to splitting open his head—a chilling reminder of how real this all was and how closely death continually nipped at their heels… and heads.

LoneWolf steadied himself in his shooting stance, firing his H&K M23 at the Bridal parade. A direct hit between the eyes took one out of commission, but the rest responded with a hail of return fire. He fought hard to resist his animalistic urge to counterattack by charging at them head-on. Instead, he loped away from the building, trying to draw their fire while the others worked to get the elevator moving.

He paused to fire off another round, lining up a Bride in his sights. A sudden shock went through his right hand—a laser had blast struck his gun, sending it flying as he watched it dissolve into red hot molten goo.

So much for his weaponry.

The others shouted to him as the elevator began descending—but with only Kid Raven and Prototype A aboard. The inner panel doors sealed shut just as they entered, giving them no chance to stop it. Without cover, Kendra and Borge, carrying Victor, ducked and weaved to avoid the incoming fire while LoneWolf ran to rejoin them.

Where to now? The only choice left was to make a break for New Castle Frankenstein. It looked like Kendra would be breaking in again after all.

LoneWolf hurriedly led them toward the sinister shadow of the steel and glass structure. "What an eyesore this is," Victor exclaimed. "Victor I obviously has zero taste when it comes to architecture."

"Hardly his most frightening creation," Borge replied. "But I do agree."

Kendra was ready to lead them in the same way she broke in previously. LoneWolf was also interested in breaking in, but with less stealth subtlety than Kendra employed, preferring to place his emphasis on "breaking." He crashed through one of the large glass-walled sections, clearing the way.

The commotion soon caught the attention of the elderly housekeeper, Minnie, who came to investigate.

"Hello, Minnie," Victor greeted her, in his eerie, echoing voice. She looked down at the cold, pale flesh of the head in the jar speaking to her, then turned to see the panting, growling werewolf beside it. Her eyes widened in terror, followed by an absurd wail. She again looked at the head, and then again at the werewolf.

Emitting a shrieking scream, she ran away, arms flapping, not to be stopped until she reached Darmstadt in the valley below. The beastly werewolf and the reanimated head shrugged at each other—well, as much as Victor could, anyway. LoneWolf was getting used to these reactions and moved on.

From the study, they took the hidden elevator down to the lab. They braced themselves for whatever fate awaited them beyond the doors.

Nothing.

That's what greeted LoneWolf and company when the elevator doors slid open. They had been on high alert, expecting an alarm would sound and all manner of grotesque and deadly things would be there to meet them. They were half relieved and half in disbelief at their luck.

In this brief moment of relative safety, they devised a plan. Borge and Victor would work to overload the Fabula Device's crystals to disrupt the Collider without triggering an interdimensional implosion—that would certainly stop the Collider, but it was a choice to be considered only beyond an absolute last resort.

LoneWolf and Kendra would work to take out... everything else.

As they walked farther in, LoneWolf could sense something, something he didn't like. Things being too easy always bothered him. It was almost an unwritten code of the spy game that if you were setting a trap, you made it too easy. Unwritten or not, the business had taught him this lesson more than once, and usually painfully.

"Does it bother you that we just took the elevator down here without a hitch?" LoneWolf asked in his husky growl.

"Not everything is a trap," Kendra replied, glancing at him in his werewolf form. She realized she was starting to get used to it—the beastly fur-covered face, red eyes, pointed ears, snout-esque nose, and jutting lower fangs. It helped to imagine him as a heavily bearded man in desperate need of a shave, not to mention an extensive amount of dental work. Much better than trying to equate him to the friendly family dog of her childhood. "Maybe it's your animal instincts in overdrive, but you're being overly-paranoid."

"It's not just animal instincts," he rasped. "My sniff says something is amiss."

Kendra dismissed this, but remained on guard, dropping back behind Borge and Victor to keep an eye on the rear. After passing through a long, empty corridor, they came upon a sealed security door. Borge attached a safecracking device, opening it with ease.

Again, too much ease for LoneWolf's liking.

Inside, the area was still under construction, a large space filled with scaffolding and exposed girders. LoneWolf's sense of scent went from overdrive to full throttle. Without warning, the lights flickered, then cut out. In the total darkness, only the glow of flashing red eyes could be seen shining from the rafters.

He recognized the smell.

"Those bitches."

He should have trusted his nose. For being made of reconstituted and reanimated corpses, the Brides had a disturbingly lovely feminine scent to them. Perhaps sugar and spice were two of the actual ingredients. The one missing ingredient would certainly have to be "everything nice."

In the pitch black, with only the red, glowing Bride eyes providing illumination, there was just enough light to see that things looked bleak. LoneWolf's animal night vision was tuned in, along with his heightened sense of hearing, and between both, they had a fighting chance.

The red eye glows intensified, followed by bright red laser arcs slicing through the dark, pieces of the metal scaffolding above falling all around them. Borge and Victor scrambled for cover behind a large piece of equipment. Frantically, Borge rummaged through his safari jacket, pulling out a small mirror. The odds weren't great, but it was a slim chance and one he had to take.

A bright red laser line beamed down next to him. Slowly inching the mirror toward it, he caught the ray in the glass, reflecting it back toward the rafters. He carefully tilted the mirror, redirecting the beam to a new target—straight back into the eyes of the sender. The Bride's head exploded, temporarily adding a little more light to the proceedings.

LoneWolf and Kendra continued this deadly game of "dodge the laser beam," both narrowly being blasted several times. Borge moved along the wall and found what he hoped he would find: the power box. He cranked the master switch and light flooded the room.

With the vast space now illuminated, the Brides lost their tactical advantage and leaped down one after another. They formed a line, marching forward like a well-trained army. This deadly doll squad advanced toward them, arms outstretched, ready to grab, and tear, and crush.

LoneWolf had no choice but to move in retreat, and did just that, leading the way to the doorway ahead. Kendra scrambled through first, followed closely by LoneWolf. On the other side, he was unpleasantly surprised to find the sneering Frau Stiglitz standing before him, holding the limp body of Kendra in one hand.

"Wolf Whitman, ja?" She examined his werewolf features, connecting the two faces in her mind. "Even if accurate, that is a stupid name to use."

He had to give her that one. Borge had now entered through the door, carrying Victor. He still did not agree.

In Kendra's haste to get through the open doorway, she neglected to check what was lurking on the other side—Frau Stiglitz, ready with a blackjack in hand, which she used to wallop Kendra over the head.

Now, she held a gun to Kendra's temple. Even if she was conscious, Kendra would find it difficult to escape this particular predicament.

"She will make a beautiful Bride, don't you think, Herr Whitman?" She stroked the delicate features of Kendra's face with what appeared to be more than just a touch of lust in her vile eyes.

LoneWolf snarled, stepping forward.

"Back, Wolfskopf," she warned, digging the gun barrel into Kendra's head. The Brides had now entered to surround LoneWolf, Borge, and Victor. Two of the Brides moved in to flank the Frau as they backed away slowly. Frau Stiglitz wisely kept the gun pushed deep into Kendra's temple, taking no chances, especially should she regain consciousness.

Volta Elettrica had returned. She silently joined the other Brides, falling into formation with the same blank, robotic expression as the others.

Then, with one quick movement, Volta whipped up her hand, using her secret service-issued pistol to shoot the Bride next to her.

"Get out of here," she yelled at LoneWolf and Borge, her eyes wild, fighting for control over herself. For now, she had it, but for how long? She didn't know. She had no idea nor could anticipate when Igor would once again assume the controls, puppeteering her as his own special, deadly doll.

Frau Stiglitz let out a screeching shriek, and fled with the Brides, dragging Kendra with them. Volta took aim, but the heavy steel door they ran through took the bullet hits. With a thud, the door slammed, the sound of the lock clicking into place.

LoneWolf gnashed his teeth in frustration. "Is there another way out of here?"

Volta pointed to a ladder along the wall. "There's an emergency exit to the stairwell through there."

Although hesitant to approach her after the earlier attack in the stables, Borge spoke up. "Can you lead us to where the Collider is?"

"I believe so. It has to be in Lab Level 6."

Borge gulped, dreading another "Bride-Out" along the way. All of this was starting to put him off the idea of marriage.

Before she could lead the way, LoneWolf stopped her. "Wait. What about Kendra? Any idea where they might be taking her?"

In answer to his question, a voice sounded over the PA speakers:
Calling Dr. Frankenstein to Bride Processing.
Paging Dr. Frankenstein, Bride Processing: CODE GREEN.

24: LIGHTNING STRIKES

The baron's eyes lit up. He had heard the page. *Bride Processing?* Frau Stiglitz must have brought in a new specimen. He glanced at his watch—there was just enough time to start the process.

He stood on the platform at the supercomputer in the vast, cavernous laboratory on the bottom floor of the massive subterranean installation. Above him, rows of electronic lights blinked away, calculating incredibly complex computations that would soon send commands to the humming Fabula Device, its crystal core glowing with the energy needed to finally and fully bring his vision to life.

With a gleam of satisfaction, he ran his hands along the cold steel railing, looking down lustily at the doomsday machine he now possessed: the Quantum Collider. Every preliminary test had passed with perfect results. Before long, he would activate the Collider and fortify his current crop of Brides with the new, stabilizing Quantum Galvanization life force. He rubbed his hands together, donned his white lab coat, and prepared to welcome a new Bride.

As he walked to the elevator that would take him to the Processing Center, he whistled a happy tune. If this was a live one, the procedure would certainly be different. They all were, in their own special ways. Assembling the Brides from the finest dead tissues, bones, and organs was always a delight to him, something he never lost his feverish thrill for. And by converting already living women into obedient Brides who would know their place, he was making true proper ladies out of them. Someday, after he had made this a better world, they would be joined in matrimony to his Nu-Men. What a super-species they would create!

The thought excited him so much that he had to take a deep breath to calm himself. But right now, there was work to do.

He also needed to get the boy back. Why hadn't the imbeciles of HIVE located him yet? Franklin was traveling with a giant, green, bolted-together monster and a head in a jar. How hard could they be to find? Though he despised the boy—his own great-great-grandson—he needed him.

That body was meant for him.

He would get the boy back, then cryogenically freeze him until the time was right. At that time, he would transfer his brain into this perfect, young body that he would make strong and powerful, even though his previous attempts to do so had inexplicably failed. The experiments tonight with Quantum Galvanization would revolutionize his work, making his transfer to this young body sustainable, and truly immortal. Until then, he must attend to this call requiring his one-of-a-kind scientific expertise.

The elevator opened just before Frankenstein reached it. Igor stumbled out, nursing a heavily swollen black eye.

"Why, Igor... what's happened?"

Igor glared at him. "I'll tell you what's happened, my *Herr Baron*," he said, his undisguised contempt spilling over. "We are under attack. And by *your* creation."

Frankenstein was startled. That miserable demon wretch was here? He would simply have to be disposed of. On the other hand, he most likely had brought the treacherous head with him. Victor III didn't deserve to be a Frankenstein, let alone have his brain housed in the head that once belonged to him. Perhaps they could capture him and find out where the boy was. They'd never risk the life of a young, physically weak boy by bringing him along.

With his usual lack of sympathy or understanding, the baron's voice grew cold. "Well? What is HIVE going to do about it? They do need to earn their keep."

Igor's eyes blazed with rage. Frankenstein had dismissed and disrespected HIVE's contributions long enough. It was not he who had successfully pulled off the heist of the Collider.

HIVE had.

It was not he who had developed a practical use for the Brides and the supersoldiers, the Nu-Men, as he called them.

They had. HIVE had.

And Igor was HIVE through and through.

What *was* Frankenstein's doing, was the forgoing of proper security. He insisted on working in total secrecy and now they had this to deal with as a consequence.

Perhaps now was not the time to make his feelings known. Soon, the Quantum Collider would be activated, and after its first successful application, it would be ready for HIVE's exclusive use. As a key leader in a new world power, a new supra-nation dominating the earth, he would achieve God-like wealth—a far better and more practical goal than trying to play God with creatures pieced together from corpses. Sure, they could be put to good use, but why settle for subhuman junk heaps when you could subjugate all of humanity?

Igor bit his tongue. Hard.

He composed himself, then spoke softly. "Frau Stiglitz can take command. I am confident she can lead the Brides to stop the intruders."

"Yes. In fact, I do believe she has a new one waiting for me now in the Bride Processing laboratory."

...

"Vot is taking Doctor so long?"

Frau Stiglitz had taken the time to dress for the occasion, wearing a skimpy nurse uniform with miniskirt. Her lumpy skin folds awkwardly spilled out, constituting a real medical emergency for anyone unfortunate enough to see it. She fidgeted with the nurse's cap while keeping her lone beady eye fixed on the captive Bride-to-be, Lady Kendra Kenton.

Kendra had regained consciousness, though the pounding ache in her skull made her wish she hadn't. The straps pinning her arms, legs, and torso to the table were tight, too tight, biting into her skin. A wide band across her forehead pressed her skull down against the headrest.

In front of her, under a red domed cage, was a conveyor platform waiting to pull her into the powerizing machine it was connected to, filled with flashing lights and eerie electronic sounds, bleeping and blooping with bad intent. It took up most of the operating room, and whatever it did, she knew she wouldn't be the same once it spat her out on the other side.

The red phone on the desk near Frau Stiglitz buzzed. She snorted, then smeared a glob of snot across her sleeve before picking up the receiver.

"Ja, Master Igor. We have them fully contained in the outer Chamber 17. Your pet Bride, Volta, went rogue. She must be reassimilated. Perhaps... I can have some time with her... alone? For persuasion, ja?"

Igor's voice on the other end was sharp and impatient. "Are you sure you have them all contained? Even the Monster?"

"There is nothing to worry about," the Frau replied confidently. "Xorror will handle it."

"You'd better be certain. As for the new Bride... the baron will be delayed. We must get the Collider activation completed. Keep her where she is and make sure the other Brides are ready. Bring them all to Lab 6."

"Sehr wohl, der Herr." Frau Stiglitz hung up the phone, her gaze creeping back to Kendra, still bound too tightly to even struggle. "Ve still have a few minutes, mein Schnuckelchen." Her tongue slithered over her toady lips.

It was only then that Kendra thought she might faint.

...

Both Frankenstein and Igor were growing impatient. The baron had wanted to start the Collider earlier, but Igor hadn't been ready. Then, just as he was leaving to create another Bride, Igor insisted they needed to activate the Collider now. Perhaps he should dispose of Igor and rid himself of this distracting HIVE business.

It was just as well. For too long, Frankenstein had waited for this moment—this chance to finally perfect what he had begun. Prototype A may have been made near immortal and also near invincible, but he sickened Frankenstein. Created to be beautiful, he had instead turned out to be a hideous failure Frankenstein couldn't bear to look at. His new creatures would soon be imbued with a power that would not only stabilize them physically, but also infuse them with an energy elevating them above even the creations of the biblical God.

Igor was growing impatient with the baron, but right now, he was irritated by Frau Stiglitz's tardiness. He had said to bring the Brides here *now*, not ten minutes from now. Finally, the lab doors hissed open, and Frau Stiglitz entered, flanked by the Brides.

He winced at her nurse's attire. "Frau Stiglitz. So nice of you to join us."

"Entschuldigen Sie," she apologized. "I came as soon as I could. I started the Bride Processor—it is set on automatic. Even without doctor's examinations, I think it will make a good girl."

Igor's hard eyes narrowed at her. "We shall see. Now, if you will line up the Brides over here."

The Brides obediently took their positions as the pointed barrel of the Collider rotated, its tip aimed directly at them. Above, Baron

Frankenstein stood on the platform, looking down at them, their vacant eyes awaiting his command. Ecstatic with expectation, his fingers caressed the controls to activate the Collider.

With the Brides lined up, Frankenstein eagerly turned the dial, watching the lights flicker on. The gauges indicated that all was optimal, and the crystals pulsed with energy from the ion particles. The cyclotrodes and superconverters whirred to life, each rotation generating an expanding swirl of pure quantum energy. A ringing hum filled the vast chamber, vibrating with perfect intonation.

It was alive!

Frankenstein sited in the charged barrel aimed at the Brides. In unison, their forehead bolts extended from their temples, standing erect, ready to channel the gathering energy.

At last, the moment of truth had arrived. Frankenstein's heart raced as he pressed the button. The air crackled as a blue beam of quantum particles streamed from the barrel. Like a conductor leading a symphony, he directed the flow into their metallic headbolts, bathing the Brides in a glowing haze of energy, infusing them with a new, supercharged form of life.

"The Power! The Power!!" Frankenstein yelled out, orgasmic in his glee at seeing his greatest work come to reality, after all this time, after all the obstacles put forth by fools trying to stop the greatest scientific mind of all time… the Baron, no, THE GOD, Victor Frankenstein.

The ocean of blue light engulfed the laboratory in its cosmic glow. Frankenstein watched it intently, filled with pure awe.

Oh my God, he suddenly thought. It was a thought and feeling which had not been present in him in many years, since the last time he had felt anything—when he grieved the loss of his beloved mother. The terrible irony of it twisted inside him—he, who had sought to conquer death, had become its servant, destroying life in his relentless pursuit of creation.

An overwhelming sense of empathy, coupled with deep remorse, came over him.

"What have I done?" he whispered, his voice trembling. "What have I done to all of these people? To my own flesh and blood?" He felt the presence of a power far greater than anything he could imagine himself as, more powerful than anything he could ever hope to create. He was seeing it, and now feeling it, and for this moment, he truly *believed* it.

"That's enough, Frankenstein."

The momentary attack of conscience was broken by Igor's voice from below. He stood on the floor, pointing a handgun at the baron.

Frankenstein switched the power off and backed away, hands raised.

"You." A look of bitter disdain replaced the joyous, hopeful expression of a moment earlier. "I should have known. Humanity has always found a way to let me down... always forsaking me."

Igor smirked victoriously. "Yes, you should have known. You should have known that HIVE is the future. I have a Yellow Jacket that was fitted just for me, and *I* will be the leader of not only HIVE Europe but *also* Frankentech. We do not need you, and the company will flourish under my leadership, making me one of the most powerful men in the world. You could have joined us—but you thought playing gods and monsters was more important."

With a nod, the Brides fell into formation around Igor. Their eyes now pulsated with a ghostly blue glow, charged with the galvanizing effects of the quantum energy. Sparks crackled from their head bolts, and arcs of lightning danced across their nipple electrodes. The infusion had seemingly stabilized and strengthened them beyond anything Frankenstein had envisioned. Igor ordered Frau Stiglitz to head to the Processor and bring back the newest Bride to join their ranks.

Igor thought about ridding himself of Frankenstein. The thought made him giddy. It was unprofessional to some degree, and unbecoming of a man of his newly minted stature to get his hands so dirty. He lowered the gun. "I could just shoot you. But I think these ladies could use the practice." Igor turned to the Brides. His grin widened as he gave the order.

"Open fire."

Aiming their bosoms toward the upper platform, the swirling static surrounding their nipple electrodes formed into pulsing lightning bolts. Frankenstein ducked as the bolts struck the metal railings around him, shaking the lab with each strike.

Damn this Igor. Frankenstein wanted to stew over the betrayal, but he needed to escape. However, revenge was always more important. He dodged another lightning strike, leaping for the control console to activate the next phase. The Collider roared to life once more, this time directing its energy into the twelve crystal chrysalises suspended above—the capsules containing his Nu-Men.

Igor stopped the Brides as the lightning strikes threatened the supercomputer controlling the Quantum Collider. His grin faded to horror as he watched the brilliant blue light surge into the magnetic poles of the Nu-Men's headbolts, electrifying each one with quantum energy.

Frankenstein smiled, but this time, there was no joy, only vengeance. His creations, his monstrous children, would embody that vengeance. With a furious roar, the Nu-Men jolted to life, supercharged with raw power. Fully energized, the musclebound creatures burst free from their crystal cocoons, leaping down in front of Igor and the Brides.

Frankenstein's supersoldiers had awakened, and they were ready for war.

25: MONSTER CLASH

Outside the door to the Bride Processing lab, LoneWolf and Volta tried to find a way in without success. The door lock was coded, and so far, their attempts to crack it had failed. When they first arrived, the mechanical door had slid open, forcing them to duck aside just in time to escape detection. LoneWolf did a double take at the rather revolting sight of Nurse Frau Stiglitz marching out, turning back to blow a kiss to the captive Kendra. Then, to make matters worse, the door slid shut behind her, trapping Kendra inside.

West had transformed back from LoneWolf. Though he still possessed enhanced strength and skills from the full moon's effects, he always felt more than a bit unruly and overly aggressive in his wolf form and wanted to stay as clear-headed as possible while focusing on a solution.

"Listen, I don't think we're going to be able to hack into this," he said. "Given how solid the door is, my own brand of brute force won't do it either. How about yours?"

Volta paused. She did have her own powers from the bizarre modifications made to her by Baron Frankenstein. It seemed, however, that they were all activated and controlled by Igor.

"How can I? I don't know how to make them work."

"Just focus. It's all connected into your neural pathways. Maybe it's like a mind-muscle connection—see and feel yourself doing it."

She closed her eyes. West felt himself starting to perspire. Kendra was inside, and who knows how far along she was in this "processing." What if it was too late?

As Volta concentrated, she felt a warmth building behind her eyes. It grew into a bright red and began to pulse lightly. She felt the rising heat, a pressure in her retinas, building to a momentous force aching to break free.

She snapped her eyes open.

West sensed the coming blast and jumped aside. A stream of laser fire shot from her ruby eyes, just narrowly missing him. The doors not only blasted open but were blasted to pieces. West hurried inside, mentally preparing for what could be a grisly discovery.

Inside the lab stood the processing machine, clearly labeled with a sign reading *Bridification*. On the conveyer beneath was the bound Kendra, electrodes and lead wires snaking across her body. She wriggled wildly, trying to rock herself off the conveyor before it fed her into the mouth of the monstrous, powerizing machinery. Tendrils of cable slithered toward her feet, ready to pull her in for the ultimate makeover into the next Frankenstein creation.

West looked over the contraption, an array of blinking lights, dials, and gurgling vials connected to giant electro-static bulbs, all controlled by a tangle of hundreds of wires and buttons. The large, round, red metal cage was lowering to enclose her, preparing its final grim procedure before swallowing her inside. He again looked at the buttons. No time to shut it off.

Quickly transforming back into LoneWolf, he slashed at the cables and electrode wires, cutting his way through to the leather straps binding Kendra to the conveyor belt. He bit at the advancing steel cable tendrils, which recoiled as if alive. With one hand pressed against the closing cage, he snatched Kendra with the other, pulling her free from the conveyor belt. Wrapping her tightly in his arms, he dove away to get clear of the death machine as the cage slammed shut.

He closed his eyes and relaxed to transform back into Val West again. As they lay atop each other, they paused to catch their breath, their eyes meeting in a shared moment of relief and unspoken tension. "Why, Kendra, I do believe with those rosy cheeks you would make for quite the blushing bride."

The unamused Kendra narrowed her eyes at him. "Watch it, or you will no longer have what it takes to be a groom, much less consummate a marriage." She followed up with an elbow to his ribs and got to her feet.

"My dear," West groaned, "you really need to find a better way to emphasize your points, other than with the point of your elbow."

They were interrupted by an ungodly wail. Frau Stiglitz had returned, hysterical at the sight. All wild-eyed bluster, she charged them in a screaming mad fit of rage. Kendra sidestepped the Frau, spinning around to land a stiff kick to the back of her head. As Stiglitz landed on the still-moving conveyor, she was immediately sucked into the hole and pulled into the jaws of the Bridification machine. Not waiting to find out what the process entailed, the three of them ran off, the horrid screeching shrieks of Frau Stiglitz ringing in their ears.

As they reached a fork in the corridor, West skidded to a stop. "Volta, which way do we need to go?"

Kendra gave Volta the side-eye. "Why are we trusting her, exactly?"

"Well, for one, she just saved your delightful posterior by blasting through the doors.

Kendra's glare only intensified. "I guess that almost makes up for trying to kill me in the stables."

Volta looked down, shame casting a shadow over her as she thought about what she had become. "I... I'm sorry. But be grateful—you were very close to being turned into what I am now: a monster."

Kendra felt Volta's inner pain for a moment. What had been done to her was truly appalling, performed unconsciously and against her will—her mind and body co-opted and corrupted. She nodded, and a silent truce was made. There was no choice but to soften her stance. She did, however, plan to run as fast as she could the first moment it seemed Volta was once again compromised and under Igor's control.

"We're just going to have to take a leap of faith," said West. "For now, we're following her lead. Once we get closer, we'll follow my nose."

...

The Monster looked around while Kid Raven tried to figure out their next move. Minutes earlier, they had exited the runaway elevator and discovered it had only descended three floors. This meant they were only halfway down. Now the question was how to get to the lower levels.

"Prototype A," said Kid Raven (Franklin insisted on calling him this instead of Adam, as his father did, explaining it was a "cooler-sounding superhero name.") "I think we're lost. There has to be a way to get down to the lower floors. But I'm sure not seeing it and we've looked everywhere."

Prototype A grunted in agreement. He liked Franklin, and in the short time since they met, he had come to regard him as a kid brother, if not a Kid Raven. In a way, they were brothers of sorts, truly cut from the same cloth.

"Wait... what's this?" He had come upon a section of the wall made up of panels. He pounded on it, and it appeared to be hollow. The Monster also pounded on it and his fist went through... and was caught by the monster behind it:

Xorror.

The wall erupted as Xorror, wounded and furious, charged forward, fists flying. Kid Raven knew Prototype A could handle the beast, so he darted through the remains of the wall to see what lay beyond. He

242

cautiously ventured in, his senses on high alert as he took in the surroundings. It was dark and cavernous and smelled of… stale popcorn? And the hint of something best left undiscovered.

Just ahead was a wall of screens over a desk with an office chair. The central monitor flickered to life, revealing the familiar smirk of Igor Zelensky.

"Intruder alert," he said in a mocking tone, watching from the overhead cameras. "I didn't know 'Code Name: LoneWolf' had a teenage sidekick, but here you are. And… there you go." With the push of a button, the floor opened up.

As the newly dubbed Kid Raven, Franklin thought he was starting to get the hang of this hero business. That is, until he ended up stuck halfway down a tunnel shaft. With his legs firmly wedged in a splits position, he looked down at the chained, fleshy-headed mutations below, staring up with black, hungry eyes and drooling mouths of jagged, rotting teeth. He thought maybe his career as a teenage crime-fighting adventurer was over before it had even begun.

Damn this Igor.

It was time to think, and fast. There was more to this than just brawn, and he meant that as no offense to Prototype A, who had no idea Franklin was stuck in this precarious position. No, he would have to think and use his brains to get out of this. Ideally, as he found out, it was a combination of both his brains and brawn. He used this combination to let go, executing a jackknife dive onto the mutants below, using them as a springboard. He launched himself upward, springing into a leap he didn't even know he could make.

Igor had shown up to gloat, and in a split second, he had even managed to pop him hard in the eye as he burst through the closed trapdoor. Not bad for a novice, he thought, as he and Prototype A worked their way down to the main lab.

Prototype A hadn't done so badly, either. Xorror had kept him busy, the two monsters battling back and forth in a contest to determine who was the dominant Frankenstein Monster.

The answer had been Prototype A.

After tossing Xorror through a wall, he reached down, tearing the mask off the metal stitches connecting it to the face. Underneath was an exposed glowing green skull screaming in agony until put out of its misery by the giant boot of Prototype A squashing it like a melon.

It had taken at least thirty minutes to get this far, and from the commotion they could now hear, they sensed they were getting closer. They had to keep moving through this labyrinth of tunnels to find their way and bring their reckoning to the Baron Frankenstein.

...

Up on a ledge some thirty feet above the vast expanse of the laboratory, Val West, Kendra, and Volta watched a raging battle of the sexes unfold between Igor's Brides of Destruction and Frankenstein's Monsters.

The Nu-Men, hulking monstrosities with bulging, green-veined muscles, ripped and tore at the Brides with ruthless aggression. Their attacks were met with counterstrikes of lethal precision. Eye-lasers cut through the air, creating bursts of sparks as they sliced through steel. Clouds of Knocker Gas™, hissed out from pointed nipples, followed by the roar of flamethrowers as the Brides' robotic-enhanced skeletons powered them forward with terrifying strength. If there was any natural attraction between the creatures, it was now overpowered by sheer, primal, destructive bloodlust.

West's eyes narrowed as he spotted Frankenstein and Igor, each watching from the shadows. No doubt, both wondered if there would be anything left of the lab and the Quantum Collider for the winner to take possession of. The baron looked to be weighing his options, thinking maybe it was time to cut and run—and also blow the whole place to hell on his way out. West had seen that desperate look of furious defeat before and it wouldn't be the first time the Baron had wiped the slate clean and started over.

West tightened his grip on the wolfskin belt at his waist, feeling the familiar tingle he always felt when savage violence was called for. Kendra crouched beside him, scanning the scene, waiting for his lead. Volta, hoping Igor was too preoccupied with the chaos below, prepared to give her all in the coming battle. West mulled over a strategy. As much as he wanted to, and salivated over the thought, he knew they couldn't just storm in. They would need reinforcements.

A sudden whirring noise caught his attention. A cable shot across from the opposite ledge, embedding itself in the rock above them. Kid Raven swung across, landing nimbly beside them, a grin spreading across his face. Before West could acknowledge the boy, a deafening crash made him turn. The solid steel door behind them buckled and flew off its hinges with a thunderous force. Out of the twisted carnage stepped Prototype A, the eight feet of trouble West was counting on.

The reinforcements had arrived.

...

Down on the main floor, Borge and Victor were ready to make a break for it. They had seen an opening with the Brides and Monsters preoccupied in combat and had managed to run as far as the base of the Collider. They would need to get closer—much closer—to stop the impending threat. To shut down the Collider, they would have to get behind it and reach the large, building-sized case containing the inner workings of the Fabula Device.

Victor's mind raced as he thought of the gravity of the situation. This battle wasn't going so well for either Frankenstein or Igor. How long would they have until the two of them fought for control of the Collider, using its destructive power to end the battle decisively? He racked his brain, trying to think of a solution. They had to find a way inside before it was too late.

There was now an even more immediate threat to deal with. Borge froze in a panic. A Bride had locked her wild, shimmering ruby eyes onto him, turning both her attentions and deadly intentions his way.

Up on the ledge, a barrage of fire blasted at the team. As the blasts approached, West transformed into LoneWolf, using his powerful form to shield Kendra from the onslaught of rocky shrapnel that exploded around them.

Prototype A turned to Volta, and in the midst of the danger, she gave him a warm smile. In that moment, he was reminded of the humanity he yearned for—the warmth of connection that had always felt just out of reach. Her smile stirred something deep within him. He moved in front of her, instinctively making his hulking form her shield.

As Volta clutched tightly to his giant arm, a sudden blast rocked the ledge, chunks of stone crumbling and plummeting to the floor below. Volta let out a scream as the ground gave way beneath her feet. Prototype A lunged, his hand reaching for her as her grip slipped through his fingers. On the way down, her arms flailed, catching onto a nearby scaffolding at the last second. She barely avoided a direct laser hit, twisting her body into a desperate slide down the rails. At the bottom, she looked up and gave a wave to Prototype A—she wasn't out of this fight yet.

Prototype A felt something snap inside him. He had seen enough as an observer and was now more than ready to enter the fray. With a roar that echoed through the lab, he vaulted off the edge of the ledge, crashing down onto two of the Nu-Men, flattening them in a grotesque splatter of green-tinted gore.

From her position on the floor, Volta knew she could help Borge and Victor. She made a break for it, dodging a hail of fire.

"Wait, hold off!" Borge shouted, but it was too late. Another Bride had joined the first, advancing menacingly from the opposite side.

Prototype A also saw this and yelled out over the sound of cracking bones as he smashed his fist into a nearby monstrosity's face. Volta, ignoring the warning, sprang into action. A laser blast was screaming straight toward Borge and Victor, and without a second thought, she dove to push them out of harm's way. The stinging energy blast struck her in the side, instantly sending her crumpling to the ground, gasping for breath.

Borge set Victor down and ran to her, pulling her to shelter behind the scaffolding of the Collider platform. He leaned down to examine her, his hands trembling as he checked her injuries. He then turned away, momentarily tuned out of the chaos of the war zone around him.

She was dead.

26: BEWARE! THE BLOBULUS

Prototype A bellowed with a hellish rage. He had barely known the beautiful Volta Elettrica but had sensed her spirit and felt her kindness. She didn't recoil at the sight of him, and like him, she was a freak—a monster not of her own making, but of the twisted designs of Frankenstein and Igor. In their fleeting moments together, he had felt something... a connection.

Now she was dead.

Now he was angry.

While Prototype A continued smashing both Nu-Men and Brides alike, LoneWolf focused on the Collider. Borge and Victor needed to get to the Fabula Device located behind it. He was ready to charge straight in, but his senses stopped him. Something was happening, and it wasn't a positive development. The Collider was vibrating, sending deep tremors through the complex. A mass of blue lightning was forming around the edge of its giant barrel.

Whatever it was doing, it didn't seem planned. A look of horror spread across Frankenstein's face. He hadn't activated the Collider—it was activating itself. The glow from it turned a brilliant, shining cobalt as sparkling energy radiated outward in steady streams, all flowing into the head bolts of the remaining Brides and Nu-Men. As the energy struck them, they jerked upright, possessed by the mysterious quantum energy coursing through them at dangerously overloaded levels.

The Brides reached out, as if asking for help.

One by one, their heads began to explode.

The Nu-Men fared no better. Quantum energy surged into their forehead bolts, causing their muscles to overgrow, expanding and expanding until they burst in a shower of muscle, sinew, and slime. With nowhere to go, the energy channeled itself to the next nearest head bolt—the magnetized electrode connected to Frankenstein's pet monster project, Blobulus.

The blobby globule of NuFlesh, still bobbing in its embryonic solution, had grown child-sized. As the infusion-blast of quantum particles hit, it swelled to the size of a man, a Nu-Man, within seconds. It held its shape for a brief moment before the energy overload made it erupt into fleshy, pus-filled pustules. Riddled with cysts, it continued to swell, expanding into a massive, oozing, tumorous mound. The glass capsule containing it shattered, and it lurched forth, leaving a trail of thick mucus behind.

Baron Frankenstein, watching from the steel walkway, decided it was definitely time to flee, but not before making his feelings known. "This is your fault, Igor!" he screamed. "Do you understand? Your fault!" He would get back up to New Castle Frankenstein, where he would activate the self-destruct code and blow them all to atoms. For now, he took cover from the carnage below.

Borge clutched Victor's glass dome tightly. He could see the Fabula Device, but reaching it still seemed impossible. The threat of the Brides firing at them and the Nu-Men tearing them limb-from-limb (at least Borge) was now over, but spreading fires now threatened the entire lab. The Collider spun wildly on its axis, hurling lightning bolts of pure quantum energy in every direction. A brief wave of relief came over Borge when he turned to see the hairy face of LoneWolf barreling toward him.

"How do we shut this damn thing down?" he growled.

Borge pointed to the large metal containment unit housing the Fabula Device. "We need to get inside, but as you can see, there's now a wall of flames in the way."

"If I can get you in there, then what?"

Victor turned his weary eyes to LoneWolf. "Then… I will do the rest. And when I do, you all get the hell out of here. And you make sure my boy is safe."

"I'll make that promise as long as I'm alive. And that means *all* of us are making it out of here alive, so let's get moving."

"Not all of us are making it out alive."

LoneWolf understood what Victor had to do. Now was not the time for arguments or sentimentality. He looked up at the steel walkway above, assessed the layout, and gnashed his teeth in frustration. How in the hell could he get Borge and Victor up there now? The stairway had collapsed in the battle. The gurgling, oozing Blobulus blocked one direction, and a wall of flames blazed from the other. Another noise caught his attention. Something whizzed past his ear, sparking off the metal grating above. A fire of a different type was now heading in their direction.

Igor, frothing with murderous rage, had pulled out an Uzi and decided he would close up operations. The Collider was beyond hope, but he had plans for escape and was certain he could pin all the failure on Frankenstein. The meltdown of the Collider would level everything for miles. Just for his own satisfaction, he would kill all these intruders who had ruined his grand coming out party as leader of HIVE Europe. He sprayed the bullets wildly, ignoring the better plan of leaving immediately.

LoneWolf threw himself in front of Borge and Victor, shielding them as best he could from the hail of bullets. He winced from an eruption of fiery pain—one of the bullets had struck his left arm. It wouldn't cause the damage it would to a normal human, but it still hurt like hell… and pissed him off. He wanted nothing more than to charge through the gunfire and tear Igor's throat out, but knew he needed to stay with Borge and Victor. The two of them were the only ones able to stop this infernal machine.

Suddenly, the gunfire stopped. LoneWolf turned to see Kid Raven whirling Igor around from behind and landing another punch to his already swollen face, his dropped Uzi sliding across the floor. Kendra's foot followed, striking him in the crotch, sending him crashing to the ground with the addition of swollen testicles.

Prototype A stalked over, glowering down at the groaning Igor. Rolling to his side, Igor pulled out a pocket pistol. The fired shot had no effect other than to further enrage the Monster.

"Listen," Igor stammered, "We can make a deal. I'm a very powerful—"

The unimpressed Prototype A grabbed Igor by his lapels and hoisted him overhead. The energy beam pulsing from the barrel of the Quantum Collider had coalesced into a giant eye of swirling energy. Igor was still pleading when the Monster yelled at the swirling eye, and then yelled at Igor to reinforce the point.

He was refusing his offer.

Prototype A launched Igor like a javelin into the heart of the energy vortex, scoring a direct hit. As Igor disintegrated, a thundering sound of flatulence erupted, leaving only the fading echoes of his final scream behind.

The resulting explosive flash of light nearly blinded Prototype A. As he turned to shield his eyes, he caught sight of Volta's body, still lying motionless on the floor. Kendra and Kid Raven looked at the flurry of sparks and quantum lightning radiating from the swirling mass, then looked at each other nervously, each thinking this was a good time to back away. Far away.

Prototype A did not. He reached out his hand, making contact with the current flowing from the Collider. Electrified by the quantum energy coursing through him, he reached down and took Volta's cold hand in his.

Instantaneously, the quantum energy surged between them, connecting the two as a circuit. Her eyes shot wide open. Energy sparked around her temple bolts, the resurrecting overload turning her skin a bluish hue, sending a shock of white streaking through her hair.

Startled at what he had done, his hand let go of hers.

She lived!

He opened his steel jaw into what was almost the thin trace of a smile. Engorged with the quantum energy, static danced over his body, lightning flashing in his eyes. The lightning in his eyes suddenly turned to fire when he saw what was happening up on the metal walkway of the computer control center above.

Baron Frankenstein had watched the carnage and bloodshed unfold, cowering behind the cabinets of the colossal supercomputer, stranded on the steel walkway. He had abandoned any hope of shutting down the Collider—it had taken on a life of its own, powered by the strange and unknown properties of the quantum energy it channeled. Still, he held on to his one hope: escape.

That hope was threatened as he spotted LoneWolf on the walkway, climbing with Borge on his back—and he was holding the cursed glass dome containing his rotten ingrate great-grandson. Even more than Igor, this was all *his* fault. The failure of his grand accomplishment was ruined by the spawn of his own loins.

What was it they were doing? They seemed to be trying to access the housing of the Fabula Device. *Let them try*, he thought. They'd likely perish in doing so, with the state of the Collider as it was, not to mention the giant, rampaging tumorous mass.

No! They would not have any chance to succeed.

Frankenstein's grip tightened around a jagged shard of broken steel he had pried from the wreckage. With a wild-eyed mania, he burst from his hiding place, lunging at LoneWolf. The sharp steel tip pierced the back of LoneWolf's neck and a sharp pain shot through him—but it wasn't the stab that caused the real damage. Frankenstein shoved him over the edge, sending him crashing fifteen feet to the floor below.

With the werewolf out of the way, the raving Frankenstein turned, brandishing the bloodied shiv at Borge and Victor.

"YOU!" The crazed eyes were red with fury, the veins in his forehead popping as he addressed the head that had once been his own. "You ruined it! You ruined everything! And to think I once…*very briefly*…had some compassion for you."

Down on the floor, Prototype A didn't think to stop and check on the dazed LoneWolf. His focus was locked on Frankenstein, up on the walkway.

So was Kid Raven's.

The metal grating shook as Prototype A landed with a thundering crash. The crazed Baron Frankenstein whipped around to meet him with a glare from hell. "You miserable, disgusting wretch. I should have full-term aborted you after giving life to your miserable carcass." He raised the shiv toward his creation, not seeming to care it would do little to stop the hulking monster before him.

Charged by the massive dose of quantum energy still surging through him, enhancing his ability to articulate his thoughts, the Monster spoke. "Beware; for I am fearless, and therefore powerful." His finger, crackling with energy, pointed at Frankenstein. "You belong dead."

Frankenstein gulped. He could feel the booming of the Monster's thunderous voice rattling his bones.

"Vengeance is Mine, saith The Lord."

The Lord works in mysterious ways and his lordship, Baron Victor Frankenstein I, was getting the feeling His wrath was upon him. His trembling hand dropped the shiv, and he turned to flee. Up the scaffold… if he could just reach the tunnel above. This was his only chance.

The frantic Frankenstein pushed his way past, scrambling up the scaffolding toward the tunnel. Below, LoneWolf stirred, licking his chops at the chance to hunt down this scurrying rat.

Cold sweat dripped from Frankenstein's face as he crawled through the dark tunnel, his mind racing. With all other options exhausted, he would need to reach the auxiliary control, where his best chance to escape would be to move the entire lab with him. Fumbling his way through the darkness, he felt his chances getting better as his fingers found the panel he was looking for: the master level to activate the riser.

The lab had been built as a multi-story hydraulic silo capable of emerging to the surface through the ruins of Old Castle Frankenstein. If he could make it above ground, he could reach his escape gyrocopter. He needn't worry anymore about activating the self-destruct from the new castle—the Collider would soon see to that. If he hurried, he could fly far enough away before the explosion turned everything within ten miles into a smoldering crater.

The complex shook violently as the silo began to rise, and the earth rumbled beneath Old Castle Frankenstein, the lab slowly pushing up through its courtyard. Frankenstein didn't care about the chaos behind him. He also didn't care about the Collider blasting through the lab's ceiling or the ever-growing mass of Blobulus, now bursting through the walls and out onto the grounds.

He was too close to freedom to care. Staying at least a half step ahead, he could almost taste the escape as he climbed out of the silo, his eyes fixed on the pad where the gyrocopter waited near the new castle.

Despite the massive failures which had just occurred, he almost let out a chuckle. He had made it once again. It may have been just by the very skin of his teeth, but he had made it.

Then he froze.

What was this??

27: NEVERMORE

Damn this werewolf!

LoneWolf smashed through the side of the lab wall, a primal force in pursuit of his prey: Baron Frankenstein. The unnerved baron raced along the top of the broken castle walls, desperate to reach the gyrocopter before this crazed wild animal caught up to him. There it was, just a couple hundred yards away. Once he was over this wall and on the ground, then it would be on to freedom.

Frankenstein's hopes of his flight to freedom crashed to the ground—hard. The Collider's destructive beam had swung over, slicing across New Castle Frankenstein and reducing it, along with the gyrocopter, to ash. Instead of a chuckle of victory, he now thought he might shed a tear of defeat.

And right behind him, the snarling werewolf was closing in.

LoneWolf knew he had him. The hunt was all that mattered, and it was nearing its end. Frankenstein was still on the run, nearing the empty tower ruins. He would pin him in there, his wolf's blood pumping at the thrilling thought of tearing out the jugular, smelling Frankenstein's fear as his life left him—permanently this time.

The salivating LoneWolf tracked Frankenstein into the ruins, his nostrils filled with the smells of damp stone and decay. He quickly filtered through the odors until he found it—the scent of his target. The baron would be able to run, but he would not be able to hide. The tower led into further ruins, some partially open to the sky and illuminated by the brilliant shafts of moonlight streaming in. Only a few more paces and he would catch him.

Dead end.

Frankenstein saw the rabid beast gaining on him and scurried up the crumbling ruins of the wall, with nowhere to go but the shattered remnants of a spire above. He didn't think it would be like this—a man of his stature and importance being cornered and mauled by a dumb animal.

Then he watched, perplexed, as LoneWolf slowed down, pausing just steps away.

"Do not toy with me, you worthless life form! If you're going to kill me, then do it!"

LoneWolf glared, red eyes glowing in the moonlight. Then, unexpectedly, he turned his back on Frankenstein and began walking away.

Frankenstein blinked, confused by the sudden lucky break, but he was going to take it. He would work his way through these ruins and still make his escape, somehow. As he crept along the wall toward the spire, he was stopped by something in his path.

"Nevermore."

Kid Raven jabbed a gloved finger into Frankenstein's chest. "And you can quote me on that."

Frankenstein turned to flee but found himself being flung hard into the opposite wall. His mouth bloodied, he spat red droplets as he faced down Kid Raven… Franklin Frankenstein.

"I don't know who you are or what you have to do with all this," he gasped, "but I am a very rich man, and I'm sure I can make it worth your while to see things my way."

Franklin stared at the face before him. It was his father's face—his father's eyes. Only now there was a mask of evil over the face, a darkness living behind those eyes, coming from the brain and tainted, soulless heart of Victor Frankenstein I, the man who had stolen his father from him. This was his own great-great-grandfather. Only a true monster would do something like this, and even more monstrous to do it to his own flesh and blood, his *family*.

Franklin wanted revenge. Now, more importantly, he wanted justice.

He triggered the gauntlet on his wrist, firing a bolo rope that snaked around Frankenstein's arms, binding him securely. Kid Raven reeled the rope in, staring down the seething baron. Frankenstein would answer for his crimes, and young Franklin Frankenstein would deliver justice.

"No!" Frankenstein bellowed, a pathetic desperation in his voice. "I deserve better than this! Don't you know who I am? Who the hell do you think you are?"

Kid Raven hesitated, his heart pounding. He brought his hands up and placed his fingers on the edge of the eye mask to peel it off. This was the moment, the reckoning he had been waiting for.

Before he could speak, the foundation shook violently, and a fissure spider-webbed up the castle wall. With a cataclysmic roar, the thunderous force of Blobulus erupted from behind it.

A titanic wave of gelatinous destruction crashed down on Frankenstein, tossing Kid Raven backward as the walls collapsed in a rain of broken stone. He dangled from the edge, clutching tightly to a marble gargoyle while the towering blob lurched past, obliterating everything in its wake.

Its mammoth weight caused the ground behind it to give way, collapsing into the deep pits below. Fragments of the castle walls tumbled silently into the darkness, swallowed by the vast, endless depths.

Only a deep chasm remained where Frankenstein had stood.

...

Kendra watched in horror as the Collider spiraled out of control, its quantum energy crackling through the lab like wild lightning. If she couldn't stop it, she would at least try to regain some semblance of control. She was in for a wild ride. After climbing atop the spinning, bucking barrel, it was not going well.

Then there was Blobulus, which was no small matter, continuing to grow at an alarming rate and consuming everything in its path, including the scattered remnants of the Nu-Men and the Brides. Kendra was at a loss. The Collider refused to respond to any of her commands. The controls flickered with a chaotic mix of warnings she couldn't decipher.

"Damn it!" she hissed, frustration boiling over. Even if she could somehow redirect the wildly spinning Collider as a weapon, it would only feed more energy into the monstrous mass of Blobulus. Time was running out, and she hoped Borge and Victor would be able to act on their end, and fast.

LoneWolf had rejoined Prototype A, Borge, and Victor on the platform. Prototype A was smashing his way through the metal housing to clear a path for them to access the Fabula Device and its array of power crystals. Inside was a labyrinth of electronic capacitors, banks of processors, and miles of wiring. It would take a small body to get through.

Borge entered without hesitation.

"It's too dangerous!" LoneWolf yelled. "Let me take Victor in."

Borge shook his head. "We don't have time to argue about this. The Collider is going to melt down if it isn't stopped and I can fit inside—you can't. We'll do this. You deal with the giant, rampaging blob."

With no more to be said, both he and Victor disappeared into the tangled jungle of twisted wires.

LoneWolf and Prototype A considered what to do about Blobulus. Kendra's bull ride with the wildly bucking Collider left her moments away from being thrown off. With no other choice, Kendra abandoned the controls and leaped off, landing on the scaffolding to join them. Kid Raven had also returned, satisfied with the measure of revenge he had witnessed.

"Any ideas?" LoneWolf asked, watching as the megablob's gaping maw opened wide. It was starving and needed to eat.

And eat.

And eat.

And eat.

Oozing away from Castle Frankenstein, it now threatened to lurch below the Odenwald Mountains, where it would destroy the city of Darmstadt, giving its pitchfork-and torch-wielding citizens something to truly worry about—beyond being ultimately turned into a smoking crater by the Collider.

It was no wonder LoneWolf would take *any* idea put forth, good or otherwise.

His only idea was to impulsively leap down onto the writhing mass of Blobulus, slashing at it with his claws. It rumbled and shuddered, bellowing with a tortured wail. Giant sentient malignant warts reached for LoneWolf with slug-like tentacles, trying to stop the assault—and pull him in to feast on his flesh. In an attempt to satisfy its ravenous hunger, the insatiable mouth was now eating anything it found before it—trees, castle ruins, buildings, electrical apparatuses, werewolves…

…and one big, juicy, delicious morsel it set its bulging blobby eyes upon:

The Quantum Collider.

The Collider had been feeding energy into it, but now the blob wanted more.

It wanted it all.

...

Inside the maze of electrical components, Borge and Victor raced to find the crystals powering the Fabula Device. An irradiated glow signaled they had found it.

"Well, doctor," Victor wheezed, "it looks like the crystals have reached mass inverse instability. I'm not surprised, with the Collider going completely haywire."

Borge set down Victor's glass dome. He shielded his own eyes, while Victor, unconcerned with the consequences, closely examined the pulsing red crystals.

"We won't be able to remove them... they've fused together. They are unstable, but not in a way that will take the Collider offline. This will now make it even more powerful. When this thing goes, it will make an atomic bomb look like Fourth of July fireworks." He thought for a moment. "Or worse—it will blast a hole through the atmosphere, destroying all life with it. The circuit needs to be broken. Now."

"By hand? That seems to be the only way."

"No. There is another. Hector, take me out of this container."

Borge gulped. This was certain death. They were already facing such a fate, but this act had a finality—an inevitability—to it. It was truly do or die. The moment was now upon them.

"Place me near the crystals. Let's hope my bite is worse than my bark," Victor said with a final weak smile. "And then may God bless you all to run like the devil to get out of here."

The implosion. Its effects would suck them all into who knows where. Death? Infinity? Another dimension?

Borge took Victor's words to heart and turned away, hobbling with his stubby legs as fast as he could toward the exit.

LoneWolf was barely keeping a half step ahead of Blobulus. It had one eye on the Collider and its others on the scrumptious-smelling werewolf in front of it, and his friends.

Which to eat first?

All of them at once, was this base creature's answer. It suddenly expanded, growing even larger. The growth spurt rocked the grounds, shaking the remnants of the castle. Blobulus's mouth slurped, sucking

LoneWolf toward it. Determined not to meet his end in this way, he slashed at the slimy, quivering tongue until it dropped him into a giant puddle of vomitous drool.

Like a giant blobby moth drawn to a brilliant blue flame, it lunged, its enormous mouth opening wide to devour the Collider whole.

LoneWolf staggered to his feet. He didn't know what was about to happen but knew he didn't want to be any closer than he had to be and pushed Kendra, Kid Raven, and Prototype A toward cover behind the lab silo.

The sound of thunder and the fury of lightning vibrated through the earth, through the time and space of all they ever knew. LoneWolf felt all of his cells scrambling. *Hold on, dammit!* He could feel the force nullifying his existence, pulling his life essence inward in a hurricane hail, climaxing in one doom-ringing interdimensional boom.

With this one long cosmic thunderclap, the maelstrom of horror was over.

Blobulus and the Quantum Collider were gone. Imploding into a black hole of dark energy, both had disappeared into the ether to somewhere unknown, or perhaps nowhere at all, atoms scattered across the endless always of all that is, was, and ever will be. Destruction and the smoking rubble of the war zone around Castle Frankenstein were all that remained.

LoneWolf sniffed around. The smell of brimstone and sulfur, mixed with other noxious chemicals released from shattered glass vials, filled the air. He took Kendra's hand to help her climb out from the pile of broken wreckage that was the lab silo. Kid Raven was up, too, dusting himself off. Prototype A was already wandering the expanse, searching.

Borge was... where was Borge?

He had been with Victor inside the Fabula Device, which was now reduced to a pile of ash and rubble. The two of them had stopped it. By destroying the crystals, the overloading collider had imploded, Blobulus shielding them from the catastrophic vacuum of the implosion, before absorbing and disappearing into it.

Prototype A was tossing aside broken sections of wall and concrete debris with great fury. Plunging his powerful hand into the pile of rubble, he grasped another hand, and the hand grasped his.

A dazed Volta rose from a cloud of dust, her eyes still closed tightly. Prototype A took a moment to look at her and thought she was the most beautiful thing he had ever seen—her soft blue skin, the stitching, those scars! He grew increasingly smitten by her white-streaked dark hair, shocked into a permanently teased towering bouffant, and the forehead bolts that matched his, gleaming in the light of the still-burning fires.

She awakened with a jolt. Prototype A was prepared for disappointment. It seemed it was all he knew and was always his only, lonely friend.

Volta paused, her senses returning to life. Her head darted around, the first noise she uttered sounding like a murderous rabid swan. Her expression went back and forth from horrified to confused. After a few moments, she appeared to get her bearings, then looked at her hand and who still had hold of it.

Used to rejection, the Frankenstein Monster braced himself, ready to back away with a single giant-sized step.

Then she smiled.

A tear of joy ran down his cheek. Volta smiled again, assuring him it was no fluke, no mistake, and they embraced. Their eyes met, then their faces. She kissed him in gratitude, then in passion, electricity crackling around their tangoing tongues.

The feeling of joy in the air was coupled with the feeling of dread. LoneWolf walked over to the pile of disintegrated wreckage that had once been the casing for the Fabula Device and sniffed around.

Nothing.

He had the scenting capabilities of a cadaver dog, and no cadaver scent was to be found.

Franklin peeled off his Kid Raven mask and joined Val West, who had transformed himself back into human form. Neither of them said a word, staring in silence at the still-smoldering remnants. The realization hit Franklin that his father was gone. He knew it would happen, and soon, with his condition. He just wasn't ready for it to be now. No one ever is. The truth of what happened, and the knowledge that his father died a hero, saving them all—and by extension, the world—helped ease the hurt just a little.

That it had all been caused by the evil of Victor Frankenstein I made it both easier and harder to swallow. Although Franklin knew the truth, the public never would. They would never know what really happened with any of this. The only silver lining was they would also never know of the insidious plans made by Victor I masquerading in Victor III's body. Now, all that was left was to go back home to FrankenCrest and take care of his mother… and himself.

As West sifted through the swirling ash, he could only feel a deep ache at the thought of Dr. Hector Borge's demise. They had been through a lot together, and it was Borge's ingenuity that had allowed him to live a life as a werewolf, under control, and to be of use to Commander 7 as a still-active agent. Borge had gone out as a hero, as a field agent, not stuck behind a computer deep underground in the ParaCommand base. It had been a noble and worthy death.

West knew he would be ruminating over this for a long while, but for now, they needed to make their exit. The authorities would soon be on their way, and none of them were interested in making a statement. Small fires continued to break out and were growing larger. Soon, the burning husk of the lab silo would collapse into the depths below, burying this all like a bad memory.

Kendra placed a hand on his shoulder. She'd known Borge since her father had helped Commander 7 start ParaCommand years ago and was also very fond of him.

"It's quite amazing, isn't it?" The exhausted and stunned group all silently nodded their heads, only half-listening. "The polymer used in this remaining piece of casing managed to withstand a supermolecular magnetitional invariance. I simply must have a sample for study to use in the—"

West slowly turned toward the voice. For a brief moment, he thought he was hearing a ghost. Then he wondered if perhaps he was seeing one.

Borge, completely covered in a layer of white dust, had emerged from under a heaping pile of wreckage. Once they registered what they were seeing, everyone rushed to help him dust himself off. West greeted him with a celebratory high-five. Prototype A and Volta went back to necking, while an overjoyed Kendra planted a kiss on the surprised Borge's cheek.

With all this kissing going on, West turned to Kendra.

"What about me?"

He closed his eyes and puckered up.

When he opened them, she was gone.

28: ANIMAL VITALITY

Two days after the Frankenstein operation concluded, Val West made his way down the steep steps to the ParaCommand base, wondering what Commander 7 and Dr. Borge were cooking up for him next.

"West," Borge said, without looking up from the electronic device he was soldering. "There's a package on your desk for you."

"We're receiving mail here now? What innovation will you think of next?"

"It was, shall we say, a special delivery."

West sat down and eyed the small box, wrapped with a red bow. Slowly, he untied the ribbon. He wasn't concerned with it exploding or having any other nefarious features—Borge would have intercepted anything like that. From the traces of scent lingering on the packaging, he already knew who it was from. He just didn't know what it was.

Inside was something he found both amusing and touching, yet it was something he would not touch. The box contained a single silver bullet, marked with the imprint of a lipstick kiss, along with a note:

Love,
Kendra.

Even though the silver would make him feel a bit weak, he brought the box closer to his nose. Tutti Frutti lipstick. A lovely scent and an even better flavor.

Franklin Frankenstein came in from the training room to join them, plunking himself down in a lounge chair near the wall of video monitors. He had returned with West and Borge to ParaCommand and had been diligently working on honing his considerable strength, speed, and agility.

With the push of a button, Borge activated the hidden bar Sir Cedric had installed. Franklin looked over the vast selection of fine and rare whiskeys and liqueurs and was slightly disappointed when Borge held up glasses for each of them—filled with kelp juice.

"I just squeezed this earlier this morning." Borge took a sip and swished it around his mouth. "Exquisite. And never mind all that other rubbish. You're much too young and in training on top of it. You won't be getting any of that from me."

"Dr. Borge is right," West said as he joined them. "You'll have to have a drink with me later, after training."

Borge clicked his tongue disapprovingly.

West grinned and pointed to the assortment of expensive bottles. "We'll start at the back row and work our way through."

"You will not," Borge chided. "Vegetable juice is the path to success, not—"

"Hold that thought." The monitor showing the news caught West's attention. He switched it to the main viewing screen and turned up the volume.

...more on the deadly incident at Castle Frankenstein in Hesse, Germany. Frankentech CFO and Vice President Igor Zelensky is presumed dead following a mysterious explosion and ground collapse at the site.

In a developing update, Baron Victor Frankenstein was reportedly not at the scene. According to a statement from a Frankentech representative, Frankenstein was seriously injured in an unrelated skiing accident on the

Schilthorn in Switzerland. We're told the baron is currently unavailable for comment as he recovers from his injuries...

West switched the television off. Franklin clenched his fists, his eyes turning to steel.

Borge thought for a moment. "You don't think... I mean, surely this is just a public relations cover."

West went cold. "I don't know... can we really rule out anything anymore?"

Franklin tightened his grip on the glass of kelp juice, crushing it into powder.

"I understand how you feel, kid. But let's not make assumptions quite yet."

At that moment, the speaker system and monitor used exclusively by Commander 7 hummed to life.

"Gentlemen, I assume you've heard the reports. Franklin, rest assured, we will be monitoring this activity as part of our global, terrestrial, and extraterrestrial intelligence gathering efforts. I also reviewed Agent LoneWolf's report from the debriefing. You were quite impressive. Very nice work, young man. I would like to extend to you a job offer. How would you like to come to work as part of the team here at Para-Command?"

"I'm fifteen," Franklin replied, taken aback.

"I am aware of that," the Commander continued. "We can make arrangements, perhaps with a boarding school. Have you ever thought of attending Eton, my alma mater? The modifications done to you have made you a one-of-a-kind specimen, with skills and talents exceeding normal human limits, making you highly valuable as an agent for this organization."

"Sir, I'm flattered. But I have to turn down your offer... for now. You see, my mom is all alone at FrankenCrest, back in the States. In fact, she doesn't even know where I am right now. And after all that's happened with my dad, I just think I should be with her... that we should be together, be a family, right now. So, thank you for everything, but I'm just going to go back home."

No one could argue with his mature-for-his-age logic.

"No, you're not," West interjected.

Franklin narrowed his eyes, confused.

"Not without this." West held up the refurbished spy suit Borge had just finished repairing and upgrading.

Franklin excitedly chattered about how he would use the suit to begin his mission as Kid Raven, cleaning up the crime-ridden streets of nearby Baltimore, and fulfilling a vow he had just sworn to himself.

"If he is still alive... I'll be waiting. I *will* take down Victor and Frankentech. And I'll find a way to come back to ParaCommand to further my training."

"Sounds like HIVE better be on the lookout, too," West said, extending a hand. "And you've got a deal. You know... I've always wanted to visit Maryland."

For the first time in a while, the boy smiled. "Then the next time you find yourself in Seyton Place, Mr. West, know you'll always be welcome at FrankenCrest."

West smiled warmly and shook his hand.

Franklin nodded to him. "Tremendous."

That evening, West and Borge returned to ParaCommand after bringing Franklin to the airport. A light spring rain fell as they walked among the familiar tombstones of London's Highgate Cemetery. They didn't mind. It was a refreshing cleansing of sorts after the rigors of the mission.

"Do you think he'll be all right?" Borge asked.

"He will. He's a strong-willed kid. Right now, he just needs time. And, in time, he will also learn to use his powers in ways he can't even imagine right now."

They rounded the corner to the mausoleum hiding the secret entrance to ParaCommand. Borge keyed in the code, the marble gargoyle's eyes glowing red as the door opened.

"But you know what I'm more concerned with right now?" West asked. "The Commander has continually been threatening to send me to Transylvania for some mission he's been keeping an eye on. Is that why he's called me back here?"

"I honestly don't know. I sincerely hope not, after the mess you made there last time."

"Now, that wasn't *all* my doing."

As they descended the stairs, Commander 7's voice greeted them through the speaker box.

"Agent West, I would like you to come see me."

This was truly a first. In all the time he had been with ParaCommand, West had never actually met Commander 7 face-to-face. It would be an honor. He didn't understand why the Commander had never been there in person, but he trusted he had his reasons.

Borge activated a hidden panel in the lab wall. West entered a dark hallway lit only by the pulsing lights of the extensive computer system he was passing through, leading deeper into the base. He continued on, weaving through cables and circuitry, until the Commander's voice beckoned him into a small chamber.

The room was little more than a small open space between circuit panels. In the center was a platform connected to the mainframe system by what seemed like miles of wires. On top of the platform sat a small, rounded glass cover, with its base wired into the system. As West moved closer, he was startled to see it contained only a human brain.

"Pardon my appearance, Mr. West," the Commander said, his voice coming through a speaker attached to the platform. "You can see now why I don't get out much."

A lump formed in West's throat. Here was one of the greatest agents—possibly *the* greatest—ever to serve, reduced to a brain in a jar connected to a computer.

"You may be curious about my condition," the Commander continued, with extreme understatement. "It was a bomb attack. One of my 'old friends' from a certain disbanded Soviet counterintelligence agency decided to send me a gift upon his escape from prison. I would have died—sometimes, I wonder if it would have been preferable—if not for the intervention of Victor Frankenstein.

"It was a Level-10 top-secret initiative, and using his advanced skills, he saved my brain, connecting it to this computer system. It would keep me alive until the time when my brain could be transplanted, either into a new human body or a synthetic one. He had said there was only one shot at it, and he needed to be certain. Now, with him dead, that chance is gone. The secrets of the Frankenstein science have likely died with him. There is no longer hope, that I know of, of being restored to bodily form."

West understood. He didn't want to disagree with the Commander, but he knew there was always hope, always advancements happening that could one day help him. The fact that he had to live as a brain in a jar, content only with his function as a spymaster, was a testament to his will to survive and thrive. Whenever West felt like complaining about his condition as a lycanthrope, he would try to remember Commander 7's attitude.

"Anyway, I wanted you to see, I wanted you to know," said the Commander. "Trust is very important, and I wanted you to understand why I believed in Victor Frankenstein. Thank you for coming, Val."

West nodded and turned to leave.

"Oh," the Commander added, stopping him. "There is one more thing, Agent LoneWolf. I'm sending you to Transylvania. Report first thing in the morning for your briefing."

...

"If you consent, neither you nor any other human being shall ever see us again; I will go to the vast wilds of South America. My companion will be of the same nature as myself and we will be content."

This was the bargain made by the Monster, Protototype A, to his creator over a century earlier. This was the deal that had been reneged, the promise that had been broken by Frankenstein.

Deep in the Peruvian jungle, the Amazon River snaked through the lush tropical rainforest, covering thousands of miles. Known as "the lungs of the earth," this seemed like the perfect place to create a new life.

Inside the little old chapel made of adobe, the elderly padre wondered if his eyesight was finally failing him. The groom standing before him was easily eight-feet tall, and his skin appeared to have a greenish hue. He had heard of people having an "iron jaw" before, but the shiny steel of the smiling mouth seemed to be something else entirely. The eyes, behind a thick ridge of brow, were smiling as well.

The bride… well, he thought her skin looked to be a smooth light blue. The rest was covered by a beautiful white wedding dress and veil, though it couldn't hide the tall hair pushing through, streaked with long white zigzagging curls. Despite their odd appearance, they had come to him with the sincere wish to be married under God, and as the padre of this church, he would do his duty.

The happy groom's thoughts drifted back to just days earlier, when he had pulled her from the wreckage after the battle at Castle Frankenstein. After embracing in a kiss, she gazed at him lovingly and asked for his name.

"Proto…"

He paused.

"Adam," he told her. "My name is Adam."

Afterward, he asked for her hand.

Rice rained down on the happy bride and groom, thrown by a throng of curious villagers. Then, just as mysteriously as they had appeared, off they went, disappearing hand in hand. They were soon borne away by the emerald jungle and lost in love and life anew.

...

"Just tremendous."

Val West was packing for his assignment to Transylvania, knowing he would leave shortly after Commander 7 delivered the early morning mission briefing. He cursed quietly to himself in his new flat on Baker Street, a place he had barely settled into before being called away on yet another assignment.

So much for taking leave. Perhaps it was for the best. He'd let himself fall a little too hard, and love was something he had always kept at a distance for the sake of his profession. Sex was different and was also sometimes part of his profession, to be used as a weapon in its own way.

He decided to turn in early. The scent—the scent of Lady Kendra Kenton... he just couldn't get it out of his head. Now, to make it worse, he smelled a strong scent of Tutti Frutti lipstick. He still wanted to taste it.

Stripping off his clothes, he tried to get it off his mind, and instead, get into bed.

When he flicked off the bedside lamp, a tingle came over him, spreading through his entire body. His ears perked up. He looked around, his enhanced night vision quickly adjusting to the darkness. Starlight filtered in through the window. A dark silhouette stood out from the shadows beside it.

West sat up. "You swore you would shoot me with the silver bullet. You lied, you know."

The silhouette, the scent, the alluring feminine aura moved closer. "Not exactly. I said I would shoot. And I did—just not at you. But there's still time."

"You won't though. It's my animal vitality. You can't resist it." West rose from his bed and stood, meeting her gaze.

"Good evening," West said, with a wolfishly mischievous grin, "Lady Kenton."

She stepped out of the shadows and turned to him, confirming her identity.

She held out her hand. He took it in his.

The glittering green eyes gazed into his, the sinful lips sending an invitation to a mouth full of mean and dangerous intentions.

Invitation accepted. Tutti Frutti lipstick. He couldn't wait to taste it.

Without any further delay, they began nuzzling.

"You think you're an animal," she teased, giving him fair warning.

He had to be up early. It was going to be a late night.

To hell with sleep.

CODE NAME: LONEWOLF WILL RETURN
IN
FROM TRANSYLVANIA WITH LOVE

Made in the USA
Monee, IL
01 August 2025

21844838R00166